FIRST NIGHT

JESSIE NIGHT THRILLER- BOOK ONE

JESSIE NIGHT THRILLER

EMBER SCOTT

THE BREAKING POINT

The Breaking Point

Even though she could hear the sirens blaring in the distance, deep down, the woman knew the man standing over her would have plenty of time to kill her before they arrived.

She lay on the bathroom floor of her house, the cool tile offering no comfort as she stared upward into the night. When she had first purchased the house, she thought the extravagantly large skylight in the bathroom a waste of money. But now, she was thankful. There were worse things one could be forced to look at as they lay dying than a beautiful, peaceful star-filled night.

She tried to moan, producing a phlegmy cough instead that bubbled out of her lips. The medication he'd stabbed her with worked so fast. She was on the floor almost immediately and hadn't moved since. At first, fear had overwhelmed her. Then that was replaced by shock and, finally, after the second breaking, acceptance. The sirens were farther away now, and she knew they hadn't been coming for her. How could they? The man had disabled her alarm system, and even if she were able to scream, there was no one to hear it.

As he stood up, looking down on her – at his handy work – she just wanted it to be over. There was no fight in her, no hope left. Where was the indomitable will to live that she had always heard humans possessed? Truthfully, it was the opposite. She had falsely been under the impression the drugs would dull the pain. But that hadn't happened.

She wanted this over.

The man leaned his head to one side, his forefinger pressed to his lips as he studied her. "Now this one is going to be tricky. The knees typically aren't meant to do what I'm about to do...but lucky for you, this isn't my first time at this rodeo."

He bent down over her, his rough hands on her legs. Was she crying? Maybe. She felt like she was crying, but she couldn't feel if any tears were actually being produced. She could feel his hands on her limbs and knew what was coming. Maybe the pain would make her lose consciousness this time, and if she was lucky, she wouldn't wake up.

But knowing something was coming, didn't mean she was prepared for it. Nothing could have prepared her for the searing pain that accompanied the harsh snap and breaking sounds that were as loud as gunshots in her ears. For a second, her breathing stopped, and she prayed that heralded the end for her.

The pain she felt was indescribable as he stood up.

His breath came in labored huffs as he smiled at her. "Wow. I know you're experiencing this as incredibly painful, but I really wish you could see it from my standpoint. It's a thing of beauty." He walked around her. She couldn't move her head to follow him but could hear the tapping of his shoes on the tile as he came up behind her. His lips were close to her ear as he whispered, "Don't worry. Not much more. If you're still alive when I get to your hips, I promise I'll make that the last pain you feel in this life."

PIG OFF THE PLATE

Pig off the Plate

J essie Night sat at the bar and stared down at the plate of pulled pork, eggs, melted cheese and Texas toast, all smothered in "special gravy" and suddenly questioned her decision to try the Pigs On A Plate breakfast special. The sign outside the Greasy Spoon Diner claimed it to be the best bang-for-your-buck breakfast in the entire south – 'a true Tennessee delight'. She should have just gotten on the road, eaten a granola bar like she had every morning for the past week, and continued on her way. But she was a little ahead of schedule and figured it might be nice to treat herself to something special.

But now, confronted with the mound the smiling waitress had plopped down before her, she was more concerned that she was treating herself to an early coronary. She wasn't sure what disgusted her more, the sight of the excess grease building along the edge of her plate, or the fact that the aroma was strangely enticing to her. One thing was for certain, she'd need a refill of coffee to tackle this. Just as she signaled her waitress, a commotion coming from the back of the restaurant caught her attention.

"No! Someone help me!" a young woman's voice called out. "He was taking pictures of my daughter! He has pictures of her on his phone!"

Jessie looked up to see a man in his mid-forties, wearing cowboy boots, jeans, a black tee shirt with a gold eagle painted on it, and a denim jacket trying to make his way towards the front of the restaurant. A young woman, no older than her early twenties, was frantically tugging at the man's jacket trying to restrain him. Behind her, a girl who looked to be around eight or nine, looked on in fear at the scene playing out before her.

The man struggled against the woman's pull, focusing instead on making his way to the front as he attempted to shrug her off.

"Somebody, please...he was taking pictures of my daughter under the table...I caught him..." she pleaded tearfully, frantic for someone to help. The patrons sitting to either side seemed to part, turning back to their meals as the man headed for the door, giving the woman a quick shove to disentangle his jacket from her grasp.

Once he was free of her, he picked up the pace and began to rush past the bar. Jessie slipped off her stool and as he passed her, stuck one foot out to catch his ankle. When he stumbled, she lifted her leg higher, causing him to crash completely onto his stomach with a thud.

As soon as he hit the ground, she was on him, one

knee in his back as she reached around and quickly fished his phone out of his jacket pocket.

"What the hell—" he started, just as Jessie held the phone's camera to his face, unlocking the device.

She stood up, quickly navigating to his picture folder. Immediately she regretted doing so. What she saw there was unsavory, to say the least. And the most recent pictures were indeed of the curly-haired girl trailing her mother. Pictures from the side, behind, and most disgusting of all, were ones that were taken under the table she was sitting at of her dress's hemline.

"Call the police," Jessie said to the waitress, just as the man stumbled to his feet. His face went red when he saw what she was looking at, but his embarrassment quickly turned to anger.

He lashed out, reaching for the phone. "You bitch! That's my private property."

The woman who was protecting her child screamed and charged at the man, swinging wildly. He covered his face but then lashed out, slapping her across the cheeks to the gasps of the diner residents. A couple of men stood up, making their way to the ruckus. But before they could arrive, the man drew his sights on Jessie again. This time, he waded in, fist clenched and drew back.

Jessie smiled, stepped back just enough that the wild swing missed her completely, and then lashed out with a roundhouse kick that connected with the side of the man's knee. There was a satisfying pop as he dropped to the floor. She stepped forward and leaned into his face. "I saw the rest of what you have on your phone. Have fun in jail, perv." Then, she smashed her fist into the side of his head and watched in satisfaction as he hit the ground and didn't get back up.

Then, she tossed the phone to the young girl's mother and walked out, aware of the eyes on her. She knew she should have stayed and made a statement to the police, but that was the last thing she wanted.

"This is why you should stick to granola, Jess," she whispered to herself as she quickly headed for the parking lot. She glanced at her watch. Still on time. She could hear the far-off sounds of sirens getting closer as she climbed into the seat of her Jeep.

3

WELCOME TO THE STRUMMING

Welcome to the Strumming

J essie gripped the well-worn steering wheel of the '98 Wrangler. It, like the seats, had been recovered, yet the leather around the ten and two positions were about three shades lighter than the rest. Her thumbs traced the worn-out grooves as she rolled her head from one side to the other, trying to relax the knots between her shoulder blades. Gray eyes swept the road in front of her while occasionally checking the rearview mirror.

She let out a breath she felt like she had been holding for the last hundred miles, as she told herself she was fine.

She was okay.

There was no one in the rearview mirror. No sedans. No black SUV riding especially low because of the increased weight from tactical armor.

She glanced down at the Whistler TRX lying on the

passenger's seat. The small, black and white screen showed that it was cycling through a variety of frequencies, and the fact that it hadn't so much as beeped since she left Colorado was small reassurance that everything was okay.

Still. Some reassurance was better than none. At this point, she would take what she could get. She resisted the urge to take it up and make sure it was still working properly. She'd had to adjust the frequency after the first couple hundred miles. All the communication from whatever local police and state trooper activities she passed by were making her jumpy.

Somewhere along I-70 in Missouri, she had changed the bandwidth, deciding it was safe to focus only on the military frequencies. She knew it was illegal, but she also knew that short of being stopped and having a trooper who knew what he was doing look at the Whistler, there wasn't much chance she would get caught. The silence the new bandwidth afforded was a soothing balm to her frayed nerves.

She finally decided it was safe enough to listen to something other than her thoughts running in a loop, and the grating sound of her almost-but-not-quite balding tires on the asphalt. She flipped through the channels, avoiding the seemingly endless pastors hawking salvation and the country stations that seemed to only play Loretta. After a couple minutes, she came to a station that played classic rock, and while that wouldn't have been her normal choice, Tom Petty's gravelly voice singing about running down a dream seemed to perfectly mirror the staccato of road noise coming from under the Jeep.

Her gaze drifted to her right hand on the steering wheel and stopped. She was strumming. Something she hadn't done in ages. The rhythm of her fingers as they tapped the wheel mesmerized her.

Pinky, ring, pointer, middle then thumb. Then it immediately reversed. Thumb, pointer, ring, middle and last pinky. Over and over the fingers moved on their own in that same pattern, while in the back of her mind she recited the accompanying numbers.

Five, four, three, two, one; counting down to the strumming of her fingers and then back up from one to five as the fingers reversed.

The sudden warbling as her tires hit the rumble strip on the side of the road snapped her back to reality and she yanked the Jeep back on course.

"What the hell, girl? Get your ass out of the clouds and back on the road before you kill yourself."

She breathed deeply, adjusting her back in the seat. She hadn't mindlessly strummed like that in a while. She knew why. She was thinking about what lay ahead.

About having to start over again.

Her knuckles grew white on the wheel as she thought about the last twenty years of her life. All spent in service to a government that thanked her by kicking her out just before retirement and stripped her of everything she had worked for.

But she knew she should be thankful that was all they had done. She wasn't doing time in Miramar at the Naval Consolidated Brig, and she hadn't been scratched off the books completely and sent to some hell hole black site. Officially, female officers only went to Miramar, which was an integrated, all branches brig. But she knew for certain that there were a few cases where women had been scratched and never heard from again.

The thought of where and what those women might be experiencing made her shudder and she glanced at the Whistler again. Still quiet.

How she had escaped with only a dishonorable discharge and not served time was a mystery to her. She knew that it had to be someone very high up who had made that possible. Had things not played out the way they did, she might have thought it was her legacy name that got her out with just the damning discharge.

But she knew better than to think that. Thanks to her, the family name was now dead in the eyes of the United States government.

A glance at her watch told her it was just before midday. She looked up, noting the position of the sun in the cloudless blue sky. Everything looked different in this part of the country, so it was going to take her body some time to adjust and start knowing the time of day just by the play of light on the topography around her. She had desperately wanted to sleep in but had made herself get up at five AM, just as she had every morning for the last nineteen years.

As road weary as she was, she was determined to finish out the last leg of the trip and make it into the mountains of North Carolina by noon. She was a little behind because she wasn't prepared for the majestic beauty that greeted her along the Blue Ridge Parkway.

The winding road cut into the mountainside snaked its way upward along impressive, and scary, slate cliffs.

The panorama of rolling mountains, cloaked in a dazzling spectrum of green hues, spread out before her like a living tapestry. To one side, the land fell away dramatically, revealing a vista of verdant valleys and sharp ridges. Below, a river traced a glistening path through the landscape, its waters sparkling under the sun. On the other side, steep slopes rose, blanketed with thickets of rhododendrons and towering trees. Forest-green pines stood shoulder to shoulder with broadleaf trees, their young leaves a bright, emerald green. Occasionally, the dense woodland gave way to clearings, where wildflowers spread their colorful blooms against the green canvas. Bursts of violets, blues, yellows, and whites spread out before her.

Occasionally, she would catch a glimpse of wildlife, including some very big, Jeep-busting deer, that reminded her to concentrate on the road and not the scenic overlooks.

She hadn't been on these roads since she was a child, sitting in the back seat of her father's spacious sedan, face pressed to the windows as she marveled at the steep drop-offs falling away from the passenger side. Her memories of the time spent with her aunt were spotty at best, but she remembered the awe-inspiring views on the drive. Her father had been stationed at Fort Bragg and would bring her and her brother up into the mountains for a few weeks at a time during the summers to spend with his sister.

That was before he had moved them across the

country to Colorado as he worked his way up the army career ladder. Once they moved, the visits to his sister had stopped. Jessie knew it was more than just distance. Something had happened there, but no one in the family talked about it.

Soon, she all but forgot the time spent eating home-made ice cream and playing along the lakefront in the town of Pine Haven. Occasionally, she would ask about when they were going to visit Aunt Gina again, but her father would grow tight-lipped and terse. Finally, she stopped asking.

Aunt Gina's name was never brought up again until the day her father sat her and Brody down, pacing the floor in front of the fireplace. He held a letter in his hand, his fist closing tight and crumpling it. It was the first time Jessie had seen her father nervous, and it was the only time she had heard his voice crack.

"Your...aunt was in an accident and has passed away. I need to fly back east for a few days to take care of some things. But I'll be back before you have to head back to school next week. You're going to stay with Patsy and Charlie until I get back."

She swallowed hard at that thought, a buzzing filling her mind and that familiar numbness starting in her diaphragm, threatening to spread. Instinctively, she started to strum, refusing to let it take her over.

She hadn't had an attack in a couple years now, and if it happened while she was driving along a road with a one-hundred-foot drop just feet away...

Something bolted onto the road from the left and she swerved, slamming on the breaks as she hit the dirt on the far side. Thank God she hadn't pulled the other way; if she had, she'd be tumbling off the mountainside.

She looked up, heart pounding as she white-knuckled the wheel. Movement in the rearview mirror caught her eye. It wasn't a deer she had nearly hit. It was too small for that. Movement in the undergrowth behind her caught her attention and she jumped out of the Jeep.

Oh, please don't let it be a person.

She made her way to the side of the road where she had seen the tall weeds rustling. Parting the brush, she froze, just as a low growl greeted her ears.

4

A BLIZZARD IN SUMMER

A Blizzard in Summer

Jessie put her hands up in a non-threatening manner, taking a couple of steps back until her boots were on the gravelly shoulder. She chanced a quick glance at the road. The curve she had just come around was a blind one and any moment a driver could cut around it, taking it too close, and plow into her.

She took a deep breath and focused on the frightened face before her.

"Easy, boy," she said, slowly bringing her arms down. She crouched down, making herself small and less threatening to the animal that peered out at her. All she had seen was a face of white fur and honey-colored eyes that watched her with caution.

The initial growl she heard was tempered now with the tiniest of whimpers. That told her the dog was open to being approached, but she still didn't want to spook the fellow. She avoided direct eye contact, looking to the side and then glancing occasionally back at the canine, letting it know she wasn't a threat. Slowly, she extended her hand, palm down, in an offering of peace and trust.

"It's okay, buddy. You're safe," she said, her voice calm, measured and warm.

She watched as the nervous dog lowered its ears, nostrils quivering, whimpering increasing just a bit. Jessie held her ground, continuing to speak in low, encouraging tones until a massive head poked through the underbrush. It was a German Shepherd. A white one, with incredibly expressive eyes. Slowly, the shepherd inched its way forward, lowering itself onto its belly until it was close enough to take a tentative sniff at her hand.

She was used to being around German Shepherds as they were often used on base, but this one was larger than most. "Just please don't bite me."

But instinct told her this dog was not aggressive. It was also very well groomed and taken care of. She couldn't make out a collar, but a dog like this had to belong to someone. As it sidled closer, a cursory look told Jessie it was a male and she reached out to give him a quick scratch behind the ears and under his large jaw. In return he licked her hand and wagged a massive tail. There was dirt marring his fur and a few chiggers attached, but for the most part, he looked amazingly clean. He couldn't have been out in the woods for long.

She stood, staring down at him. In return, the shepherd sat and stared up at her.

By her calculations she was only a couple of miles from the town limits, so chances were good that the dog belonged to someone in town.

"I bet someone is missing you something fierce, boy. What say we try to find out who your human is?" She took steps towards the Jeep, looking back to see if he would follow. The dog whimpered, looking back at the protection of the bushes and then at his new friend. She patted her thigh lightly, encouraging him to follow, and smiled when he did.

Reaching into the back of the Jeep, she fumbled around in one of her duffel bags until she found a bottle of water. Cracking it open, she poured some into her hand, holding it down for the big boy to greedily lap at. She repeated the procedure until most of the water was gone.

"Okay. Hop in, and let's get you to town. Surely someone will recognize you."

She opened the driver's side door and slid her seat forward, motioning for him to climb in. He looked wary at first, but with a little more coaxing, he hopped into the back seat, stretching out in a prone position.

"Poor thing. You must be exhausted." She climbed behind the wheel, fired up the engine, and eased back onto the road.

In just over a mile, she was greeted with a sign announcing they were entering Pine Haven. The letters were painted in gold above a picturesque scene of a tranquil lake dotted with beautiful houses. "A Perfect Place To Be", was the tagline painted at the bottom of the billboard.

She huffed quietly to herself. Pine Haven certainly looked perfect, just like so many of the small towns that dotted this stretch of the Blue Ridge. And, she supposed, it was. If you could afford to live in the houses on the lake.

Glancing in the rearview mirror, she could see her passenger was sleeping, ears twitching every so often as he dreamed about whatever adventure had led him to be lost along a scenic stretch of deserted mountain roadway.

The dog raised its head lazily when the Jeep rumbled over the train tracks that acted as a boundary into the town proper, before settling down and drifting back to sleep. Before her, the road to either side became overgrown with large pines and red oaks whose tops stretched towards one another to form a canopy of green that split and dappled the sunlight.

As she left the wild serenity of the mountainside, signs of civilization began to emerge. The dense, towering forests began to thin out, making way for modest houses, their rooflines peeking through the thinning tree line. The houses on the outskirts of the town proper were emblematic of mountain-town architecture; a blend of wood and stone blended in with the surrounding nature. They were painted in somber earth tones, though here and there Jessie could catch a glimpse of a vibrant blue or green, sometimes seeing the pop of a red door or the canary yellow of a porch swing.

Gardens offering up an array of foliage were hemmed in by picket fences and encircled many of the homes. They echoed the lived-in warmth and down-home comfort one would expect from a lakeside town built in the side of a mountain.

As she rolled deeper into town, the road smoothed out and the homes started to appear a little statelier, sitting farther back from the road, with expansive, well-manicured lawns. She could also see the beginnings of small businesses appearing – a family-owned grocery store, a post office, a couple of large Victorians with shingle signs hanging from the porches.

Traffic had also picked up, and she took a left, following the slow-moving cars making their way onto the town's picture-perfect main street.

She slowed, memories flooding her as she entered the main artery of the town. It was lined with a variety of mom-and-pop shops as well as some of the town's more prouder homes. Grand old establishments that were a mixture of private homes on the upper levels, but business and specialty shops on the ground levels. While many might argue that the lake, with its expansive views of the surrounding mountains, was the heart of Pine Haven, Jessie knew that it was Main Street that drove the town.

There was an undeniable charm about the tree-lined sidewalks interspersed with park benches and gas lamp posts. From the outside, it looked like a community that cared about its members. Of course, Jessie knew that that care could be dependant on which side of the tracks you lived on in Pine Haven.

She angled the Jeep into one of the on-street parking slots and hopped out. Her eyes swept the length of Main Street out of habit, but everything looked like you would expect. A few kids on bikes dashed by, a shirtless jogger ran past, and here and there she saw locals going in and out of the specialty shops. The smell of fresh baked bread and coffee caught her attention as she pushed the seat forward to let the dog out. He immediately ran to a grassy area in the town center to do his business, reinforcing to Jessie the idea that he was well trained and cared for.

She ushered him back into the Jeep when he came jogging back to her side. "You wait here. I'm going to grab a coffee, and a snack for you. I'll also see if anyone knows who you belong to."

With the top down, she knew he would be fine; she just hoped he'd still be there when she returned. Stepping up onto the wooden porch outside of Angel's Bakery, Jessie looked over her shoulder as she placed a hand on the door. The dog was still in the back of the car, head cocked to one side as his eyes followed her every move. She smiled. "Good boy."

Stepping through the door, Jessie was overcome with the warm smell of fresh brewed coffee, sugar and yeast. Her eyes were drawn to a glass counter that nearly spanned the width of the space. In it was an array of delicate pastries, cakes and golden loaves of bread. At one end sat a wooden counter with a cash register and one of those small silver bells that you tapped for service.

The interior of the bakery was cozy and inviting, with cream-colored walls, wood trim, and a large chalkboard behind the counter listing the day's specials. Vintage photographs and old signs and license plates adorned the walls, adding to the place's charm. There was a large picture window facing out on Main Street with a couple of small tables and chairs arranged to take advantage of the view.

Jessie walked up to the register and tapped the little bell. There was a set of wooden swinging doors that must have led to the kitchen, because the closer she got to them, the stronger those amazing smells were. In seconds, a middle-aged woman came through the doors, all smiles and hand waves at seeing someone new coming into her store.

"Well, hey there, how can I help you?" she asked.

Jessie had forgotten just how happy everyone was in these small communities, and she found herself trying to mimic the woman's affability. "Hi. Everything looks wonderful. But could I have a large cup of whatever house brew you have on hand? Black, please." Her eyes drifted to a small plate sitting by itself on the counter with small, golden treats shaped like bones. "Are those dog treats?"

The woman smiled as she began dispensing a cup of very strong-smelling coffee. "Sure are. Grain- and preservative-free. I bake a fresh batch every morning."

Jessie smiled. "Could I have a few of those as well?"

"Coming right up. You visiting from somewhere? Haven't seen you in here before."

Jessie's mind spun. She wasn't quite ready to announce she was potentially a new member of the community. "Yes. I just pulled in from out west." She saw the woman give her a look that wanted to know more as she punched in numbers on the cash register. "I used to visit my aunt here when I was a kid, so I...kinda wanted to revisit; stroll down memory lane." That wasn't entirely untrue.

"Well, welcome. My name's Angel. If you're around, stop in anytime."

Jessie smiled as she fished in her pocket for a bill.

Angel held up her hand. "Nope, this is my welcome to Pine Haven gift. You like it, come on back and pick out something else."

Jessie wavered but knew there was going to be no arguing with the woman. So, she just nodded and said she would definitely be back as she cast one last glance at the display of goodies. She turned for the door but spun on her heel. "Can I ask you something? On my way in, I found a dog outside the town limits. No collar but seems pretty well taken care of. I was wondering if maybe you recognized him. He's a white German Shepherd. I have him in the back of my Jeep."

Angel's brow dipped as she walked around the register and followed Jessie over to the window.

"That's Blizzard. He belongs to Jeb Thompson; older man who lives just at the edge of town up on Elmwood. What in the world? They are never apart. Guess Blizzard must have run off and Jeb's in no shape to catch him. Here—" She went back to the counter, retrieved a pad and began scribbling on it. "Here's the directions to Jeb's place. It's about a half-mile up the turn-off I marked here – just keep going and you'll get to it. I don't know his number, or I'd give you that."

Jessie took the piece of paper and thanked her. "I'll return him to Mr. Thompson. Thank you so much for everything. I'll definitely be seeing you again."

She left the bakery and walked over to the Jeep. "Blizzard, huh?" The dog's ears stood even straighter, and he barked a quick reply. "Okay then. Let's get you home. I'm betting Jeb is worried sick about you." The mention of his owner's name caused Blizzard to whine loudly, his tail suddenly going a mile-a-minute.

Jessie looked at her watch as she climbed in. She had plenty of time to get Blizzard home and still make her appointment.

It took just over twenty minutes to make her way out of town and to the winding dirt road that led to Jeb Thompson's place. The house was set at the edge of an overgrown field, isolated from foot and car traffic. It was one of those places that if you didn't know where it was, good luck finding it. It was a small dwelling, unassuming, with an old Ford Thunderbird in the driveway and a small barn sitting out back.

No sooner had Jessie eased her Jeep to a stop than Blizzard jumped out, barking and running to the small front porch. He scratched and whined furiously at the door before running back and forth, desperate to get inside.

"Easy, boy," she cooed, walking up to the door. She knocked and tried to calm the shepherd down. When no one answered, she knocked again, this time calling out. "Mr. Thompson? Are you home? I found your dog." She leaned in, listening, but heard nothing. Blizzard was all but vibrating with nervous energy at this point.

There were two windows flanking the door and Jessie moved to one, cupping her hands to peer through the glass. Her breath caught at what she saw.

There, lying on the floor just inside the doorway, was an elderly man. He wasn't moving, and from where she stood, Jessie couldn't be sure he was breathing.

5

KICKING IN DOORS

Kicking in Doors

J essie pulled out her phone and dialed 9-1-1. She spoke rapidly, giving the dispatcher the name of the road and owner of the house where she was located. The dispatcher assured her someone was on their way, and asked Jessie to stay on the line. Instead, she tucked her cellphone back into the lightweight jacket she wore and examined the door.

An older farmhouse like this had doors made of solid oak or pine, which made them incredibly sturdy. But upon closer inspection, she saw that the frame in which it was set was not as impressive. There were signs of warping from age and weather, which meant breaching it was a possibility. Her eyes settled on the worn doorknob and lock.

That was the weak point.

She stepped back, measuring the distance, and placed her weight on her right leg. With her left, she struck out, slamming the heel of her boot into the lock. The door creaked, giving a little but held. She took a deep breath and struck again, driving through the lock and adding as much pressure to the kick as she could by pushing off her dominant leg.

This time the door gave way, the weakened frame splintering as the door burst inward.

In seconds she and Blizzard were at the man's side. He was elderly, in his mid-eighties, gray hair and full beard, with pale, clammy skin. He was on his back, arms outstretched. In one hand, he had a loose grip on a pill bottle. She bent down and picked it up, turning the label towards her.

Nitroglycerine.

Moving to his side, Jessie shook the man's shoulders. "Sir...Mr. Thompson? Can you hear me?" She spoke in a loud voice, trying to see if he was at all responsive. She placed two fingers on the side of his neck, carefully feeling for a pulse. It was there, but just barely. Thready and irregular. While she was feeling for a pulse, she was watching for any signs of his chest rising. Once she established that he had a pulse, she bent close, her ear almost touching the man's mouth and nose.

If he was breathing, she couldn't perceive it.

Her mind raced back to how long it had been since she found Blizzard, trying to work out a rough timeline as to how long the man might have been down. That would definitely help the paramedics when they arrived. She quickly, but carefully, swept her finger into his mouth to make sure his airway was clear, then tilted his head back slightly and began giving rescue breaths. His heart was still beating so there was no need for compressions. At least not yet.

She gave one breath every five to six seconds for two minutes then felt for his pulse. It was weak, but still there. Beside her, Blizzard was whining nonstop and pacing the floor. She tried to ignore the dog as she continued to try and resuscitate the man.

Her mind was racing. *Where the hell is rescue?*

Another breath. Another pulse check. Was it getting weaker? Finally, the wailing of the paramedic's siren drifted through the house. In no time, she heard the crunch of the ambulance grinding to a stop on the gravel just outside the house.

Seconds later, a man and a woman burst in through the door, greeted by Blizzard's less-than-welcoming growls. Jessie sat up, breathing hard from her exertions. "It's okay, boy. They're here to help." She noted the look of fear in the man's eyes as they locked on the dog. A thought struck her, and she turned to the shepherd. "Blizzard. Crate!"

Immediately, the dog spun and ran out of the room, heading for the back of the house.

The paramedics kneeled next to the man, placing a large tackle box of supplies next to him. Jessie turned her head to see a third paramedic, a male, pushing in a gurney with a life pack and monitor sitting atop it.

"Hello, ma'am," said the first man. "Are you a family member, do you know what's going on?"

"Not family," Jessie replied, stepping back as the female paramedic began to examine Mr. Thompson. "Elderly male, mid-seventies, found unresponsive. Very weak pulse, breath sounds not detectable by ear, I administered rescue breaths. Have gone through three cycles of breathing. He's on nitroglycerine—" She pointed to the bottle next to him. "No idea how long he's been down, but I found his dog wandering outside town about two hours ago. Brought the dog home to find the man unresponsive on the floor."

The paramedic looked up at her approvingly before they began placing the monitoring equipment on the unconscious man. They talked rapidly among themselves, tossing around words relating to the readings they were getting. Then, moving with practiced care, they lifted him onto the gurney, raised it to full height, and began pushing him out the door.

They nearly ran into a police officer who appeared out of nowhere and quickly stepped aside.

"How's he doing, Bradley?" the officer asked.

The paramedic who had taken lead onsite spoke quickly. "Not good, Alex. Jeb's a tough one...but this looks bad. County General has a team on standby waiting for him. We need to move."

The officer just nodded and stepped aside.

Bradley turned quickly, looking at Jessie over his shoulder as he gave her a nod, then gave one last glance to the policeman. "You can thank her if he lives. That was some top notch work she did keeping him breathing until we got here." And then they were out the door, pushing the man into the back of the ambulance before speeding off.

In the sudden quiet that followed, Jessie could feel her hands trembling as the adrenaline that fueled her started to burn out of her system. She closed her eyes, taking deep breaths as she forced her pounding heart to slow.

The police officer stood there for a second, thumbs hooked in his belt, before walking over to her and extending a hand. "Alex Thomas."

She opened her eyes and nodded, returning the handshake. "Jessie Night."

He frowned a bit before slowly nodding. "You're taking over the old Rawling's place out near the lake, right?"

She hesitated a moment, taking the officer in out of habit. He was maybe an inch over six feet, broad shoulders, strong build, but not the kind that came from working out. More like the kind built over a lifetime of slinging hay bales and working a farm. Right-handed, strong, steady gate. Jessie tightened her lips, reminding herself that this wasn't the military. She didn't need to assess everyone that stepped up to her. "Yes. It used to belong to my aunt, Gina. She left it to my father when she passed, and well...here I am now."

He nodded, giving her a pleasant smile. "Nice welcome to town for you. Sorry you just had to go through all that." She didn't answer, opting to hold his gaze for a second. "So, do you mind telling me what happened? How you came to be here, I mean." His eyes drifted around the room, lingering slightly on the door.

"I found his dog. A lady – Angel – in town was nice enough to tell me who Blizzard belonged to and where his owner lived. I drove up, saw him lying on the floor and...well, tried to help him."

Alex was nodding, still staring at the door. "You did that?"

Jessie felt heat rising in her face. "Yeah. Adrenaline. Sorry. I'll definitely pay for it."

The officer held his hand up. "Not a problem. We'll get it all fixed up. Thank you for stepping in the way you did."

She was about to say something when she remembered the dog. She turned and made her way out of the room, retracing the way she had seen Blizzard go. There was a small kitchen off the living area, and a mud room off to the side. That was where she found the shepherd, sitting in his crate, panting heavily.

"Hey, come here, boy," she said, clapping her hands. He trotted up, tail wagging, and nuzzled his nose into her hand. A quick glance around revealed a doggie door cut into the door leading out of the mudroom. "So that's how you got out, huh."

"Poor thing must have run out for help when Jeb collapsed. The two of them are pretty much inseparable. I can't imagine him leaving Jeb for any other reason," Alex said.

"Well, it's a good thing he did. Otherwise, I would have never found him." She frowned. "Mr. Thompson didn't look in the best of shape. I really hope he pulls through. What about him?" She glanced down at Blizzard.

"Well, I'll call animal control. They'll come take him to a shelter until something can be worked out."

Jessie looked at the animal, his honey-brown eyes staring back up at her. "He's just been through a traumatic event, unsure what's happening and where his human is. You lock him up in a cage now and I'm betting he's going to have a terrible time."

Alex let out a sigh. "Probably. But unfortunately, there isn't much else we can do. I mean...I would offer to take him, but with my hours, I don't know it would be a good fit."

She was already shaking her head. "No, he's been through enough already." She took a deep breath. "I could keep an eye on him, I guess. Just until Mr. Thompson gets back on his feet."

Alex's green eyes lit up. "That would be pretty kind of you, Miss...er...Mrs...?"

Jessie cleared her throat. "Jessie. Just Jessie."

He nodded. "Jessie. That would be mighty kind of you indeed. Do you have experience with shepherds?"

She shook her head. "Not exactly. I have been around them, but never owned one."

Alex didn't say anything as he studied her. "Well, I should probably head back to the office to fill out the paperwork on this. I'll also swing by County General and see how Jeb's doing."

Jessie dug out her phone. "Here. Let me send you my number. Please let me know how he's doing and certainly let him know not to worry about Blizzard. I'll take care of him until they can be reunited."

Alex did the same, taking out his phone and swapping numbers. "He'll appreciate that. And, please, don't worry about the door. I'll have someone come over and secure that before nightfall."

"Just a second," Jessie said, going back into the mud

room. She looked around and finally saw what she was looking for. With a grunt, she lifted the big bag of dog food that was sitting by the door.

"Here, let me," said Alex. He took the bag from her as they headed out of the house.

Hanging on a hook next to the door was a collar and leash. Jessie snagged them and ushered Blizzard out, doing her best to close the broken door as tight as possible. Alex dropped the bag in her Jeep, and they said their goodbyes. Once the tan and white police cruiser had pulled out, Jessie looked down at Blizzard.

"Okay. Looks like we're going to be stuck with each other a bit longer. Don't make me regret this." She glanced at her watch. "Shit. Gotta go, boy. Hop in."

She'd have to hurry, but she was just going to make her appointment. There was a realtor waiting to give her a key. One that was going to unlock the dusty silhouette of memories and lost time.

6

A KNIFE UNDER THE PILLOW

A Knife Under the Pillow

By the time Jessie made her way back to the town's only real estate office, the wind had picked up considerably. It whipped around her as she stepped out of the Jeep, rustling Blizzard's fur and making her pull her breaker a little tighter around her.

She stepped up to the glass window of the office where there were a few pictures of houses for sale or rent. The majority of the listings were for the more modest houses as you came into town, not the luxury properties that dotted the lakefront. She imagined those were more private listings that didn't get advertised. The one sign that wasn't displayed was anything stating dogs were not allowed in the building.

"Guess you're in luck," she said, looking down at her new friend. "Ready?" She wasn't sure if that was aimed at Blizzard or herself as she pushed open the door, jingling a little bell that hung above it.

The office was set up with two rows of waist-high cubicles on either side of the room with a comfortable walkway between them. It was basically one big open space and Jessie could see all the way to the back of it, where there was a large table with two copiers, a large coffee machine, stacks of paper cups, and an assortment of small snacks and crackers. Off to one side was what looked like an office, but there were no lights on inside so she couldn't make out what exactly the room was.

"Hello?"

There was a rustle of papers from the back of the room, followed by a man's voice. "Hey there." A bald head leaned out from the last cubicle and the man stood up, waving in her direction. He made his way towards her at a fast clip, hand extended.

Blizzard let out a low rumble, the hair on his back rising a bit. The man stopped, doing a double take at the sight of the large shepherd.

"Blizzard, no," Jessie said. "Be good. He's alright, just had an adventurous day." She tightened her grip on Blizzard's leash to reassure the man.

He reached up, pushing a pair of wire-rimmed glasses up on his face and then gave her another smile before offering his hand, this time moving much slower. "You must be Jessie?"

She nodded. "And you're Jordan Myer, right? It's nice to meet you in person."

He nodded. "Yes indeed. Email is great for a lot of things, but unfortunately, I can't hand you over the keys via email." He laughed at his own joke, and Jessie just nodded in agreement. "Well, come on back. Just have a couple things for you to sign and then we can get you out of here." He led the way back to the cubicle. "Can I get you anything? Coffee? Water?" He squeezed in behind the desk and offered her the seat opposite him.

She hesitated, pulling the seat out and placing it at an angle near the corner of the desk. Old habits die hard, and she wasn't comfortable having her back completely to the door. Especially since it was the only way in or out of the office that she could see. She sat down, watching as the realtor took a stack of papers out of the desk drawer and applied them next to a framed picture of himself and an attractive smiling woman.

"I understand you've signed everything with your lawyer, so no need to go over all that. But I thought you might like some of the paperwork that breaks out the utilities details and where to find the emergency water shutoff, breakers, etc. Your father had set up a management company to go by every so often and keep the place in order. You won't have to do much, maybe some light dusting here and there, but otherwise, everything is in order. And with that—" He reached into the top drawer and took out a set of keys. "I can happily turn your new home over to you. Oh, and there's a number on that top sheet to the guy who owns the property management company. If you run into anything you have questions about, feel free to call him."

"Thank you so much for doing this. I'm sorry to bring you into the office on a Saturday. I really tried to get here earlier in the week, but it just wasn't possible."

Jordan held a hand up. "Think nothing of it. Here in

Pine Haven, we go that extra mile to help our new residents."

"So I'm seeing." She stood to leave, reaching to shake the man's hand. "Oh, a couple of last things. Is there an alarm code in here?" She held out the packet of paper she had picked up. "And are these the only set of keys out there to the house?"

The man's eyebrows dipped as if she had just asked a question he didn't quite understand. "There isn't an alarm system. I'm pretty sure your aunt never had need of one. And yes, those are the only keys out there to your house." He offered her his smile again, and she nodded.

"Thank you. For everything. I'm sure I'll see you around." She gave Blizzard a nod and the two of them left the office, heading back out to the Jeep.

Opening the folder, Jessie put the address to her aunt's house – now *her* house – into her cell phone and eased the Jeep onto the road. While she had vague memories of the home, she had no idea how to get to it. That was always the wonder of traveling as a child. She was free to stare out the window and let her imagination run, not paying attention to traffic signs and road names. For her, the destination was always what mattered; not how they got there.

Jessie guided the Jeep down the winding road that followed the curve of the lake. The evening sun cast long, shadowy silhouettes of the luxury homes that dotted the lake's edge, their glassy reflections shimmering in the water. These modern testaments to affluence stood in stark contrast to her destination. Ahead, the small, modest home she remembered emerged as an enigmatic contrast to the McMansions that preceded it. The home was located near the mouth of the lake, set back quite a bit from the water's edge, and nestled among the overgrown undergrowth surrounded by towering pines. It was an area that she knew wasn't as desirable as the spots on the water that commanded the sweeping views up and down the lake.

But it was hers. For now, at least.

The stairs creaked as she made her way to the comfortable porch. The front door was painted a bright, robin's egg blue and sitting in front of it was a gift basket with a folded note attached.

She picked it up, scanning the handwritten note. "Welcome to your new home, the Pine Haven Realty Group," she said, reading the note to Blizzard. "Huh. Wonder why Jordan didn't just give it to me at the office?" She shrugged and inserted the largest key into the lock and pushed on the door.

She braced herself for a flood of memories as she stepped across the threshold, expecting them to over-whelm her senses. Only it didn't happen that way. Instead, they trickled in, more quiet whispers carried on the wind rather than thunderous explosions. They flitted around the edges of her mind, flickering in and out of focus like the fireflies she and her brother used to catch down by the river. That was a clear memory. The fear she had at keeping them in jars for fear they would suffocate.

Looking around, she realized the realtor was right. The place definitely needed some cleaning. Dust parti-cles fluttered in the stream of late day sunlight that streamed in through old lace curtains. The air was slightly musty, tinged with the faint, sweet smell of old timber.

She sat the gift basket down on the coffee table in the living room and made her way into the little kitchen. She tested the water, made sure the lights and oven were working, then turned her attention to Blizzard.

"I think I should feed you before doing anything else." The dog wagged its tail in agreement. Rummaging through the cabinets, she found a large bowl, then hauled Blizzard's food in and placed a couple of cups into the bowl. Filling a second bowl with water, she placed it next to the first and then bade the dog to come on over and eat. He attacked his food ravenously before lapping greedily at the water. Once that was done, he made his way to an area in front of the old, wood burning fireplace, circled a few times, then plopped down in contentment, eyes lazily starting to close but also remaining focused on Jessie.

"Alright, now that you're taken care of, my turn," she said. "So, before you get too comfortable, let's go."

Blizzard lifted his head, ears perking, as he got up, stretched and followed her out the door. Once outside, she walked the perimeter of the house, checking the immediate vicinity for any signs of recent activity. To one side of the house was the root cellar she remembered, and she was happy to see the doors were chained and padlocked. One of the keys on the ring she was given was probably for that, but she could explore that the following day.

The back lawn trailed gently into denser overgrowth

where the worn, wooden walkway began extending down to the floating dock at the lake's edge.

Making her way back to the front of the house, she was about to go back indoors when something caught her eye. Nearly hidden in the weeds, half under the front porch, there was half of a blue sign. She pulled it out and could see the letters 'AT' on it and the beginnings of a D where the sign had cracked. The unique shape of the sign, and the logo, belonged to an Anti Theft Deterrent; the national remote security company that was popular because of its low pricing and ease of set up.

Jessie frowned, looking at Blizzard. "I thought Jordan said Aunt Gina never had an alarm system." She shook her head, dropping the fragmented sign on the porch. "One more thing to look into tomorrow. But for now, the inside."

Moving through the house, she began to re-familiarize herself with the layout. The inviting living room was anchored by the stone, woodburning fireplace, and it flowed directly into the small, warm kitchen. A dining room and half bath completed the main living area. There was an expansive sunporch that spanned the back of the house. The back wall was almost all windows, taking in the marsh-like lake views framed by weeping willows, tall pines, and expansive oaks.

The stairs were aging but sturdy, leading to the second-floor landing that expanded to two bedrooms on one side of the house with a bath between them, and the primary suite on the other side. Between them was a comfortable and cozy seating area with a small bookcase squatting by a well-worn wingback reading chair.

Jessie checked every room, making sure the doors all closed securely, and that every window could open and shut smoothly and quickly. But most importantly, she checked every lock in the house, making note of the couple of doors where the lock didn't fully engage or had wobbly doorknobs.

Once she was satisfied that every nook and cranny in the house had been checked, she allowed herself to sit down for the first time all day. Blizzard parked himself in front of her, staring up at her with inquisitive eyes.

Jessie reached out and scratched the top of his head. "What? Just because you're paranoid, it doesn't mean people aren't talking about you." She sat up, looked around, and stretched her arms over her head. "You know what? It's time for bed. Unpacking can wait."

Trudging into the kitchen, she looked through the drawers until she found what she needed and then retired upstairs. She cracked the bedroom window to let in the cool evening air, then locked her bedroom door and placed the butcher knife she'd taken from the kitchen between the mattress and box spring, handle facing out, before falling into bed. She was only slightly aware of Blizzard climbing onto the bed and curling up at her feet before she succumbed to exhaustion and drifted off into dreamless slumber.

7

A BOATHOUSE WITH A VIEW

A Boathouse with a View

I t was the scream that woke Jessie from a dead sleep.

Her body reacted before her mind was fully engaged, and by the time the sleep cobwebs had fully been burned away, she found herself standing at the side of her bed, knife in hand, listening for any creak of a floorboard or hushed whispers that might alert her to the presence of someone inside the house.

But she was alone. Well, except for Blizzard. The shepherd was standing stiff at attention, his eyes and ears focused on the window.

That was where the scream had come from. Outside the house. Then, there it was again, this time, joined by a second voice. As she quickly pulled on a pair of jeans and her boots, her mind was already working out the logistics of what she had heard.

Two distinct voices. Both male. Both young. Probably

early teens judging from the timbre of their vocals. At least one of the voices hadn't completely dropped yet, so that told her the youngest might be prepubescent. Racing down the stairs, she grabbed her jacket as soon as she hit the landing and ran out of the house. Her subconscious had already worked out where the screams were coming from. Behind her house and to the right, down towards the lake.

She moved through the muddy marshland that bordered her property as quickly as possible, with Blizzard staying on her heels. She hadn't told him to follow but was pleasantly surprised when he did so. She was more than glad for his company, considering she had no idea what could have made two boys scream like that.

She exited the marsh onto a clearing that faced a small beachhead with an overgrown, rotting boathouse at the lake's edge. She looked up the hill that bordered the property and saw a tiny, white farmhouse sitting even farther back from the lake's edge than her own house. From the looks of the unkempt fence and property, she guessed the house to be abandoned.

Movement caught her eye at the same time Blizzard began to bark furiously. Two boys had come running from the boathouse and were racing towards her, eyes wide in panic. They skidded to a stop when they saw the large white dog planted firmly in their path, growling a warning. They nearly fell onto their backsides trying to backpedal away from the shepherd.

"Hey, it's okay," said Jessie, holding her hands up to show she meant them no harm. "He's friendly. Blizzard, good boy. Sit." The dog did as he was told and the two boys looked up, as if they were just then registering that there was a person there.

Jessie took them in with a glance. They were pale as ghosts. The youngest was probably twelve, the older maybe touching on fourteen. Slight of build and with matching tousled, sunburnt hair, Jessie took them to be brothers.

"What's going on? What happened?" she asked.

The younger of the brothers began to cry, and the older one jabbed him in the ribs with his elbow.

"Back there...it...it's..." began the older of the two. Then, he bent over, hands on knees, and emptied the contents of his stomach.

Jessie's eyes drifted to the boathouse. "You boys stay here. Do you have a phone?" The younger one nodded, trying to bite back tears. "Good. Then call 9-1-1 and tell them we need the police." She then turned and headed for the boathouse. "Blizzard. Come."

Steps from the boathouse, Jessie swept the lakefront, looking for anything that might signal the presence of someone else. She ordered Blizzard to stay where he was as she took a tentative step onto the little wooden landing strip next to the house. She wondered how the edifice itself was still standing. Its wooden frame bore the scars of countless seasons – the sun-bleached wood, warped and chipped, covered with a network of cracks like an old sailor's weathered hands. Moss and lichen clung desperately to the roof, giving the building a ragged, melancholic look. It was missing shingles, which only added to the sad, harrowed appearance of the place.

The door, if you could call it that, hung half off its

hinges – a useless, nearly rotted-out guardian too weak to keep vigil.

Inside, the silence was solemn. The space was cavernous, much bigger than she expected. The scent of damp wood, stale water, and the faint hint of diesel fuel lingered in the air. The floor was a slick mess of old, weather-worn planks, littered with rusty nails and chipped paint. The walls were splintered and covered with aged boating equipment – fraying, faded ropes, corroded hooks, and brittle life jackets. An old beat-up rowboat sat in one corner, having been hauled out of the water ages ago.

Jessie was careful as she walked around the opening that ran into the center of the boathouse, the brackish waters of the lake rustling below.

Her ears burned with the sound of flies buzzing. The smell had hit her even before she opened the door. She had tried to push it away so that it didn't blind her other senses and maybe cause her to miss some important detail. But now, as she approached the rowboat, there was no denying the stench.

It was a fetid mixture of sweet, rotten meat and spoiled eggs that hung in the air. It was the unmistakable smell of death, and Jessie steeled herself for what she would find in the little rowboat.

Whatever it is, you've seen worse.

She held her breath, bracing herself, and walked up to the boat, peeking over the side. For a second, darkness creeped into the periphery of her vision. The world spun and she closed her eyes, backing away, willing herself not to pass out.

Air.

That was what she needed. She ran from the boathouse, bursting into the open and pulled in lungfuls of the mountain air. The dizzy spell passed, and she motioned for Blizzard to follow her back up the trail to where the boys were still standing, ashen-faced.

"Is that...is it real?" asked the younger of the two.

She hesitated, unsure what to say. A glance at his older brother was no help because it looked like he wanted to ask the same question.

She took a deep breath. "Did you call 9-1-1?"

They both nodded, not taking their frightened eyes off her.

"Okay, good. That was very brave. Now, I know what you saw in there was upsetting; but I need you do something for me. Now, before you forget anything, I need you to think hard and answer this question. Did either of you touch anything in there?"

They both shook their heads, but then the younger burst into tears. "He made me do it!"

"Uh-uh!" wailed the older.

"You dared me! Said I would be forever chicken if I didn't do it!"

Jessie took a deep breath. She would forever be in awe of parents who dealt with this on a daily basis. "Boys. Focus. What happened? And what were you doing out here?"

The younger of the brothers took a breath. "We are going to be in so much trouble. Dad is going to kill us."

"No, he isn't," Jessie said. "Now tell me what

happened." There was the wail of multiple police sirens in the distance, growing closer with each breath.

"We snagged a couple of my dad's beers," said the elder in a rush. "We were just going to taste it, that's all."

Jessie frowned. "Did you touch it?"

The younger started crying again, this time nodding his head. "But only to see what was under the tarp. Jerry said to pull it off and see what was under it that smelled so bad."

Jessie's brows furrowed as she thought back. There wasn't a tarp over the body or next to it. "Where is the tarp that was covering it?"

"We...I...dropped it. Into the water. I didn't mean to, I just pulled it off and when we saw what it was, I fell back, and it fell into the water." His watery eyes fell to the ground.

Great.

"It's okay. But I want you to think hard about what the tarp looked like – the color, the feel, everything about it. And when the police get here, tell them every detail you can remember, okay? That will be a big help."

They both nodded strongly, before the older one looked up. "Are we going to jail?"

This elicited a wail of horror from the little one.

"No. No you're not. The police are going to need your help with this. And I think you need to call your parents as well."

They exchanged horrified looks and Jessie knew that they were infinitely more afraid of their father than anything they had seen in the boathouse.

The first of the police cars pulled up and Alex

climbed out. He nodded at the boys in a way that let Jessie know he not only knew them, but also had had encounters with them before. Then he turned his attention to Jessie. "Well, twice in two days."

She blushed, not quite sure how to take that. "Officer Thompson," she said, squinting in the early morning light to read his badge.

"Please. Just Alex. So," he looked around, "What's going on? We got a call from those two, but one was wailing so hysterically we couldn't make out what he was talking about. Just said to send everyone to the boathouse out by Alpine Pasture."

Jessie nodded grimly towards the water. "They found a body in the boathouse."

Alex's face dropped, his eyes scouring the scene. "You see it?"

"I did."

"Great." He clicked on the small communicator fastened to his shoulder and requested paramedics and a coroner. "Male or female?" He started to walk down the trail to the boathouse.

"Female. I think."

He stopped, half turning and giving Jessie a questioning look.

"The body doesn't have a head," she said.

8

ROOKIES TOSSING COOKIES

Rookies Tossing Cookies

Jessie stood on the trail close to the lake's edge and watched as one of the deputies exited the boathouse and promptly vomited on the trail. He bent over, staggering to make his way to the water where he then vomited a second time.

Two more officers were in and out of the little house taking photographs and wandering around the wooded area near the trail. She opened her mouth to say something, but then thought better of it. Instead, she turned her attention to the paramedics examining the two boys. They had managed to get the ambulance over the field and as close to the boys as possible. They were shining penlights into their eyes and giving them oxygen to help calm their breathing and nerves.

An old Ford pickup truck rumbled down the clearing and came to a sliding stop near the ambulance. A man and a woman jumped out, rushing towards the boys. The woman had tears in her eyes, but the man was seeing red.

Deputy Alex came out of the boat house at the same time, his face pale and sweaty, but to his credit he was holding in his breakfast. Jessie got his attention and nodded in the direction of the family chaos that was about to ensue. Alex rushed up the hill, arms raised just as the father was starting in on the boys. Jessie followed, curious as to how the officer would handle things.

"Chase!" he said, firmly enough to get the man's attention, but not so much as to startle the kids. "Not what they need right now."

The man he had called Chase was red-faced, his eyes swinging wildly from the boys to the policeman. "What the hell were they doing up here?"

Alex hesitated, hooking his thumbs into his belt. "I believe they were sneaking a little bit of your beer. All in good fun, I'm sure."

Now the red spread from the man's face to his ears as his lips pressed into a thin line. "Jesus Christ, boys. It's Sunday! And the morning. And you're chasing beer?"

Both boys trembled, and Jessie frowned. She had seen this kind of anger in men before.

"Look, Chase, the issue right here and right now is that they have been through a traumatic experience. Take them home once the paramedics clear them, get them some food, and just talk to them. I'll be by later just to check in and see if they remember anything else. Also, we have a crisis counselor on call that you can—"

"Ah, hell, Alex – they don't need none of that. Soft

enough as it is. Look at 'em; all weepy eyed over what...a body?"

"Actually, sir, they were very brave. I know grown men that couldn't stomach the sight inside that boathouse." She stepped closer, her voice remaining calm yet firm. "Their reaction is normal. It's human. I've seen soldiers – grown, trained men and women break down seeing what those two just saw. What they need now is understanding and support. Not judgement."

The big man drew back, staring at Jessie. He mumbled something under his breath as he turned away, motioning for the boys to get in the truck. His wife gathered them, offering words of compassion as the family climbed into the Ford and started backing out.

Alex stood next to Jessie as she watched the truck pull away. "That was pretty impressive, disarming Chase like that. He's mostly all bark and no bite, but he likes to think of himself as the biggest dog around."

"Well, I've known men like him. And I can tell you from experience, it's not always just bluster."

He gave her a questioning look. "What you said about trained men and women. You military?"

A tingle moved across the base of her neck. "I used to be. Retired now."

He just nodded slightly, sensing from her tone that she didn't want to get too deep into those woods. She nodded towards the boathouse and all the commotion.

"Can I say something without offending?" she asked.

"Of course. Please do."

She took a deep breath and dove in. "Your crime scene is being contaminated left and right. You got deputies in and out of the site, without booties on, one of them just threw up twice, once on the trail, and I've seen at least four officers tramping up and down the trail where the un-sub could have travelled in to bring the body. Because judging from the lack of splatter in the building, she wasn't killed there." She looked away, briefly. "Removing a head is messy business. That was done somewhere else. And where are your detectives? And the coroner?"

Alex looked at her again, this time open appreciation flooding his face. "That officer who threw up? You could say he's the department's acting detective."

Jessie couldn't hide her reaction as she swung around to face him, eyes wide. "You're shitting me."

The look on his face told her he was not. "That's the chief's nephew. He's a walking idiot, but no one would say that to the chief. In his eyes, the nephew can do no wrong."

"Well, he's doing quite a bit of wrong. How many cases does he have under his belt?"

"Counting this one?"

Jessie rolled her eyes. "Say no more."

They were interrupted by another police cruiser rolling up, and another sedan that was all black with semi-tinted windows.

"Well, looks like the chief has decided to visit this one." His voice lowered and his eyes narrowed. "And he brought company."

Jessie wanted to say more but could tell from the shift in Alex's body language that now wasn't the time to discuss matters further. To her surprise, the officer leaned in close. "Did you get a close look at that body?"

"No. As soon as I saw what it was, my first thought was to get out of there so as not to contaminate the scene and also to get those boys back in sight. You never know who might have been watching and waiting for the discovery of the body."

He nodded but didn't reply, only walked over to the two cars that had just pulled up. He greeted two men who got out of the first car, one was obviously the chief, judging from the way he was dressed and the way he carried himself. He barely acknowledged Alex as he made his way to the passenger side of the black sedan and opened the door.

A woman stepped out. She was petite, in her early fifties, with auburn hair stylishly cut short. She was dressed in a bright blue pantsuit with a white blouse. Green earring studs and a silver chain with a cross dangling from it were the only jewelry she wore. She smoothed her suit, nodded to the chief, and walked around to the front of the car. Jessie watched her shake Alex's hand before running her hand through her hair and starting down the trail towards her.

The sedan's driver side door opened and a slender man that couldn't be more than mid-twenties climbed out. He was dressed in jeans and a short-sleeved, button-up shirt. Jet black hair, pulled back in a man bun, sat piled on top of his head as he reached into the back of the car and hauled out a large camera.

"Great," Jessie muttered. "The press is here."

The female reporter stepped up and looked her up and down. "And who are you?"

Her directness startled Jessie and for a second all she could do was stand there slack-jawed. "Um, well..."

"This is Jessie Night, Mayor. She's new to town as of yesterday and she was the one who stumbled across the body," Alex interjected.

Jessie nodded. *Mayor? Interesting.*

The mayor turned to the police chief. "I thought you said a couple of kids found it?"

The chief looked flustered and turned a set of steely eyes on Alex. Jessie cleared her throat, getting his attention. "They did find it. I heard them scream and came over to see what was going on. I had the boys call 9-1-1 and went to see what had upset them so."

The chief turned his eyes on Jessie. "Came over? So, you live close by?"

She nodded. "Next lot over."

Alex interjected at that point. "Chief Walker, Jessie just inherited a place here in town and will be staying for —" he glanced over at Jessie— "A bit."

The chief scratched his head. "You mean Gina Brody's old place? That must make you her niece. She used to talk about you."

Jessie hoped she hid the look of surprise that she suddenly felt.

"What? You think I don't get to know everything I can about new people moving to my town?" Even though he stood a good foot taller than her, and outweighed her by more than her body weight, Jessie felt like he was sizing her up.

The mayor rolled her eyes and lifted a hand. "Enough of the chitchat. What's going on here?" She motioned for the man with the camera to step up, encouraging him to snap her picture. "Will, how's the light look for me?"

"You look great as always, Madame Mayor," the man replied, shooting the camera and clicking a few shots.

"That's enough," she said, striding towards the boathouse.

Jessie gave Alex an alarmed look and the officer quickly moved to block her path. Something that the mayor clearly wasn't used to as she abruptly stopped, raising one hand to her chest.

"Um, Mayor Beaumont, I don't think you should go down there. I mean, we are just now securing the scene, and...well, it's messy. You don't want to see that. And you have such nice shoes on today as well."

This brought a quick smile to the mayor's face, and Jessie cringed as the woman actually glanced down at her footwear.

"Well, if you and the chief are both standing up here, who is running the show down there?" the mayor asked.

"That would be Todd Freeman," Alex responded.

Chief Walker cleared his throat loudly. "That's Police Lead, Officer Freeman." He leaned into the man with the camera, nodding.

The cameraman drew out a small, scratchpad and started scribbling notes.

"Christ, Trent," the mayor said, rolling her eyes in the chief's direction. "You know how I feel about that boy. Barely has two brain cells to rub together and you went and made him a lead anything."

Chief Trent Walker's ruddy cheeks deepened in color, and he shot Alex a nasty look. But he also kept his mouth shut.

"Fine. Tell me what's in there," the mayor said.

"From what we can tell, the victim is a female of yet-to-be-determined age. Her body was found..." He hesitated, looking at the photographer eagerly waiting, pencil poised over his notepad.

Mayor Beaumont turned to the photographer and gave a subtle shake of her head. Without hesitation, he closed the notepad and stuffed it back into his pocket. Once that was done, the mayor nodded for Alex to continue.

"The victim has been decapitated. And there's no sign of the head," Alex continued.

Jessie watched the mayor closely. The woman's face blanched a little, but she quickly regained control of herself, tugging at the waistline of her jacket. "I see." She turned to the photographer. "Will, this does not get printed. Until we know what the coroner has to say, this is a blackout." She turned to Alex. "I want those boys who found the body to understand that if they so much as breathe a word to a single living soul about what they saw, I will cancel their Little League team day so fast it will make their—" She caught herself and stopped. "Do I make myself clear?"

"Yes, ma'am," Alex answered, as the mayor turned, heading back towards her car and motioning for Will the photographer to follow.

"And I want a full briefing on this first thing

tomorrow morning," she called out, not bothering to turn around.

"Hey, what should I do?" said Chief Walker, hurrying up the hill.

The mayor stopped, turning to him. "Your job, Trent. Your job. And keep that numbskull nephew of yours in check."

As the chief escorted the mayor, Jessie turned to Alex.

"Well, that was tense," she said.

"Going to get a whole lot worse. Look, this is beyond me, but I just got a call that the coroner is finally on his way. Had to come from the next county over. If you're up for it, I'd like a second set of eyes on the body when he gets here."

Jessie remembered what he had whispered to her and gave him a puzzled look. "What did you see?"

He was starting to break out in a sweat under the rising sun and raised a forearm to mop at his brow. "I might be wrong, but it looked to me like that poor woman's arms and legs were turned around backwards."

9

MADE UP TITLES

Made up Titles

The sun was hanging low on the horizon as Jessie stepped lightly over the dewy grass, her eyes fixed on the ominous boathouse. Alex trudged next to her, his heavy footfalls breaking the silence between them.

"So, what's the deal with your mayor? Was it my imagination or was there a little tension between the chief and her?" Jessie finally asked.

Alex sighed. "No, not your imagination. Those two tend to butt heads on occasion. If you believe the rumor mill, there was once something between them, many, many years ago. Ended badly from what I heard, and the chief has never gotten over it. The night Maggie – Margaret – got elected mayor, I heard the chief went on one helluva bender."

Jessie nodded along as he spoke. She could see that developing. The way Chief Walker tried to carry himself, the tone he used – all of it spoke to a man that didn't like not getting his way. And to suddenly have someone who spurned him become his new boss...well, that was a recipe for disaster.

"And the camera guy?" she asked.

"Will Mason. He's the mayor's press secretary and personal photographer. He's also the editor and reporter of the Pine Haven Crier. The town paper."

Jessie gave him a buzzed look.

Alex laughed lightly. "Small town. People wear multiple hats around here. Mason's mom died of breast cancer a couple years back. Maggie kind of took him under her wing, made sure he had everything he needed. He has a fancy degree in journalism, but opted to stay in town, taking over the paper after the old editor-slash-reporter quit."

Jessie bent down, examining an area of the trail not far from the boathouse.

"Find something?" Alex asked.

"No. The problem is, we don't know how long the body's been out here. We don't know if we are looking for fresh forensics that the killer could have left, or if it was so long ago that everything could have been washed away by now. When was the last time it rained here?"

"Three nights ago. Just prior to your arrival in town."

"Figures. If the body was brought in before then, there's a good chance any forensic evidence could be lost. Did your team recover the tarp the boys said fell into the water?"

"Sure did. It was snagged on one of the support posts under the house. It's been bagged and tagged." He watched as Jessie stood, hands on her hips as she looked out over the water. He could practically see the wheels turning in her mind. "You're thinking what if the killer brought the body in by boat."

"Honestly, it would make the most sense." She walked towards the lake's edge. "The view is almost completely obstructed here from any of the lake homes. I mean, I'm right next door, and unless I was standing out on my dock, I wouldn't have seen anything."

"Can I ask you something?" She nodded her encouragement. "Why do you know so much about all of this?"

"I watch a lot of *Law and Order*." She offered him a half smile. "Sorry. I'm not very good at humor. I am – or rather I was – a military investigator. So, I made my living by doing exactly what we are doing now. Looking at crimes, finding motives, finding criminal activity that was hidden, and bringing people to justice."

Alex pursed his lips in admiration. "Well, that explains how you were able to put Chase in his place back there without making it too obvious. It's funny, you're not what I would expect a military investigator to look like."

Jessie arched a single eyebrow. "Oh really?"

A deep blush spread over Alex's face as his eyes dropped to the tops of his shoes. "Oh...well...that's not what I meant... I mean...you're so young."

"Ha." Jessie threw her head back. "Good recovery. I happen to be older than I look. We're just able to retire a lot earlier in the military than in the private sector." She wanted to remark that he looked too young to be a police officer, but she thought better of that.

"I can't imagine being able to retire. I've been at this for six years now. Retirement seems so far away."

Jessie clamped her lips tight. Had this man just read her mind?

"So, have you seen this before? Headless bodies, I mean."

"Unfortunately, I have. I've built cases against military personnel that have committed some pretty heinous crimes." Memories, unbidden and raw, rattled their cages in her mind. Despite the heat, she felt a chill creep up her spine. "Tell me about Todd. You say he's a Police Lead? I've never heard of that title."

"It's because it's made up. He's not really a detective. Or a lead. He's second year out of the academy. Chief Walker doesn't have any children of his own, so he dotes on Todd as a replacement. Chief's sister was on him to give Todd enough of a raise to get him out of the house. The only way the Chief could do it was a promotion." He sighed, shaking his head slowly. "He decided the department needed a Police Lead on the payroll. So, there you go. Closest thing we have to a detective." He cracked a smile at her. "Welcome to Smallville."

"Wait, you've never had a detective?" Jessie asked incredulously.

Alex lifted his shoulders. "There's never been a need. I mean, we have the occasional drunk driver, or someone taking a neighbor's bike or something like that. Minor crimes that typically solve themselves. During peak tourism season we might see a little more action, but we've never had anything like...that." He indicated the boathouse.

Jessie didn't respond, trying to hide her amazement. This might be a sleepy town, but in her experience, those were the ones that had the deepest, darkest secrets. Plus, it was still a tourist's destination. The lake attracted people from all over the western Carolina range. In the height of summer, the population could almost double.

"Todd is way over his head on this one," said Jessie. "No offense, but this town has a serious problem that just announced itself."

They reached the entrance of the boathouse just as Dr. Jefferson Lindquist, a portly man with tortoise-shell-rimmed glasses, thinning white hair, and wearing a black windbreaker stepped out. His hands trembled slightly as he removed his glasses, wiping the lenses with a cloth from his pocket. When he arrived, he had ordered everyone out of the boathouse, including Jessie and Alex, as he began his initial investigation.

"Doc? You okay?" said Alex.

The man gave him a quizzical look. "What? Of course I'm not okay. Who the hell would be okay after seeing something like that? You know, people think that because I work around death all the time, I must be made of stone, or gotten so 'used to it'" – the last part he put in air quotes. "Well, the truth is, I'm as human as the next person, and that shit in there disgusts me." He closed his eyes, taking a couple of deep breaths and exhaling loudly. When he opened his eyes, he seemed to have regained his focus. "I'm sorry, Alex. I didn't mean to go off on you. It's just – it's not death that upsets me. That's a normal process, a result of living. It's nature in action. But that in there? That's not nature at work. That's the results of a very sick person."

"So, we're dealing with a murder," Alex said. Immediately he realized what he said when he saw the look the medical examiner gave him.

"Well, her head didn't just happen to fall off," said Dr. Lindquist. "Sorry. Lord, I want a cigarette. I should have never quit smoking."

"Any way of identifying her?" asked Alex.

The examiner shook his head. "Not yet. I'll need to get back to the office to try that. From what I can tell, she's in good shape, probably in her mid-thirties, but again that's hard to pinpoint here in the field. Also, no identifying scars or tattoos that I could make out."

"What about fingerprints? Maybe we could get a hit on her from those," Alex offered.

He shook his head. "Her fingerprints were seared off by an incredibly high heat source. So, no luck there."

"What could you tell about how the head was removed?" asked Alex. "Was it a clean blow, like an axe or guillotine would produce?"

"No. The blade that was used to remove it was serrated," the doctor replied.

"Like a saw?" asked Alex.

"Exactly," said Dr. Lindquist.

"Well, she definitely wasn't killed here or the immediate vicinity," said Jessie. "Okay, what about the limbs?"

Dr. Lindquist blew out sharply. "That was the most disturbing part. They were rotated around backwards. Her joints, and I mean all of them – shoulders, elbows, hips, knees and ankles, were broken, and then her limbs twisted around. I won't be able to tell if that was done pre or post-mortem until I get her back to the office."

"Can you establish a time of death?" asked Jessie.

"Initially I estimated the time of death to be around twenty-four to thirty-two hours. But...I need to do some deeper tests to make certain of that. Look, I know this isn't what you wanted to hear, but with a case like this, there is a lot to be done from a post-mortem aspect. I'm sorry I can't be of more help right now."

"Doc, you've done everything you can for us right now. And that's all we could ask of you," said Alex.

"You've actually told us a lot," said Jessie. The two men turned their attention her way as she continued. "We know that our killer is familiar with the area. Contrary to what they show on television and movies, dead bodies are very heavy and hard to move. Yet the unsub knew enough about the town to get it from one place to here unseen. We also know that this was premeditated."

"How so?" said Alex.

"He removed the fingerprints. And by removing the head, he made sure that we couldn't use dental records. That means he knew what he was doing and was prepared for the kill. This took time to do to someone. That means he worked someplace relatively isolated." Her eyes drifted back to the interior of the boat house. "And also, we know that whoever did this is physically very strong. Dr. Lindquist, do you have any idea how the joints were broken?"

"Extreme physical force is all I can say right now. I'll know more later."

Alex looked around. "Where the hell is Todd Freeman?"

"The other police officer?" asked Dr. Lindquist. "He left a while ago. Said he had to write this up and prep the chief with preliminary findings. I told him I'd give him a call as soon as I learned more. And don't worry. This jumps to the top of my heap. I'll pull an all-nighter and have some more answers for you tomorrow."

Jesse was nodding before turning to Alex. "You have a very serious problem on your hands here, Alex. There is a madman loose in Pine Haven. And anyone that does this to another human being has killed before and will most definitely kill again."

10

OSSO BUCO AND ALE

Osso Buco and Ale

Alex walked Jessie back to her house just as the sun was starting to drop out of view. They didn't speak, each wrapped in their own thoughts as the sun began to disappear. Molten golds and burnished coppers spilled across the tranquil surface of the lake. The only sounds were those of the scurrying woodland creatures and the snap of twigs under Blizzard's paws as he padded along beside them.

Back at her house, she made her way up to the porch and turned to say goodnight to Alex. "I'm not sure what the proper etiquette is here. I mean, saying thank you for the day seems so...wrong."

Alex laughed, trying to hide his smile. "Hey, have you eaten?" He pinched the bridge of his nose. "What am I saying, of course you haven't. Cos you've been with me all day. I guess, what I'm saying is would you like to grab a bite? It's too late to worry about cooking something. At least for me it is."

Jessie considered his words, weighing things in her mind that he couldn't see.

Alex held up a hand. "Only in a professional capacity, I mean. I'd like to hear more of your thoughts on what we're up against. Also, I gotta admit, being able to pick the brain of a military investigator is more than a little appealing."

Jessie stood there, her head ticking back and forth as she made a show of debating what to do. Staying in was the smarter choice. She wasn't yet up to mingling with the community. But she also had planned to go food shopping today and that had not happened for obvious reasons. All she really had in the house was the contents of the welcome basket she had received, and to be honest, a meal of crackers, hard salamis and warm white wine wasn't the most appealing.

"Sure. Sounds good," she answered. "Come in while I feed Blizzard. Then we can head out."

Alex watched as she retreated into the house before following up the steps, closing the door tightly behind him.

"I KNOW it's not a fancy five-star French bistro, but it's the best we got here in town."

Nestled in the heart of Pine Haven, Alex brought Jessie to a charming establishment known as 'The Haven's Hearth.'

Despite its rustic, timber-framed exterior that blended seamlessly with the surrounding pine trees, it was obviously an unexpected gem in the Pine Haven establishments.

An inviting warmth radiated from both the wood-burning stove nestled in the corner and the effusive hospitality of the staff. Golden light spilled from wrought-iron chandeliers hanging overhead, illuminating the polished wooden floors and the array of snug booths lining the walls. Each booth was separated by a low partition, offering both privacy and the comforting hum of ambient conversation.

The center of the restaurant was made up of rich, dark wood tables, covered in contrasting white tablecloths, lending an air of refinement to the otherwise cozy ambiance. Charming features such as exposed timber beams and a lovingly maintained antique counter gave the space an air of nostalgic charm. Yet, tasteful modern touches – the art hanging on the walls, the crisp linens, and the sparkling glassware – elevated it to a level of sophistication that was more akin to an upscale eatery one might find in any major city.

Walking in, they were greeted by the hostess. A young woman named Sandy whose bright smile went up a few megawatts when she looked up and saw Alex. That same smile dimmed considerably when he asked for a booth for two, indicating that Jessie would be joining him.

"Of course," came the curt reply, followed by clipped steps to one of the booths hugging the wall. "Your waitress will be right with you." She turned without waiting for a reply and clipped her way back to the welcoming station.

"What was that about?" asked Jessie, sliding into the seat facing the door.

Alex gave her a puzzled look.

"That hostess. She went from hot to subzero in record time."

"Oh that," he said, brushing it off. "That's just Sandy. We went on a quasi-date once. It was terrible, and I told her that I thought we would be better staying friends. She was fine with that, I thought. But who knows?" He shrugged, offering Jessie an easy smile.

It was a good thing they were keeping this on a professional level. There was certainly something very easy-going about Alex, and that smile he had a habit of flashing only added to his charm. But seeing Sandy, and her statuesque physique, reminded Jessie that she had way more miles on her than these newer models rolling out.

"So, what's good here?" she asked, opening the leather-bound menu.

"Honestly, you're not going to go wrong with whatever you order. Everything is fresh and locally sourced," said Alex, perusing his menu.

The restaurant's food was an exquisite blend of local favorites and inventive cuisine. Everything indeed sourced from local farmers and fishermen to ensure unparalleled freshness. The aroma of delicious food – fresh caught fish, hearty stews, or their famous pine nut pie – wafted enticingly from the kitchen, a testament to the talent of the chefs. A tasteful bar area off to one side offering an impressive selection of local wines and craft beers, caught Jessie's attention.

Alex followed her eyes to the bar. "Would you like a bottle of wine?"

She shook her head. "Thanks, but no thanks. But I won't say no to a really nice beer."

"Now you're talking. May I suggest a Gaelic Ale? It's local and amazing."

They finished going over the menu in silence, as a waitress brought them water and asked if they needed more time to make a selection.

"I'm good," Jessie said, looking at Alex. When he nodded, she proceeded to order the pork Osso Buco, and Alex had the wild striped bass.

"Oh, and two Gaelic Ales," he added, before the waitress could walk away. "Well. Here we are." His tone was a bit awkward but engaging. "What should we talk about?"

"The case," Jessie replied, watching as he picked at the corners of his napkin, folding and then unfolding it before finally placing it on his lap.

"Oh, yeah, of course," he replied. "But first, what made you join the military? What kind of training and background does a military investigator need?"

She regarded him for a moment as she took a sip of water. Everything about his body language told her he was nervous. If talking about her experience either reassured him or calmed him, then he would probably retain more information once they began to discuss the case. Still, now it was her turn to fidget a little. Talking about herself wasn't something she did with others. But she wasn't in the military anymore. She needed to become more comfortable in her civilian life.

And that meant learning how to speak to civilians.

She cleared her throat. "Well, I come from a military family. My father was a high-ranking colonel in the army. He was career, so the fact that me and my brother both ended up enlisting was almost a foregone conclusion in the family."

"You have a brother? Older or younger?"

She stared at him for a second, reminding herself that he probably wasn't interrupting her, but rather was taking an interest in what she was saying. "Yes. Brody. He's two years younger than me. But he was also the rebel. Instead of joining the Army, he enlisted in the marines."

"And where is he now?"

"The Middle East, I believe. He went into MARSOC – the Marine Special Operations Command – they're special forces. So now he gets deployed all over the world doing...whatever Uncle Sam tells him to do. After going through basic training, I opted for the Military Police. My CO was a hard ass, but he was also impressed by my attention to detail and my stubbornness. Two qualities that he said were hallmarks of a good military investigator. So that was the direction I went. And I found that I had a knack for investigating and maintaining law and order in the military community." She took another sip of water and gave Alex a shrug. "So, I put my time in, and well, now here I am."

She tried to make it sound as complete as possible. There were things she wasn't ready to talk about. Certainly not to a police officer. And since when did she open up like this to anyone? Especially someone she had only met under a couple of less-than-ideal occasions.

"And your father? Is he still back west?"

She felt a hitch in her breathing and her stomach dropped. "No. He...he passed away not long ago. I'm kind of starting over out here." She could see the look forming on his face. One that said he was about to throw a pity-party in her honor, and that was the last thing she wanted. "Now, what about you? What drove you into law enforcement?" she asked.

The waitress arrived with their beers, telling them their food would be out shortly.

"Perfect timing." Alex took a deep breath, pushing himself back into the worn leather backrest of the booth. "I wish I could say something altruistic drove me to my profession – a desire to help the community, or following in my father's footsteps – but it was nothing like that in my case. My parents died when I was very young. We were out camping up the mountain a ways, and it started raining. My dad said it would be okay and we stayed. Then it really started raining, and before we knew it, there was a flash flood. I just remember hearing what sounded like a freight train running towards us in the middle of the night. When the water hit us, our tent was swept up. My mom disappeared almost immediately, and my dad grabbed me and somehow managed to get the life vest on me from the fishing gear before that all vanished. He held onto me as long as he could, but there was just no way. We were tossed around in the water, and I remember hitting something, a rock, or a tree stump maybe. That was it. The next thing I knew, I was being fished out in the morning by search and rescue. They never found my parents' bodies." His voice grew low, and his eyes were focused on something Jessie couldn't see. Something she was glad she couldn't see.

"My God, Alex...I am so sorry," she said.

His focus returned and he offered her that charming smile again. "Thanks. It's okay. Happened a long time ago. But my grandmother took me in so that I didn't end up in the system. Growing up, I had a bit of a rebellious streak in me." He chuckled lightly. "I don't know how my Gram put up with me. I had my issues – nothing major, but some underage drinking, a misdemeanor trespassing charge – but those, combined with my bad grades, meant that I really didn't have a shot at getting into college. And this being the mountains of North Carolina, my options were limited. About that time, we had a break-in at the house. Just some kids causing trouble and looking for quick cash. They thought the house was empty and took off when they realized Gram was there. But it scared her so bad she had a heart attack." His eyes grew misty as he sipped on his beer. "She hung on for another year, but then passed. That was a wakeup call for me. So, I went into the academy. Chief Walker gave me a job, and well... here I am."

He held up his glass and Jessie clinked hers against it.

Dinner arrived and they both gazed longingly at the presentation before them. The rest of the evening was spent enjoying food, more beers, and a shared laugh or two. Jessie knew they should have discussed the body, but she was reluctant to bring it up. It had been far too long since she just sat and enjoyed the company of another. Turned out, she didn't need to bring it up.

Alex did.

"Thank you. I know we were supposed to talk about... what you found in that boathouse – and we will – but I think I need to ease into it." He glanced down at his empty plate as he folded his napkin and placed it next to it.

"I understand. In my time, I've seen some things that I hoped to never see again." She leaned forward, dropping her voice to a whisper. "But I have to tell you; what we saw today is right up there."

He swallowed hard. "I'm scared, Jessie. Not of a killer or what it's going to take to find this maniac. I'm afraid that there are two victims today. That poor woman out there, and this town. Something tells me, Pine Haven is never going to be the same again. Or maybe it's me that won't be the same again."

Jessie stared at the officer. He was right. As someone that had looked evil in the eye, she knew it changed you. He wouldn't be the same. All she could hope was that he was strong enough for what was to come. Hunting killers wasn't for the faint of heart. Whoever had done that to the woman in the boathouse, had set up shop in Pine Haven.

She shouldn't get involved. But she also knew the man sitting across from her wasn't prepared for the storm that was coming. It was time.

Time for her to dust off skills she had hoped to never need again.

11

ALL KINDS OF FUN

All Kinds Of Fun

There were so many things he was good at, but one skill in particular had become indispensable for him in this town.

It was invisibility.

Not literally of course. Rather, it was his ability to not be noticed by those around him. Years spent lying perfectly still in fields, waiting for the right moment when his target would appear in order to squeeze off the perfect kill shot. Walking through hostile village after village and sitting unseen by locals as he eavesdropped on conversations. It all served him well in this little Pine Haven.

Never more so than now as he watched her from a distance. She had caught his attention the moment she entered town. Everything about her intrigued him. The way she moved spoke to the training she had undergone. The strange tics she sometimes experienced told him she wasn't truly comfortable in her body, and he was determined to find a way to exploit that. The way she seemed just a bit ill at ease around the townsfolk told him that she probably wouldn't be around for long, so he would have to move fast if he wanted her.

The dog surprised him. He wasn't expecting that. Dogs, especially German Shepherds, could prove unpredictable in their actions once they bonded with a human. But this dog wasn't hers. That meant the bond hadn't formed yet. Still, he'd have to rethink his strategy now.

Not a problem. He liked a challenge.

He had already been through her house, her things. Found her weapons stashed around the rooms. The knife beneath the mattress was a surprise. Why wouldn't someone like her have a gun? Unless she did have one and he hadn't yet found it.

His mind drifted as he watched her standing there, and his eyes lost their focus for a moment, combing the ground where she stood. That break in attention nearly got him caught. He was so still he hadn't noticed a large doe foraging just to his left. More importantly, the doe hadn't noticed him. The cracking of the branches caused the woman's eyes to sweep in his direction.

Her intuition was sharper than he expected. He didn't move, not wanting to alert her even more to his presence. The slight breeze placed him downwind of the dog, and for that he was grateful. He waited until the tension seemed to leave her body and they moved on, heading back to the house. He followed at a distance, a part of the woods that detached itself and moved with the shadows behind her, trailing her home. Even after the door locked behind her, and the house grew still, he waited for a full hour before shrinking from the edge of the woods.

He melted into the shadows, careful to leave no footprints that she would be able to track if she ventured to where he had been crouching.

This was going to be interesting. Bringing her into this would liven up the dullness that had crept into him lately. His employers might not like it. But screw them. Their check had already cleared, so now he was free to have some fun.

And this one looked to be all kinds of fun.

12

A LUCKY BREAK

A Lucky Break

I t wasn't the first rays of sunlight breaking through the wooden shutters that woke Jessie. It was the call of the birds in the trees outside her bedroom. Sleeping with the window cracked had let the cool night air in, but it also let in the shrill chirping of Robins, Bluebirds and Carolina Wrens, among others.

How the hell do animals so small make such loud noises?

She was buried under a large comforter, the weight of which kept her body heat trapped. The chill in the bedroom, coupled with the warmth of the blanket, created a perfect cocoon for sleeping. She felt something cold and wet pushing against her neck and turned over to see the large white shepherd nuzzling her awake, his tail fanning furiously.

"Okay, okay, I'm awake." She lazily reached out and scratched at his head. "I'm betting you need to go out. Then some breakfast for you." She sat up, swinging her feet over the edge of the bed and into her waiting slippers. "Then, my friend, you and I are going for a run."

They made their way downstairs, where Blizzard attacked his food bowl as soon as she sat it down for him. Watching him eat, she felt guilty about not asking how Mr. Thompson was doing. Alex had said he would check in on him, but he didn't mention if there was any change in the old man's condition. She made a mental note to find out, just as Blizzard finished licking the inside of his bowl.

After throwing on some joggers and a tee shirt, she grabbed Blizzard's leash and the two of them headed out. She needed to move, to stretch her muscles and push her body. To say that the past couple of months had been stressful was an understatement.

The scenery around her blurred by as she ran along a trail that hugged the lake. She passed the occasional fellow jogger, and there were a few kayaks out on the water, but for the most part it was peaceful and serene. The sound of the water, the breeze ruffling the treetops, all of it was just what she needed to take her mind off everything that happened and led to her leaving Colorado and moving to the other side of the country.

She did let her mind drift back to the scene at the boathouse. As disturbing as it was, she preferred that to where her mind really wanted to go.

She replayed the scene over in her mind. There was something she was missing. She just couldn't quite put her finger on it. The sound of a twig snapping caused her to stop in her tracks. She stood still, looking in the direction of the disturbance. The undergrowth off the trail was so thick she couldn't see very far into the woodlands around her. Other than the chirping birds, the forest was quiet. But whatever had caused that snapping was big and heavy.

She glanced down at Blizzard and saw that he was trained on the same area she was. They listened for a moment more but heard nothing else.

"Come on, boy. Probably a deer." Still, she knew that she would now be hyper focused on her run back to the house. But having a hundred pounds of fang and claw running at her side did make her feel a little better.

Just as they reached the house, her arm buzzed. She pulled her cell phone out of its holder and looked at the screen. It was Alex. Dr. Lindquist had found something of interest. She hurriedly typed a reply, asking Alex to send her the address of the medical examiner's office and she would meet him there.

She picked up the pace as she headed back to the house. Upstairs, she showered and changed quickly, before heading for the door. She stopped and stared at Blizzard, trying to remember how long a dog could remain inside before needing a potty break. She sighed, looking at the location of the medical examiner's office on her phone. "I think you better come with me. I might end up being gone longer than I think."

It was a forty-five-minute drive to the coroner's office, located in the next county over from Pine Haven. The drive took her through some winding passes away from the lake and higher into the mountainous terrain. Finally, the GPS told her she was approaching her destination and she took a deep breath, steeling herself for whatever might have been found.

The medical examiner's office was a standalone building that had once been a classic brick and mortar warehouse, now renovated to serve its somber purpose. From the outside, the building retained a certain utilitarian charm. Brick walls, painted a clean, crisp white, rose three stories high. A small sign, polished stainless-steel letters spelling out 'County Medical Examiner,' hung above the broad entrance. The pavement around the building was well-maintained, its tar surface soaking up the warmth of the sun. Large, verdant trees lined the building, their leaves rustled softly and created an almost deceptive backdrop to the grim work done within.

Jessie eased her Jeep to a stop next to Alex's patrol car. She looked around but didn't see the officer, so climbed out, attached Blizzard's leash, and headed for the entrance. Alex stepped out of the sliding doors, greeting her as she approached.

"Jessie," he nodded. Then bent down to ruffle the fur on top of Blizzard's head. "Thanks for coming. I figured you might want to hear what the doc has to say." He started back into the building but turned to face her. "Oh, and uh, Todd is here as well. The doc called both of us."

"Well, he is running the show. I'll keep quiet and stay in the background." She resisted the urge to have her fingers crossed behind her back when she said it. This wasn't her case. The more she thought about it, the more she should probably just mind her own business.

But she followed Alex into the office building, nonetheless.

Inside, the building was a study in efficient minimalism. The reception area was immaculate, with neutral beige walls devoid of any decorations, save for a couple of framed qualifications and licenses. The sterility of the space was echoed in the bright, overhead, fluorescent lighting. There was a desk in the reception area, with an attractive woman in her early twenties sitting there, typing furiously. Behind her, a wall of two-way mirrors hinted at the office spaces beyond.

"We're ready to go back," said Alex to the woman.

"The dog can't go in. Health codes," she said, eying Blizzard.

Jessie hesitated, but then wrapped Blizzard's leash around the arm of one of the chairs in the reception area. "Could you maybe just keep an eye on him?"

She smiled but didn't speak. Slipping her hand under the desk she depressed a button, creating an audible buzz and the metallic pop of locks receding.

Alex motioned for Jessie to follow him and together they passed through the doors into a chilly, open space that led to a bank of doors. Jessie could hear the distant hum of refrigeration units as they walked past, making their way to the final door at the end of the space. After pushing through, they found themselves in an antechamber where shoe covers, masks and yellow paper gowns hung on a wall.

Jessie knew the drill and began pulling everything on before they made their way into the examination room. The space was a study in function over comfort. An overhead surgical light cast an intense white glow on the polished steel autopsy table at the center of the room, causing it to give off a near-blinding sheen. Around this central island, the room spread out in an ordered array of machinery and medical instruments. Cabinets lined one wall, their glass fronts revealing neatly stacked and meticulously labeled supplies.

The room was significantly colder than any other place they had entered, and Jessie could feel the bite from the high intensity, commercial air conditioning units. It penetrated her light clothing and brought goosebumps to her flesh.

Standing at the table was Dr. Lindquist, dressed in a green surgical gown, mask, and gloves, he offered a solemn nod in Jessie and Alex's direction. Next to him stood Todd Freeman, looking a little green around the edges as he tried desperately not to look at the body displayed on the cold, surgical table.

"Hey, doc," Alex said. "What have you got for us?"

"Yes, Dr. Lindquist. What have you been able to find out?" echoed Todd, quickly. He fumbled around and removed a small notebook from his pocket and began to take notes, focusing solely on his paper.

"Well, as you can see, I have not finished the autopsy, but I did find a couple of crucial pieces of forensic evidence that I thought you should know about."

Alex moved closer, staring down at the body. Staples in the form of a 'Y' showed where the coroner had opened the body to remove and examine the organs.

"Going by the internal organs, I'd say the victim is in her mid to late thirties and was in very good physical shape. Muscle tone is healthy and there are no signs of disease present in any of the organs. I was trying to establish a definitive time of death and found something interesting." He rolled the body up onto one side so that they could see her backside. There were several small patches of purplish marks on the skin. They were surrounded by areas of bluish-white, and the skin where they appeared seemed to be of a different consistency; almost wax-like.

"Looks like bruises," said Todd, looking away quickly. "Probably where the victim fell backwards. Or was dragged or something."

Dr. Lindquist pursed his lips before continuing, trying to contain any annoyance he might have felt. "Yes, that is a possibility. However, in this case, those aren't bruises. It's frostbite."

Todd looked up from his notes. "It's not winter. How could she have frostbite?"

Jessie was staring at the body, her voice little more than a whisper. "He kept the body on ice."

Dr. Lindquist gave her an appreciative smile. "I believe so."

Alex opened his mouth to speak but was cut off by Todd.

"Was that to keep the body from stinking?" the young man asked.

Jessie and Alex exchanged looks before encouraging the medical examiner to continue.

"No. I believe our killer did this to delay decomposition, in order to throw off how long the victim has been dead. Now that I have seen this, there are other tests I can perform that will tell me when she died, but it will take a little longer than normal."

"This is a big help, doc," said Alex. "It tells us a bit more about our killer."

Jessie was nodding, still staring at the body. "What about the joints? Any further details as to how that was done?"

The doctor held up a finger. "If I had to guess I would say it was done by hand."

"Christ," said Alex. "Whoever did this must be built like a tank. Definitely someone who would stand out in a crowd."

Jessie didn't speak, pressing her lips into a thin line. The color was starting to drain from her features, but she shook her head at Alex when he gave her a questioning look.

"Oh, but all of that is not the big news," said Dr. Lindquist. "I think I may have a way of identifying her. At least until the head shows up." He turned and made his way to a computer that sat against the wall behind the exam table. He scrolled through some images, finally bringing up some digital X-rays. "I was about to give up hope on making an identification when I came across this." He pointed to the image. It was of the victim's lower leg. The opaque white of the bones was interrupted by something on her ankle that the X-rays could not penetrate.

"She's broken her ankle and had a pin placed," said Jessie.

"Yes, indeed," replied the doctor. "I thought it was strange upon initial inspection that this was the only joint on both legs that hadn't been manipulated by her attacker."

"And that helps how?" asked Todd.

Everyone ignored him as the doctor continued speaking. "Surgical implants such as pins, screws, rods, and plates usually have markings on them that serve as identifiers. Those markings can include serial numbers, batch numbers, or the manufacturer's name. These identifiers are important for tracking and quality control purposes and can provide useful information in a variety of situations, such as recall of a particular batch of devices, research, or legal cases."

"Or murder," said Jessie.

"I have already reached out to the manufacturer to start the ball rolling. Hopefully, they can tell me where the implant was installed, and from there – with the police department's help – I should be able to find the surgeon who put it in and identify our Jane Doe."

Alex reached out and gave the doctor an appreciative clap on the back. "Excellent work, doc. As soon as you hear something, you call...us. All of us."

Todd had his phone in hand and was reading the screen. "In the meantime, the chief and the mayor are back in his office. They want an update. Now."

Alex shook his head as they followed Todd out of the building. He gave Jessie one last questioning look, but she kept her eyes glued straight ahead.

She was in her own world as she picked up Blizzard and headed for the Jeep. The more she was learning about this case, the more uneasy she was feeling. Why did she have the sneaking suspicion that identifying who the victim was would bring them no closer to catching this killer than they were?

13

A PROFILE AND AN INVITE

A Profile and an Invite

Once back at the police station, a single story, square brick building on the backside of Main Street, Jessie sat in the waiting area as a burly, balding, police officer sat behind the sign-in desk reading a folded magazine. He would occasionally look up, his eyes moving from Jessie to the white shepherd at her side, then back to his magazine. It was eerily quiet inside the department, and Jessie imagined this was what it was like most of the time. Even though it was tourist season, there wasn't much trouble for people to get into in a town like Pine Haven.

Other than murder, that is.

She could hear voices coming from somewhere behind the reception area, the loudest of them being that of the chief. Leaning over to Blizzard, she whispered. "Wonder who that's about."

Finally, Alex appeared at the reception desk and

motioned her back. "Sorry about that. The chief was concerned that you might leak something to the public. Since you're not a member of the department."

Jessie looked around his shoulder at the small conference room where he had been standing. Inside was the chief, his nephew, Mayor Beaumont, and her photographer slash reporter, Will Mason. "There's literally a member of the press in there with them."

Alex could only shrug in response. "Come on. Todd is about to present his findings."

Together, they squeezed into the small space that consisted of a desk at the front of the room, a large white board behind it, and an arrangement of chairs scattered around for attendees to sit. The mayor and her reporter were seated in the very front, only a few feet from Todd, who stood alongside the chief behind the desk, facing the room.

"Okay, now that we are all here, let's get down to it," said the chief. He gave a nod to his nephew and then moved to have a seat close to the mayor. Jessie didn't miss the fact that he didn't even glance her way.

Todd cleared his throat and looked nervously around the room. The mayor was sitting with one leg crossed over the other, her support knee anxiously bouncing away. "Well, we all know, there was an incident at the boathouse yesterday. A couple of kids found a dead body."

On the outside, Jessie remained calm and collected, while her insides were reacting as if he were scratching his nails across a chalk board. She knew better than to glance Alex's way but sensed that he was feeling it too.

"The deceased is a female who previously was in relatively good shape. Our coroner, Dr. Lindquist, has not been able to determine a time of death because the killer applied ice to the body. So, without the head or the fingerprints, we are waiting for the coroner to identify some, um, surgical implants. Then once we know who the victim is, we will proceed to finding our killer."

Jessie bit the inside of her cheek as she watched Todd wrap up his presentation. She had to remind herself she was a guest in their house. One that the Chief of Police already didn't like for some reason, and speaking out of turn wouldn't win him over to her side. So, she stood there, in the back of the room, fists clenched till she feared her nails would puncture her palms.

Chief Walker cleared his throat loudly. "Excellent work, Todd. Thank you for taking the lead on this."

The mayor frowned, looking around. "What? That's it? How exactly do you plan to 'proceed to finding our killer"? Did I miss something, because this literally told me nothing about what's going on in my town. Christ, I should have called in the FBI or at least reached out to the police department in Chicory. At least they have some real detectives on their roster."

By the time she finished speaking her face was fiery red and there was a tiny vein running down the side of her neck that pulsed with each breath.

"Now, Maggie – Mayor Beaumont, we can handle this," said Chief Walker. "This is Todd's first case, after all, so he deserves the chance to prove himself."

"Oh bullshit," she replied. "This isn't a missing cat or some *Nancy Drew* mystery." She looked over at Jessie.

"Hell, right now I'd settle for *Nancy Drew*. We have a mutilated woman, who may or may not be part of our community, and the son-of-a-bitch who did it is walking around laughing at us. I don't give a good goddamn what Todd deserves. The only person that deserves anything right now is that poor woman lying on a coroner's slab. She deserves to have her killer brought to justice."

The young photographer leveled his camera at the mayor, but before he could snap a picture, she gave him a look that would have stopped a locomotive. He wisely lowered his camera and went back to scribbling in his notebook.

"Mayor Beaumont, I don't think you can fully appreciate the intricacy involved in a case like this," said Chief Walker. "Now, we are all here for the same thing, and given time, I have all the faith in the world in my team to bring this monster to justice." He gave a sly look to Alex.

Alex drew himself up and gave Todd a quick nod of his head. "Todd, you know I think that the ideas we discussed at the coroner's office were sound. After what we learned from the condition of the body and from the crime scene, you were probably right about us needing help profiling the killer. I mean, that would be next steps, right?"

Todd shifted his weight from side to side a bit and squeezed his right hand into a fist a few times. "Absolutely, Alex. That is the next step."

"Oh?" said the mayor. "And what kind of help do you require? I can get on the phone and have someone sent in if needed."

"Actually, I think we already have someone who is

familiar with...acts of this nature and can probably provide us with some insight." Alex leveled his gaze at Jessie.

The chief's body went rigid. "What? Her? No. We aren't involving civilians in our investigation. Mayor, you said yourself that we need to keep a lid on this until we know what's going on. No offense, Missie, but we don't know you."

Missie? Jessie balled her fists, gritting her teeth so tightly she was afraid one might crack. How she would love two minutes alone with this jackass.

Not my house, not my house, not my house. She willed her pounding heart to slow, refusing to give in to what she imagined she could do to the chief.

"Chief Walker, I need to be blunt," said Alex. "We are in way over our head. What was done to that woman, I've never seen anything like it. None of us have." He turned to the mayor. "And yes, you can call in the FBI. But how long does that take for them get involved?"

"Longer than you have." Jessie spoke quietly, but all eyes turned to her. "Every minute you wait, is a minute the trail is getting colder. And that's another minute that the unsub is getting bolder."

"Unsub?" asked the mayor.

"Unidentified subject," replied Jessie. "It's a term for a killer who has yet to be identified. And the longer you take to capture or eliminate him, the greater the likelihood he will slip away. Or worse yet, decide to hang around awhile and do it again."

"What is the first thing we need to focus on?" asked the mayor.

"Well, the first thing you need to do is identify that victim. Once you know who she is, you can start to look for anything that might give you a clue as to why and where she might have been killed. That will be how you ultimately catch this guy."

"We need a profile of this guy," added Alex. "We need to know what we are up against."

Chief Walker huffed. "Well, that's what we are working on, but it's hard until we can identify the victim."

That was the last straw for Jessie. "You're looking for a male, Caucasian, probably in his late to mid-thirties, possibly a bit older."

Once again, all eyes fell on her. Chief Walker folded his arms across his chest. "And just how do you know any of that, little lady? Why are you so certain it's even a man? Isn't this the 'me too' era?"

Jessie's left eye flinched. She could practically hear the sound of flesh on flesh as she imagined the edge of her hand cutting across his glaring face. But she decided to strike in a different way. "He's most likely Caucasian because most killers who commit a crime like this rarely do so outside of their own race. I say he, because what was done to the victim takes strength. Strength to do what he did to kill the victim, but then to move a dead body after the fact and place it in a confined space with ice. And I gave you the age range for a couple of reasons. What was done to the body – the beheading, the breaking of the joints, the removal of the fingerprints – all point to a calculated and methodical individual. Such traits typically develop with age and experience. Also, what he did took time; it wasn't a quick kill. That takes control over one's schedule, and it requires a degree of professional training and exposure. Someone with medical or military training. That usually doesn't happen for someone in their twenties."

The chief's face reddened slightly but he didn't speak. The mayor turned to Jessie, her brows pinched together. "What else do you know about this killer? How detailed of a profile are you capable of giving us?"

Jessie hesitated. She hadn't meant to say as much as she did, but the way the chief was treating her had plucked at the final nerve she was holding back. She looked briefly at Alex, who nodded for her to continue.

"Well, I've given you the basics already. But before I say more, I need everyone to understand what profiling is. It is an act that allows law enforcement to infer behavioral, personality and demographic characteristics about the unsub. It is based on analyzing crime scenes, the victim and the manner in which the crime was committed. Given the brutal nature of this crime—" She stopped and walked up to the white board and picked up a black marker, pointing to the board. "May I?"

Everyone looked to the chief, who only grunted and nodded.

Jessie took a breath and began speaking while writing key words and phrases. "We are looking for someone methodical and patient. The killer took time to do what he did. The amount of detail and patience to break joints and rearrange someone's limbs after death is highly unusual. This level of mutilation tells us it is someone who enjoys exerting control and power over their victims.

"The killer is also experienced. This isn't his first kill.

They removed the head and burned off the fingerprints to prevent or delay her identification. This means we are possibly dealing with someone with knowledge of law enforcement or at the very least a very keen interest in police procedural shows.

"The unsub is also a high risk taker. We can tell from the brutality and gore involved with this, combined with the time needed to do it. They are also calm under pressure. This tells us he is not easily rattled. This kind of emotional control means we are most likely dealing with a psychopath.

"Lastly, I would say that this level of extreme mutilation suggests a form of personal motivation. The killer may have known the victim or felt a deep-seated resentment or anger towards them or what they represent. Whoever did this, is most likely going to do it again unless they are apprehended quickly." She cleared her throat. "And of course, Police Lead Freeman was right. The next big lead we get will be in the identification of the victim."

The room was so silent, Jessie wasn't sure people were still breathing. Her face heated, and she hurried back to her place at the back of the room.

The mayor turned to Chief Walker. "Well, Trent?" She cocked a single eyebrow his way.

The big man narrowed his eyes, seeming to choose his next words very carefully. "That was very insightful, Miss – uh, Ms. Night. Thank you for that. It appears that you have some experience in this area that my team...and I, could utilize. Maybe we can work out a consultant position for you. Just until this case is closed. You'd be under my direct supervision of course – and Todd's." He nodded in his nephew's direction.

"What do you say?" asked the mayor. Her eyes were all but pleading with Jessie.

In her mind, Jessie knew she couldn't say no. All she could picture was the woman in the boathouse, and she knew there was no way she could deny helping capture the monster who did that. She nodded.

Alex smiled. "Welcome to the Pine Haven police department. Let's go get you squared away with some credentials and logins. Looks like we are about to be spending a whole lot of time together."

14

AN UNWANTED VISITOR

An Unwanted Visitor

The drive back to the house was a quiet one. Jessie drove on autopilot, her mind replaying everything that had transpired at the examiner's office and the police department. Movement in the rearview mirror caught her attention and she smiled at Blizzard, his nose rising and quivering as he filtered out the scents he captured in the air.

She frowned, remembering that she was supposed to be checking in on his owner. Why did that keep slipping her mind?

"Well, that's an easy fix." She glanced at her phone mounted on a heads-up display attached to the windshield. "Hey, Suri, text Alex. Hi Alex, I was just wondering if you had a chance to check on Mr. Thompson? How is he doing?"

The digital assistant in her phone read her text back

to confirm it was correct and then sent it. In a matter of moments, her phone dinged with a reply.

"Hi, Jessie. I'm sorry. I meant to let you know. I checked in on him last night. He's not doing well. The strokes he suffered are still evolving. The docs will know more over the next seventy-two hours. Are you able to keep Blizzard a little while longer?"

Jessie nodded and responded to her electronic assistant. "Not a problem. I just hope he's okay. Talk later." She glanced into the mirror. "Well, buddy, looks like you're stuck with me a bit longer." The thought made her smile. She had never considered herself a dog person. Having a pet of any kind had never been something she had ever given serious consideration to. In her previous life, it wasn't something she felt she could dedicate enough time to, considering she never knew when a simple workday could lead to hopping on a flight to investigate a potential crime scene multiple states away.

But this was a new life. A life where just maybe she could consider dedicating her time and energies to something other than hunting down people who did really bad things in a misguided belief that they were serving the greater good.

Try as she might, she couldn't stop her thoughts from circling that old band wagon. She had moved to Pine Haven to start over again. To get away from the darkness that had nearly swallowed her whole.

"Who are you kidding? You moved here because you had no other choice," she mumbled.

She had to be careful. Helping out a police department had the potential to put her name out there. She had no reason to think anyone would be looking for her; but you could never be too careful when dealing with the monsters she had left behind.

At least she hoped they were behind her. Instinctively, she glanced at the portable radio on the passenger seat. All quiet.

She pulled into the long drive leading to the house and immediately felt that something was off. The security sign half under the porch had been moved slightly, and there was dried dirt on the steps leading to the porch.

Taking a deep breath, Jessie slowly advanced up the stairs. She grasped the handle of the front door and it clicked, opening with a gentle push. It was unlocked. She frowned. No way she had left the door to her house open like that.

Pushing the door open, she stood there, letting her senses feel out the space. Blizzard stood still at her side, ears trained ahead, straining for any sign of disturbance. "Go, boy."

The dog pushed into the living room, sniffing immediately at the floor, then making his way into the kitchen, sniffing intently at the floor. Jessie followed behind him, moving to the counter where she withdrew one of the large kitchen knives from the drawer. She cursed herself for not keeping a gun, suddenly regretting her decision to leave all the aspects of her old life behind.

She didn't need any reminders of the world she had once inhabited; but she also knew that having her military-issued Sig Sauer P320 would have given her considerable peace of mind at the moment. Climbing the stairs, she hugged one wall, and grasped the knife with the blade edge out and up against her forearm in a reverse grip that would give her more flexibility than just a straight thrust if needed.

She glanced down at Blizzard, noting the fact that he didn't seem particularly troubled. That put her a little at ease knowing there was no one in the house. Still, she advanced on the upper floor cautiously, systematically checking each room and window, until she came to her bedroom.

She entered, head down, knife at the ready. She stood still and listened. She trusted Blizzard's senses far more than her own, but still listened to her own instincts. There was no one there, but that didn't mean someone wasn't in her personal space earlier. She could smell something – a musk that smelled different from the woodsy aroma the breeze carried in through her cracked window.

Out of habit, she looked for the knife under her mattress and was relieved to see that it had not been disturbed. A quick check of her few belongings told her nothing had been moved. Maybe it was just her imagination at work.

But she knew better than that.

Taking out her phone, she made a reminder to have a security system installed as soon as possible before returning downstairs and placing the knife back in the kitchen.

She had just placed a bowl of water on the floor for Blizzard when she was startled by her phone buzzing. For a split-second, she looked at it in confusion. It had been so long since anyone actually called her that she had almost forgotten it was capable of receiving calls. She glanced at the number displayed and frowned. She could have sent it to voicemail, but knew that would only result in an immediate second call.

"Dr. Anderson," she said, stabbing at the screen to turn on the speaker function. "How are you?"

"Jessie. I'm doing well and I hope you are." The tone on the other end of the phone was cordial, with just the right amount of caring mixed in. "I wanted to check in. You were supposed to call me when you arrived in North Carolina." As usual, her voice was light and free of any discernible accent. Something the military taught all of its shrinks so that they could more readily fit in with whomever they may be actively counseling.

"Oh, yeah, I'm sorry about that. I just got in a couple of days ago and it's been a real whirlwind." Jessie glanced over at Blizzard as he headed for the door, standing patiently and giving her the 'I gotta go' look. "Okay, hang on, boy...here you go." She swung open the door, letting him out.

"I'm sorry, what?" said Dr. Anderson.

"Oh, I'm sorry. That wasn't for you. I was letting the dog out." As soon as she said the words, Jessie regretted them.

"A...dog? Interesting," the woman replied.

Jessie could practically hear her scribbling in her notebook.

"It's a favor for someone. Long story. Like I said, it's been a whirlwind couple of days."

"And how are you dealing with the stress?"

Jessie hesitated. Dr. Anderson could always smell a

partial truth, and Jessie was sure she would be able to still do it from halfway across the country. "It's been...tiring. I'm not as young as I used to be." She waited for the doctor to answer and then continued when no reply was forthcoming. "If you're asking if I've had any more episodes, I haven't."

That was true. What had happened during her drive into town was an *almost* episode.

"That's excellent news, Jessie."

If that was true, why did she hear a 'but' coming?

"You know, Jessie, there is no shame in taking medications. Catatonia can be a severe, debilitating condition if left untreated."

Jessie sighed. "And you know how I feel about those particular meds. I can't be wandering around wasted on Ativan or some kind of barbiturate on the off chance that I might...*might*...have an attack."

Silence on the other end. More scribbling, no doubt.

"Yes, you have made your stance on medications quite clear in the past, Jessie. I just want you to remember that an episode can be triggered by sudden stress or extreme emotional events. And if—"

Jessie cut her off. "And that's why I left Colorado and everything that happened behind me. That's why I'm starting over again. New life. Less stress." She purposefully blocked the image of what she saw in the boathouse from her mind.

Dr. Anderson was silent, and when she spoke, her voice had softened, and Jessie could hear the human beneath the physician. "Jessie. I'm speaking to you as your friend now, not your therapist. I only want the best for you: and what I'm about to say is coming from your friend, not a representative of the United States Army. You made the right decision in leaving all this shit behind and starting over. And if you ever need me...not Dr. Anderson – you just have to call."

Jessie breathed a sigh of relief, closing her eyes in a silent thank you for the support. "Thank you for that. And yes, I will call if I need to."

"Good." And just like that she was speaking to one of the military's top psychiatrists. "And because I knew you would say no to any medications, I took it upon myself to find a therapist specializing in your...condition, that's about an hour away from where you are in North Carolina. She has agreed to take you on as a client and I'm texting you her contact information. I expect you to make an appointment within the next two weeks. Understand?"

"Is that coming from my therapist or my friend?"

There was a slight pause. "Yes."

Jessie smiled, and let it show in her voice. "Thank you, Jasmine. I will give her a call."

"Good. And don't be a stranger!"

Jessie promised to stay in touch and wished her friend well before clicking out of the call. Immediately, her phone buzzed again. "Hey, I said I'd call, alright."

"What? It's me, Alex. I thought you might like to know; Dr. Lindquist just got an ID on our victim."

Jessie felt her heart skip. "I'm on my way."

15

COINCIDENCES AREN'T REAL

Coincidences Aren't Real

Th
e sun had set when Jessie pulled into the police station. The fading light painting the fractured concrete with the warm, soft palette of twilight.

Inside, the deputy sitting at the reception desk didn't even bother to look up as she walked by, holding up the laminated consultant's card that Alex had snagged for her. She breezed by him and headed right for the small conference office they had crammed into earlier. She braced herself for the mass of people that would probably be waiting but was pleasantly surprised to find only Alex and Todd Freeman in the room.

"What? No mayor and her personal reporter? Or the chief?" She managed to say the last part without sounding like she had just swallowed something bitter and tough.

"We – I mean I – thought it might be best for us to

focus on this, come up with a game plan, and then present findings to the chief. From there, he can decide how to proceed with the mayor."

Surprisingly, Jessie found herself nodding in agreement with the plan. It was a smart move. Keep the brass out of the weeds, let them know what was happening on an as-needed basis. While she doubted they would have true free reign – especially where the chief was concerned – it would at least give them breathing room to shape the investigation as needed.

"Alright, what do we know?" asked Jessie.

Todd flipped open his ever-present notepad and read aloud. "Dr. Lindquist was able to track the model number and maker of the plate on our victim to Hillsdale Memorial Hospital, which is a couple hours away. Furthermore, he spoke with the doctor who performed the surgery, and after a bit of back and forth the doctor admitted that he did operate on a woman fitting our victim's identification. He said she suffered a serious trimalleolar break of her ankle, and the only way to set it was to put a plate in. Her name, was Jordan Myer."

Jessie flinched, her eyebrows furrowing.

"Something wrong?" asked Todd, looking up from his notes.

"No...not really," said Jessie. "Weird coincidence. That's the same name as the realtor I was working with and met in town a couple days ago to get the keys to my aunt's house."

Now it was Alex who frowned. "I'm not really a believer in coincidence."

"Honestly, neither am I," echoed Jessie. She watched

as Alex took out his phone and began to type furiously with his thumbs.

He looked up from his screen, eyes wide.

"What is it?" asked Jessie.

The policeman held his phone screen out for them to see. "It says here that Jordan Myer is a realtor with Pine Haven Realty." There was also a profile and accompanying business picture of the realtor, looking confident standing in front of the lake.

"That definitely isn't the Jordan Myer I met," said Jessie. "That Jordan Myer was a man." The little warning spark that had popped up in the back of her mind was now a full-on four alarm fire.

Alex looked at his watch. "The realty office will be closed now. We could probably find the owner of the company and pay him a visit."

Jessie shook her head. "Or we could just wait until first thing in the morning and pay the office an unannounced visit. Something is very off there, and if we notify anyone, even the owner, we might inadvertently tip someone else off. We could lose the element of surprise."

"Good point," added Alex. "So, we do nothing in the meantime?"

"No. In the meantime, we find out everything we can about Jordan Myer. Social media, home address, business listings...everything. How long do you think it would take to get a search warrant for her house?"

"We could probably have it tomorrow, maybe just before midday," answered Todd.

It was clear he wanted to contribute, and Jessie found herself not wanting to alienate the man.

"Good. That will give us time to visit the real estate office first. Try and get a feel for what is going on," said Jessie. She turned to face Alex. "I don't suppose you have a composite sketch artist on staff here?"

Alex huffed. "We don't even have a detective, remember?"

Todd snapped his finger dramatically. "What about Will?"

Jessie frowned. "The reporter who trails the mayor everywhere?"

"Yes," Todd said. "He's not just a reporter and photographer – he's also an amazing artist. His portraits booth at the county fair is always one of the most popular attractions every year."

Alex was nodding. "He's right. Will has a gift when it comes to drawing. If you can give a detailed description, he might be able to help."

"How soon can you get him over here?" Jessie asked.

"Well, it's late—" began Todd, before seeing the look Alex and Jessie gave him, "—but I'm willing to bet he can get here pretty quick. I'll make the call."

"We'll go fire up the coffee maker in the break room," said Alex. "It's shaping up to be a long night."

Sipping on her second cup of coffee, Jessie looked over Will Mason's shoulder as he carefully added some finishing touches to the sketch.

"Yes, that's it. That's the man I spoke with at the real estate office," Jessie said. Alex and Todd were correct.

Will was extremely talented. "That's an amazing job. You might have missed your calling."

The young man looked up and smiled. "It's only possible because of the incredible detail you provided." He put the finishing light strokes to the sketch and handed it to Jessie. "I hope this helps."

"It definitely will," she said. Placing it on one of the desks, she took out her phone and snapped a couple of close ups of the drawing, then turned to Alex and Todd. "Have you found anything?"

Alex looked up from the laptop he had been scrunched over. "Her social media is pretty much locked down tight. She has a business page for real estate on a couple of platforms, but that's it."

"Go through the comments on them if you can. See if anything stands out as stalkerish or creepy," Jessie suggested, before turning to Todd.

"I've run her name through multiple databases. Not so much as a parking ticket and her name has never come up associated with anyone else's in any report. She's clean."

Jessie began to pace back and forth in front of the desk where Will had been drawing. The chances that there were two people of different sexes, with the exact same first and surname, working in the same office was too astronomical to calculate. It just added another layer of questions to an already complex case. In her past life, peeling back the layers had been much easier. Typically, there was a crime, and it wasn't too hard to discern who had committed it, or why. The trick had been *proving* the suspect had committed the crime.

But here, she had the evidence of a crime and a potential suspect. But what was the motive?

"Hey, do you guys need me for anything else?" It was Will. He was beginning to pack up his sketch pad and array of charcoal pencils.

Jessie eyed him suspiciously. "Don't you want to know what's going to happen next? What our thoughts are and...whatever else it is that reporters always feel entitled to know?" For a brief second, she saw a look of hurt flash across his young features.

Then he offered her a tight-lipped smile. "Most reporters want to know everything about a case like this because they need to be the first to report. They don't want to be scooped." He looked around the office. Who's going to scoop me here? I am the only editor and reporter of the only paper in Pine Haven. I figure when you know something that you want me to get out, you'll tell me. Or Maggie will." He stood up, throwing his backpack over his shoulder. "I hope you catch this guy. That's really all I want to report on." He headed out, nodding to Alex and Todd as he exited the room.

"Well, now I feel like a heel," said Jessie.

"Don't," said Alex. "Will's a good kid. He knows you're not from around here."

Jessie frowned. "That's not an excuse though. Where I am from, the press was always looking for a reason to tear you down."

Alex regarded her for a moment. "Doesn't sound like you're too fond of where you were. You'll find the longer you're here, the more you'll get used to the quirks that come with a community like Pine Haven."

Jessie hesitated, not sure how much she wanted to say. "Well, I'm not so sure I'll be here long enough for that."

Alex stared for a brief moment but then dropped his eyes back to the laptop. "Yeah, well, Pine Haven isn't for everyone I guess."

Jessie took a breath, trying to figure out how to clarify what she meant, when she saw him stiffen in response to something on his screen. "What is it?"

He pointed to the screen, spinning it around. "Jordan has some pictures here of recent sales she made. There's one here of a very nice house on the lake. Lots of the usual congratulatory comments. But the last one on this pic is from John Bartley." Jessie saw Todd's head snap up at the mention of the man's name. "The comment reads, thanks for cheating me on this one."

Jessie watched the two police officers exchange looks. "Okay, I'll bite. Who's this John Bartley?"

Alex turned to her, his face hard. "He lives across the tracks. He's the head of a motorcycle club that runs a lot of illegal goods through Pine Haven. We've had run-ins with him before. Not the most pleasant of guys."

Jessie narrowed her eyes. "Unpleasant as in potential murderer?"

Alex set his jaw hard. "From what I've heard, it wouldn't be the first time he's killed."

16

GETTING REAL WITH THE REALTORS

Getting Real with the Realtors

Sleep didn't come for Jessie. After hours of tossing and turning, she finally got out of bed, let Blizzard out to do his business, and then settled on the couch and began to put together the laundry list of offenses on John Bartley that Alex had shared. The man was definitely bad news, but the stuff they had on him was weak.

She opened the case marked 3921-AP. There were a couple of cases of public intoxication and disorderly conduct, and some calls against the man for trespassing. Certainly not the worst record Jessie had ever seen compiled on someone. There also wasn't anything in it to suggest he was capable of the kind of cold-blooded, calculated murder they were investigating.

And then she picked up a second case folder. This one was marked 3921-AP-C.

It had the same mugshot of John Bartley attached to

the first page, but this report was very different. It appeared that the Pine Haven police department was keeping an off-the-records file on Mr. Bartley. And it read entirely different from the first.

Suspected drug trafficking, possible firearms dealing, assault and battery that couldn't be proven because the victims would never come forward and make a statement about what happened to them. Or who did it. There were surveillance notes on him entering and leaving known drug hotspots, but nothing that would stick. Jessie continued poring through the file, but there wasn't anything that said this was their guy. Granted, John Bartley was not a nice man, but that didn't mean he was capable of committing the heinous act she had witnessed.

Then, on the last page, one last note stuck out at her. John Bartley was one of the prime suspects of an arson. An old mill just on the outskirts of town had burned down and the owner had refused to cooperate with the police as to just what may have been the cause. Eventually the case was dropped, and the owner moved out of town with an insurance settlement, which was strange. Most insurance companies don't payout until they know the exact cause of a fire.

There still wasn't anything linking Bartley to the murder, but if he were a closet firebug, that added another layer to his psyche that could link him to the killer's profile. Thrill seeking and de-personalization were two traits that the killer and an arsonist would share.

Further searching and she saw that the cause was

finally marked as accidental. The other interesting thing about it was who had signed off on, and closed, the investigation.

Chief Clint Walker.

Interesting. The fact that his name was on the document in this file meant he probably didn't know the file existed. She filed that away in the back of her mind. One more thing to discuss with Alex when they were alone. Not that she wanted to be alone with him. More like she needed privacy with him. Professionally speaking, of course.

She shook her head, trying to get that easy-going smile of his out of her mind. The image folded and was replaced with the look on his face that flashed by when she said the jury was still out on her staying in Pine Haven.

She checked her watch and realized she would have just enough time to grab a quick bite for breakfast and walk Blizzard before Alex would be by to pick her up. The plan was to swing by the realty office as soon as they opened and speak with the owner. After that, even though she had a feeling Alex wouldn't like it, she wanted to swing by this John Bartley's residence and question him. She plugged the address in his file into her phone and it came back with directions to a part of town that she only vaguely remembered.

The railroad tracks that ran through Pine Haven divided the town, literally, in half. While the tracks were the lifeblood for getting supplies into and out of town, they also represented the demarcation between the haves and the have-nots. On one side sat the lake and all the luxurious properties that dotted it. The town proper was also mostly on that side of the tracks as well, with its perfectly sculpted Main Street and mom and pop bakeries and shops that were tailor-made for window shopping. Ironically, many of the owners of those mom-and-pop shops lived on the opposite side of the tracks, where the shotgun houses and small, craftsman style bungalows were more affordable.

The working class, and those who were barely scraping by, having inherited their tiny homes from a parent or grandparent, mostly kept to themselves. While only a few miles from the property of the lake, the rail-road tracks might as well have been the gates to another world. The sad thing was the two sides of the town were symbiotic in nature; one wouldn't be able to sustain itself for very long without the other.

Even though her house was a mere shadow compared to the rest lining the lake, Jessie knew just how lucky she was to live there. But she also knew that no matter how long she stayed, she'd never truly be accepted by the lake crowd. Not that she cared. A lifetime in the military had put layers of scar tissue on her, and good luck to anyone who tried picking at those scabs.

She had just returned to the house, changed out of her sweats, and was making sure that Blizzard had enough water in his bowl when she heard the crunch of Alex's tires across the gravel driveway. When she saw him approaching the front door with a large coffee in hand, she could have kissed him. She immediately started to blush at the thought and took a moment to collect herself when he knocked.

"For you," he said, ceremoniously handing her the cup.

"You must have read my mind. My aunt has some weird-looking kettle thing with a glass knob on top for making coffee. I've no idea how to use it and haven't made it to town yet to buy something made in this century."

Alex laughed. "I figured you for one of those K-cup drinkers."

Jessie smiled as she bent down to ruffle Blizzard's head before stepping onto the porch. "Those things are bad for the environment."

WHILE THE REAL estate office looked the same as when Jessie was there on the weekend, the bustle of a few agents, loud conversation and ringing phones transformed the space. There was a woman sitting at the front desk reception area who smiled politely as they approached. Jessie wasn't sure, but she thought the smile brightened a little when Alex stepped forward.

"Hey there, Alex. What can I do for you today?" she asked.

"Hi, Tess. We were wondering if we could speak with Mr. Evans, please. It's rather urgent."

Tess seemed a bit startled, sitting up straight in her chair as she reached for the phone. She pushed a button and then whispered quickly into it. Replacing the headset, she beamed up at Alex again. "He says come on back. It's the first door on the left. Can I get you some coffee?"

"Thank you, but no." Alex nodded as he and Jessie made their way past the desk. The office door was open, and the plaque tacked to the wall next to it read Clive Evans in large, gold letters. Jessie couldn't recall if she saw that on her first visit in the office. As they walked into the room, she turned her head to get a glimpse of the cubicles down the hallway, hoping for a glance at the realtor who had presented himself as Jordan Myer.

"Alex, my boy, what can I do for you? You finally ready to buy you a place on the water?" Mr. Evans rose from behind his desk and offered his hand to the officer. "And who's this pretty thing with you?" His eyes roved over Jessie in a way she didn't care for and then they widened as he looked back to Alex. "Don't tell me you've finally settled down? Looking for a place to start a family, huh?"

Jessie saw the tips of Alex's ears go red and he quickly readjusted his wide-brimmed hat, pulling it lower on his head.

"Uh, no. On both of those points. Clive, this is Jessie Night. She's new to the area and is working with the department as a consultant."

"Nice to see you, Mr. Evans," Jessie said, nodding at the man.

"Please, call me Clive. And what can I help you with if you're not looking for a house?" He plopped back into his chair, motioning for the two of them to take a seat opposite his desk.

"Clive, we need to ask you a couple of questions about an investigation we're running," said Alex. "Do you have an employee named Jordan Myer?"

"Sure do. Our top agent. What's going on?" His brow furrowed, and he leaned forward in his seat.

"When was the last time you saw her?" Alex continued.

"Friday a week ago. Just before she left for vacation."

Jessie sat forward. "When is she due back?"

Clive looked around his desk, pulling out a paper calendar and placing it in front of him. He flipped through a couple of pages until he found the one he wanted. "She's due back tomorrow. She was out a week, driving down to the Outer Banks to visit the beach and then coming back. She took an extra day – today – to recover from the drive. Why?" He looked from Alex to Jessie and back to the police officer. "Oh no. Was she in a car accident? Is everything okay?"

Jessie caught a glimpse of Alex from the corner of her eye. His leg was bouncing uncontrollably, and it was all she could do not to put a hand on his knee to steady him. What had to come next was hard for even the most seasoned of officers to do. He removed his hat and looked Mr. Evans in the eyes.

"Clive, I'm sorry to be the one to tell you this, but... well...we found a body and have every indication that it is Jordan Myer."

Jessie watched the older man closely. His reaction would tell her if he had any idea ahead of time what the officer was going to say. But she saw the color drain out of the man, his body lurched forward, his spine no longer able to support him in a seated position. His breath caught and then released in a shuddering gasp as he struggled to understand the horrific news. He grasped the side of his desk, knuckles white, as he looked up at Alex. "That's not funny, Alex. Not at all. Now you take that back."

The quake in his voice told Jessie that he knew what Alex was saying was true, but he wasn't ready to bring himself to accept it. He dropped back in his chair, sweat breaking out on his forehead.

"We are so sorry for your loss, Mr. Evans – Clive," Jessie said.

"I just can't believe it. She was so excited about a deal she had just closed and was using the commission to treat herself to the trip." He looked up, more confusion in his eyes. "Where...how did you find her?"

Alex shuffled in his seat, glancing at Jessie before he spoke. "We aren't ready to release the details just yet. We still have a couple more things to do, including notifying her next of kin. Would you happen to have information on them?"

Clive shook his head, reaching into his jacket pocket to take out a handkerchief and mop at his brow. "She... she didn't have any. No kin that I know of, and she never listed any on her employment application."

"Clive," said Jessie, leaning forward to focus on the grieving man. "We are going to need her computer and the names and numbers of any clients she may have been working with lately."

The man started to stand, then reached and punched a button on his phone. "Tess, could you come in here?" He turned his attention back to Jessie and Alex. "Tess will get you anything you need. My God. I just...what am I going to say to everyone?"

As Tess entered the room, Jessie turned to Mr. Evans one more time. "There's one more thing I need to ask you about." She took out her phone and brought up the picture Will Mason had drawn. "Do you know this man?"

Evan stared before shaking his head. "Never seen him before. Is he the...killer?"

Jessie put her phone away. "He's the man I met in here on Saturday who was using Jordan's name and credentials. So yes...he's a person of interest."

Tess knocked on the door and was beckoned in. There was no way around telling her what had happened and minutes later, a sobbing receptionist was leading them out of the office and to the workspace of a murdered colleague.

17

SECRET RELATIONS

Secret Relations

"Tess, I know Mr. Evans said Jordan didn't have any family that he was aware of. How well did you know her? Do you know of any next of kin she might have?" Jessie asked. The shocked receptionist had led them to the last cubicle in the office. The one that Jessie had visited with the impersonator. Her skin crawled as she rounded the corner where she had sat with a possible killer.

Tess was dabbing at her face with a tissue between sobs as she shook her head. "Jordan was probably my best friend here at work. And no, she had no one. She had a sister who passed away ten years ago. Car accident. But that was all."

"What about a boyfriend?" asked Jessie. "Or girlfriend? Did she have anyone special in her life?"

Tess seemed to tense up at the question, wrapping one arm across her torso to hug the other. "She was seeing someone. But she wouldn't say who. She said it was still too new to talk about and she didn't want to jinx things. She is – she *was* superstitious about stuff like that. All I know is she was head over heels for this guy, but I don't know who he is."

Jessie thought back to everything on Jordan's social media. There was nothing that mentioned or hinted at a relationship. It wasn't much, but it was certainly worth looking into. "Thank you. That's definitely something we will follow up on."

The energy in the office had changed dramatically as word of the passing of one of their coworkers had quickly spread to the agents. Many were sitting at their desks, heads hanging low, and a few were openly sobbing while trying to comfort one another.

"Hey, uh, would you mind if I sent everyone home?" It was Mr. Evans who had come up behind them. "I can't imagine anyone getting work done today."

"Um, not just yet, Clive. I need to get some statements from everyone in the office. After that, they can go." Alex looked at Jessie and she nodded. "I'll set up in the break room. Can you ask everyone to come in one at a time so I can just ask a couple of questions? And this is everyone at the agency?" He looked down at a list Tess had provided him.

Mr. Evans nodded. "Yeah. That's everybody, and it looks like everyone is in the office as well. Here, I'll show you to the break room."

They stepped away, and Alex turned to Jessie. "You got this?"

She nodded and gave him a slight smile before

turning back to the desk where only days before she sat across from someone pretending to be a realtor. The desk was barren. The first thing that Jessie looked for was the smiling picture of "Jordan" and his spouse that was sitting on the desk. It, and everything else she had seen, were all gone. The only thing remaining was the computer.

"Was this the only computer Jordan used?" Jessie asked. Maybe they would get lucky, and all her business dealings would be contained.

"No. She only used that when she was in the office. The rest of the time she used her laptop. As a matter of fact, she preferred her laptop, even when she was in the office. Most of the agents do. These computers are dinosaurs. Everyone was always complaining to Clive about upgrading them, but he always said he'd get to it later. And later never came." She burst out in another round of tears, and Jessie waited until they subsided.

She took out her phone and showed the picture of the man she had met with. "Tess, have you ever seen this man before?"

The receptionist stared at the picture. "No. He doesn't look familiar at all."

"You're sure? Could he have been one of Jordan's clients?"

"Not that I know of. If he was, she never brought him here to the office."

That perked Jessie's ears a little. "Do the agents have clients they don't bring to the office? That they maybe only meet at the properties they are selling?"

"Some yes. I know that Jordan handled a few high-profile clients, for rentals usually, and they would not come to the office. She usually did everything by email and then would go to them to hand over the keys and sign the paperwork."

"Thank you. That's very helpful. But the transactions record you pulled for Officer Thomas will still show their names, correct?"

She frowned. "I believe so. Although some are handled through trusts and may only be under the lawyer that represents the trust, or something like that. But there aren't many of those." The woman moved to sit down, reaching for the chair.

"No, don't touch anything," said Jessie, stopping her. The woman's eyes grew round as saucers. Jessie softened her tone. "It's okay. We're going to need to have forensics sweep this cubicle and I'd rather not have it be anymore contaminated than it possibly already is. Also, is this the only place Jordan would have kept any personal belongings?"

Tess nodded.

"Do me a favor. Without touching anything, can you look at her desk and bookcases and see if anything is missing?"

Carefully, almost as if she were stepping across a minefield, Tess made her way around the desk and to the bookshelves against the wall behind it.

"Her picture is missing, but that's all," Tess said, pointing to an empty spot on the bookcase.

Jessie frowned. "What kind of picture?"

"It was one of her in front of the old Tarrif place. It was the first house she sold here in Pine Haven when she started fifteen years ago."

Jessie felt the skin on the back of her neck prickle up. "Thank you, Tess. You've been a big help. Why don't you go and see if Alex is ready for you? And here—" she handed her a business card, "—If you think of anything... anything at all, you call me."

She waited until Tess had left the cubicle before she looked at the empty spot on the bookshelf. Taking out her phone, she snapped a pic and texted it to Alex. Surely someone on staff had the ability to lift fingerprints, and while it seemed like a long shot, maybe they would get lucky and find something they could work with.

Once she'd finished her inspection of the room, she made her way back to the break room where Alex was consoling Tess. She couldn't hear what was being said, and sensed the timing was not right for her to intrude, so she waited outside the door until Tess stepped out.

Tess shook her hand. "Thank you for helping with this, Jessie. Please catch the monster who did this." Her tears started flowing again and she walked off, headed back to the front of the office.

"That was the hardest thing I've ever had to do," said Alex, his voice heavy with fatigue.

"You did a great job," said Jessie. "I hope you never have to do something like this again in your career."

They both knew that was unlikely, but it sounded good in the moment.

"I sent a message to Todd earlier. Told him what was going on so he could give the chief and the mayor a heads up. It won't take anytime at all for news to spread through the town. I'm betting the mayor's office will be fielding a lot of calls soon."

"You think panic is going to take over the town?" Jessie asked.

"Well, half of it probably. The half that lives on the lake." She sensed a bit of resentment just below the surface, but it wasn't the right time to pry. Besides, he was entitled to his feelings. Not asking certain questions assured the two of them stayed firmly planted in the professional arena.

"Did you get any leads?" asked Jessie.

"Not really. No one saw or heard anything out of the ordinary in the time leading up to Jordan leaving for vacation. No one recognized the picture of the man you met here. No one really seems to be that close to Jordan."

"Tess was, and she told me something interesting. She said that a picture was missing from Jordan's bookcase. A photo of her in front of the very first house she sold fifteen years ago. And get this. It's the Tarrif house."

Alex's eyes widened. "As in Chase Tarrif's house? The father of the two boys who found the body?" Alex was up and heading towards the door. "Looks like we should stop in and see how those boys are doing."

"Normally, I would say that can wait," Jessie said. "The first step, now that we know where Jordan lived, should be to check out her house. Tess told me she had a laptop that she relied on more than the computers here. Maybe we'll get lucky and it's there. However, it's not like her house is going anywhere. Whereas, there is nothing stopping Chase from uprooting the boys and his wife and running off. He needs to be the priority."

"Good point," Alex replied. "I can 't see him running, but just in case, I'll have Todd send one of the other officers to sit outside his gate and keep an eye on things until we can get over there."

Jessie nodded appreciatively. Alex was thinking like a detective, whether he knew it or not. As they walked out of the office, she saw Clive Evans, the owner of the agency, still sitting alone in his office. His head was low, and she saw a small glass with a pour of a brownish liquid in it. She felt for him. Small businesses like this often had a family atmosphere to them. And today, this man had just found out that a member of his family had been murdered.

If having a morning drink was what he needed, then who was she to say anything? But the sight of him, broken, hurting, mourning the loss of a friend...it helped her resolve. They were one step closer to a killer, and hopefully they would find something in Jordan's house that would shorten that distance a little more.

18

ONE HELLUVA DRUG

One Helluva Drug

"So how do we handle this?" Alex asked as he maneuvered the car through the light morning traffic. "Good cop bad cop? But Chase is a pretty mean old dude. So maybe bad cop worse cop?"

Jessie was staring out the window, watching the peaceful scenery whizz by. "Chase seems like the kind of man who will shut down if confronted in too aggressive a way. My read on him is he thrives on being in control. If he senses that we are accusing him of anything, shit might go south. However, if we need to play hardball, then that's what we'll do. Especially if he clams up or becomes evasive. We need to find out if he had any ongoing contact with Jordan after the sale of his house."

"You think he could have done it?"

Jessie hesitated. Choosing her words carefully. "In my experience, under the right circumstances, people are capable of great acts of violence. The trick is to figure out what set them off. No matter how dark the act, everyone has a motive."

Alex stared at her in wonder. "You must have lived in a very dark place."

She gave him a half smile. It was nice of him to think of that in the past tense for her.

They climbed into Alex's car just as his phone began to ring. He switched over to the car's speaker system and answered as he pulled out of the Pine Haven Realty parking lot. "This is Officer Thomas."

"Alex, it's Todd. Is Jessie with you?"

"I'm here," Jessie answered.

"What's up, Todd? We're headed over to Chase Tarrif's house to follow up on something."

"I thought you might want to know; Dr. Lindquist has found something he wanted me to pass on to you guys. He rushed the lab work on our victim and found something very interesting in her system. He found a drug called—" there was a shuffling of papers and some mumbling before Todd spoke up, "—Vecuronium. It is considered a neuromuscular blockade. It works by blocking the signals for the nerves to the muscles, resulting in a state of complete paralysis. But it has no effect on the consciousness, and it does not block pain sensation."

Alex was frowning as he concentrated on the road before him. "So, what does all that mean in the context of our victim?"

"It means she couldn't move at all to defend herself during the attack. She was awake and fully aware of everything the unsub did to her. She would have felt everything and not been able to utter a single scream the entire time," answered Jessie.

"My God, who could do something like that?" asked Alex.

Jessie didn't answer. Her mind was spinning. She had a hunch that there was more to come but waited for the acting police lead to speak up.

"And there's one more thing," Todd said.

Jessie felt a chill run up her spine as she waited for more horrors.

"The doc says the woman was alive when her joints were broken and her limbs twisted around like that." Again, he could be heard rustling his notes. "Apparently, there was active bleeding in and around the areas of the broken joints. He said that it's a very strong indication the person was alive when it was done. He also says that since there are no massive contusions showing impact at the site of the injuries, the wounds weren't inflicted by a piece of equipment, like a hammer or something. He is now certain they were done by hand." The car was so quiet that Todd finally had to clear his throat. "You guys still there?"

"We're here," said Alex. "Look, do me a favor and send us everything the doc found. In the meantime, we are heading over to the Tarrif place. If your officer gets there first, just have him sit outside the gate to their property and let me know if anyone leaves the house."

"You got it. I'll email you the full autopsy report from the coroner. We also started the paperwork to obtain the warrant to go into Jordan Myer's home. I submitted for that as soon as we learned her address." The line went dead, leaving Jessie and Alex to sit in silence, digesting the latest information they had received.

"That was smart with the warrant," Jessie finally said. "I'm sure it will be a no-brainer for the judge."

Alex agreed. "Todd's not a bad guy. I think his strength is going to be in the office however, not the field."

Jessie didn't respond, pressing her lips into a thin line. She had worked with men who were better at strategizing than field operations and she knew they were still capable of causing a lot of damage. Especially if their eye was on a prize other than serving the greater good.

"Is he a lock to take over his uncle's position? Any time frame?"

"I guess it's just more a given than anything else," replied Alex. "The chief has one foot out the door already, so I'm betting he'll retire end of the year." He let out a deep sigh. "Then Todd will officially be my boss. Should be fun."

"You need to establish boundaries with him now," said Jessie. "And decide what you want your working relationship to be. Otherwise, he'll establish it based on what he wants out of it; and trust me, you don't want that."

Alex shifted in his seat then changed the subject. "Have you ever seen or heard of someone doing that to a body with their bare hands?"

Taking a deep breath and exhaling slowly, Jessie turned to face Alex. "I've never seen it myself. But during my time in the military, I heard whispers of black sites using drugs like the one found in Jordan's system as interrogation techniques. It's illegal, of course, but much of what happens on those sites is off the books. Only the worst of the worst were committed to those sites. Enemies of the state that would never see the light of day again..."

"Jesus. Sounds like there is more to it."

"We need to focus on the atrocity at hand. Maybe one day we can swap war stories," Jessie said, returning her gaze out the window.

They rumbled across the railroad tracks, and the difference between the two sides of town were immediately felt. The increased rumble in the roughness of the highway echoed the feel of small, one-story homes, some of which appeared to be little more than shacks.

"Here we are," Alex said, pulling up to a modest house with peeling paint and an unkempt lawn. He shut off the engine and they stepped out into the late morning sun.

They approached the house and Alex knocked at the door. A television blared in one of the rooms and the sound of a baying dog barked somewhere in the house. The door creaked open and Chase Tarrif's bloodshot eyes swept over them.

"Alex," he said, giving the officer a nod. His eyes drifted in Jessie's direction, but he only acknowledged her with a stiff raising of his chin. "What can I do you for?"

"Chase," Alex said in greeting, "we were checking in to see how the boys are doing, and also to ask a couple of follow up questions. Would that be okay?"

The man hesitated for a moment then turned to

shout over his shoulder. "Dina, put the dog out back, and boys, turn that noise down. There's someone here to see you." Stepping aside, he let them enter the small living room. The space was dominated by a large television fixed to one wall with a couple of loveseat-sized sofas and a La-Z-Boy recliner facing it. Heavy blinds were drawn, adding to the almost claustrophobic feel of the room. The boys looked up, eyes large as Alex and Jessie entered the room. "Hi, boys, remember me?" Jessie said, keeping her tone non-threatening. They both nodded in unison. "Well, me and Officer Alex here just came by to check in and see how you're doing."

"They've been fine," said Chase, looking at the boys.

The boys exchanged shy glances before cutting their eyes to the floor. There was a commotion from the kitchen and Dina Tarrif stepped out, wiping her hands on a dishcloth. Dark, heavy bags weighed under her eyes. "They're not fine. They're having nightmares, waking up screaming every night." She stared defiantly at her husband, daring him to deny it.

"Did you call the therapist I recommended?" asked Alex.

For once, Chase seemed to lose his bravado. "Not yet. But maybe it wouldn't hurt."

He didn't meet Jessie's eyes, and it was a good thing. Anger flooded every inch of her being as she witnessed what the man's cruelty had wrought on the children. The boys were probably suffering from post-traumatic stress and their ass of a father had probably been telling them to "shake it off".

Ten minutes. That's all she wanted with the man. See

just what he'd be able to shake off by the time she finished with him.

Jessie gave a knowing nod to the boy's mother. Dina Tarrif turned to the children with a smile. "Boys, go outside for a bit while the grownups talk, alright?"

She didn't have to tell them twice. They clearly would have preferred to be anywhere other than in the presence of a police officer and Jessie. The back door out of the kitchen banged shut behind them as Alex turned to Chase.

"Look, I'm sorry I didn't take this as seriously as maybe I should have. But you know we can't afford some fancy shrink when the kids had no business being out there in the first place," Chase said.

Alex held up both hands, trying to deescalate the situation. "Chase, there won't be a bill. The crisis counselor who works with the station will see them free of charge. Now, if they need any deeper therapy to deal with the issue, we can cross that bridge when and if we come to it. The town has some discretionary funds that the mayor sets aside and I'm sure we can work something out. The main thing is to get them kids the help they need before things get even worse for them. Agreed?"

Chase was suddenly sheepish and couldn't hold Alex's gaze as he slowly nodded his head. "We'll make an appointment for them tomorrow." He glanced at his wife, her face hardening as she struggled to hold back emotions. She nodded and headed back into the kitchen.

"Look, Chase," said Alex, "We didn't come her just to check on the kids."

The other man's eyes grew hard as distrust seemed to creep into his steely gaze.

"We've identified the body your sons found as Jordan Myer. Did you know her?" Alex asked.

The man flinched, his lips drawing tight. "No. Can't say that I do."

Jessie stepped forward. "That's strange considering she was the realtor who sold you this house." She watched the man closely, looking for any changes in his body language that might suggest he was hiding something.

Chase's shoulders slumped. "Look, do you know how long ago that was? Dina and I were just starting out. The kids hadn't come along yet...a lot has happened since we bought this place. I honestly don't remember the name of the person that sold it to us."

Jessie narrowed her eyes at him. "It's just that this is a very small town. I find it interesting that you don't remember ever seeing her again in all the time you've lived here."

"I don't think I like what you're implying," Chase said.

"That's okay. You don't have to," Jessie replied.

"I think we are done here," said Alex, moving to step between the two of them. "We'll be leaving now. If you do happen to remember anything, give me a call, okay?"

As they were leaving, Dina appeared back in the doorway. Her eyes met Jessie's, holding her gaze for a split-second too long. Then she disappeared back into the kitchen.

Before walking out the door, Jessie turned. "One last thing, Mr. Tarrif. Are you familiar with Vecuronium?"

The man looked genuinely puzzled. "What's that?"

Jessie gave him a little smile. "Nothing. Not important."

Once outside, Alex stopped on the porch. "What do you think?"

"He's not our killer. Something may have gone on between him and Jordan, but he definitely didn't kill her."

Alex's phone buzzed and he glanced quickly at the screen. "Looks like we got the warrant to search Jordan's house."

"Good," said Jessie, heading for the car. "Time to see what our victim can tell us about who murdered her."

19

ARM BAR FOR THE WIN

Arm Bar for the Win

J ordan Myer's house was on the right side of the tracks perched atop a hill with distant views of the lake. Surrounded by rolling acreage of mature trees and heavy undergrowth, it wasn't the type of place that someone would just stumble across.

"Someone cherished their privacy," said Jessie as they pulled up to the house.

The house itself was a blend of rustic charm and contemporary appeal. The exterior was a mixture of warm caramel-hued woods and large glass panels allowing glimpses of the large great room that dominated the center of the house.

"Maybe," said Alex as they exited the car. "But it also reminds me of living in a fishbowl."

He was right. Jessie scanned the landscape and saw multiple points along the tree-lined property where someone would easily be able to watch the home's occupants without fear of being discovered. She made a mental note to check the area after sweeping the house. If someone had been lying in wait there, they would have most likely felt a degree of comfort that could have made them sloppy.

Together they made their way down the stone walkway to the expansive, covered porch. Jessie was looking at the ground, glancing up and down the landing leading to the porch as they approached.

Alex looked at her questioningly. "What are you looking for?"

She didn't look at the officer as her eye continued to play across the lined sidewalk before finally landing on something. "This." She made her way to one of the rocks that made up a decorative boundary and lifted it. "This rock didn't quite match the others and it's hollow." The top of the fake rock lifted off in her hands to reveal a door key hidden inside.

The large, double front door seemed solid enough as they stepped across the porch. Alex inspected the jam before knocking loudly. "Doesn't look like it's been tampered with."

Before Jessie could push the door open, a shadow flitted through the house, barely visible through the large transom windows to either side of the door. Jessie glanced at Alex, her heart jumping a few beats. She leaned close to the officer and whispered. "Go around back and check for signs of a break in. If someone is in there, they didn't use the key to get in the front. I'll go in here and try to flush them your way."

Alex hesitated, giving her a doubtful look.

"If we both go in here, and there is a back door, we could lose whoever it is."

Reluctantly, Alex agreed. He nodded and silently disappeared around the side of the large house.

Jessie slid the key into the lock and pushed the heavy door open. An alarm chimed when she pushed it open, but no security alarm went off.

The doors opened to a large, high-ceilinged great room. From there, the house divided into two wings, with the kitchen just beyond the main living area. The house was a mix of styles, but the main level was pretty much one large room. Through the spacious kitchen, Jessie could see a set of French doors leading to a patio.

She saw Alex slowly make his way onto the flagstone that led to the doors. He pushed lightly and one of the doors gave way, giving off a second chime from the alarm system. As he stepped inside, Jessie slowly made her way towards him, listening for anything that might give away an intruder's presence.

Alex made his way towards her, crossing the kitchen, and passing by an opening that led to one of the wings to the right of the house.

Too late, Jessie saw the intruder as he rushed Alex's back, striking the officer with what looked like a small, wooden art object. It struck the police officer's back with a thud, sending him sprawling to the ground. Jessie sprang forward, just as the intruder turned to run for the patio door. The figure was dressed in gray pants and a black, long-sleeved sweatshirt, which Jessie was able to grab just before he made it to the doors.

He pulled free, but she slowed him just enough to get

close enough to wrap her arms around his waist. The man grunted, turning around and swinging at her wildly. Years of military training kicked in as she sidestepped the blow, knowing the man would be thrown off balance by the miss. She could tell he wasn't a trained fighter, and as he stumbled, his right arm crossing his body, she reacted with a quick punch to his side.

He grunted, but turned on her, trying to grab her around the shoulders. His eyes were wide, and spittle flew from his lips as he attempted to shove her away to continue his escape. Jessie crossed her left hand across them, grabbing onto his wrist. With a sharp torque of her body, she bent him double, his hand bent up and back in a manner that put enormous pressure on his arm. Her mind raced and she realized if the man didn't stop, she would be forced to break his elbow. He struggled against her, and she shook her head, steeling herself for the sharp snap of bones that was to come.

"Stop." It was Alex's steely voice that made the intruder freeze. That and the barrel of his Glock 22 pressed against the man's temple. "John Bartley, don't make me put a hole through that pea-sized brain of yours."

The man went limp in Jessie's grasp, and she slowly relaxed her grip on his wrist.

"On the floor, now," said Alex, grabbing the man by the neck of his shirt and shoving him down. Once he was on the floor, Alex placed a knee in his back and heaved his arm painfully upward. "What the hell is wrong with you, man?"

The man he called John Bartley grimaced and

grunted a reply. "Thompson? That you? I swear man, I didn't know it was you."

"You're under arrest, John," Alex said with a growl.

"What? What for?"

"Well, for resisting arrest and assaulting an officer to begin with. And then there's breaking and entering as well as the possible the murder of Jordan Myer as well," replied Alex.

John Bartley's body became as stiff as a statue. His voice dropped. "Murder? She's dead? Oh God..."

"Yes, she is. And you just became my number one suspect."

"No man, I swear, I didn't. I would never do that. It can't be true..."

Jessie stared at the man, her breathing finally slowing. "What were you doing here? Why did you try to run if you had nothing to do with her murder?"

The man was gasping for air, and at first Jessie thought he was having an asthma attack, but then, she saw the look on his face as he tried to turn and look up at them. He was afraid...and more than that. He was in shock.

"I tried to run because I thought you were the people that did that." He jutted his chin over his shoulder. "Back there in the bathroom. I...I would never..."

Alex gave Jessie a look, her eyes following the direction John was indicating. It was towards the hall of the wing where he had been hiding. She gave Alex a nod. He pulled out a set of handcuffs and snapped them on John's wrists, cuffing them behind his back.

"You move from this spot or try something – anything

at all – and I won't hesitate to shoot you where you lie. Understand?"

The man nodded, dropping his face against the floor, his body limp. Jessie watched as he slowly began to shake. Whatever he had seen back there had been enough to nearly traumatize him. Together, they headed towards the back of the house, Alex leading the way, gun pointed ahead and down as they eased through the hallway.

The room opened into a large, primary bedroom, and as soon as they stepped across the threshold, they were hit by an unmistakable smell. It wasn't as bad as the boathouse, but it carried the same, rancid undertones, biting at their eyes and stinging the nostrils.

Alex pointed to an open door to one side of the room.

Jessie's adrenaline surged as they approached the master bath.

The smell got stronger as they approached, and when they stepped inside, Alex heaved as he struggled to control his stomach. Jessie felt dizzy as she took in the sight before them.

"Jesus Christ," Alex said, turning his face to the side.

20

WHAT'S IN THE FRIDGE?

What's in the Fridge?

The house had filled up with police officers as Jessie watched Alex question John Bartley once again, trying to find a crack in the man's story.

"Okay, John, tell me again. What were you doing here?" He had out his notepad and was comparing John's answers to the first time he had questioned him while they were waiting for backup and the medical examiner to arrive.

John exhaled sharply, his leg bouncing uncontrollably. "Man, I told you. I came looking for Jordan because she hadn't answered any of my texts while she was on vacation, and I knew she was due back in town. So, I called her. And then texted again. Still no answer and her phone kept going straight to voicemail. I decided I would drop by to see her in person. I arrived just before you did, I swear it."

"And the bathroom?" Alex asked.

Sweat broke out on John's forehead and his skin turned ashen. "I swear to you, I had nothing to do with that. I might have done some messed up shit in my time, but that…hell no. I swear on my mama."

Alex scoffed. "I happen to know you'd sell your mama down the river if it meant saving your own hide."

John continued shaking his head. "No, man. Not me. We've had our run-ins, and I know you think I'm responsible for a lot of the bad shit that goes down in Pine Haven…but I would never do that. And I would never…would never hurt Jordan."

Jessie caught something in his tone. "John, how did you get in here? The extra key was still in its hiding place when we arrived."

He looked sheepish and stammered something they didn't catch.

Alex rolled his eyes as he reached out to haul the man to his feet. "Okay, enough. I'm charging you with two murders, John. Jordan, and whoever that is in the bathroom."

"Okay, wait," he said, taking a deep breath.

"I came in the back. My car is parked at the bottom of the hill, opposite the lake. I have a key and I came in through the back door."

"What are you doing with the key to a murder victim's house, John?" Alex asked.

He hesitated, taking another deep breath. "Because we were in a relationship. I loved Jordan, and I would never do anything to hurt her." His voice broke and he began blinking rapidly as he looked up to the ceiling, struggling to hold back tears. "I loved her."

Jessie stepped closer to the man and shoved her hand in his pocket. Both he and Alex looked at her in shock when she pulled out and felt around in his other pocket, before drawing out a key and holding it up. She didn't have to try the key to know it would fit into the patio door locks. As much as she hated to admit it, John was telling the truth. At least about that much.

"And our friend in the bathroom?" Alex asked, again.

"You gotta believe me. I don't know anything about that."

Alex motioned to another officer to come over. "Wesley, can you take John here down to the station. Charge him with assault on a police officer." He looked at the man, holding his gaze. "If we find anything connecting you to that—" he motioned over his shoulder, "—you're going to regret not speaking up when you had the chance."

Just as the policeman was about to lead him away, Jessie stopped him. "John, why didn't you park in the driveway?"

He looked at her like he didn't understand the question, his face deepening in color. Finally, he answered. "Because Jordan didn't want anyone seeing me come up to her property. She wasn't ready to tell anyone about us, so she had me always come in the back way. But that was my key, not a spare."

Jessie nodded, and the officer took the man out of the house. She and Alex turned just in time to see Dr. Lindquist come out of the primary suite hallway. He had a grave look on his face and was rubbing his eyes.

"That is a mess," he said. "Another headless body

with the fingerprints burned off. At least this time the limbs weren't turned around."

"The body was also left in a tub of water," said Alex. "What is the significance of that?"

The coroner shook his head. "My guess? It was a tub of ice that melted. Another attempt to hide the time of death. But with this one, I'm betting it was a much more recent kill."

"Doctor, what about the blood splatter?" asked Jessie. "That was a considerable amount of blood, even for a beheading."

Alex looked at her out the corner of his eye. "You've seen your fair share of beheadings?"

"Only the aftermath," she said, grimly. "But there was blood everywhere in that bathroom. The walls, the fixtures, the ceiling." She brushed past Alex and the doctor and headed into the bedroom, looking around. "But there isn't a drop in the bedroom."

"What are you thinking?" asked Alex.

"There is no way someone was this messy in the bathroom—" she turned and studied the bed and dresser, "—yet left not a drop of blood in here. There aren't even any footprints. He must have put down a tarp or something. Because if he did that in there, he would have left some cross contamination somewhere. No way he didn't step in blood. So that means he was prepared for what he did. Definitely took his time."

She slipped on a pair of yellow crime scene booties and carefully stepped into the bathroom, averting her eyes from the naked, headless man lying in the tub. She walked over to the walk-in shower and inspected every inch of it, her eyes stopping on the bar of Dove soap. It was ivory in color, but the underside was slightly pink. She pointed to it, turning to the coroner. "He showered after doing his dirty work. Then managed to get back out of the room without leaving footprints." Her gaze drifted around the room, locking onto the blood covering nearly every surface in the room. "There's so much blood because all of this did not come from that one body. Dr. Lindquist, I'm betting if you run as many samples as possible, you'll find two different blood types. This is where he killed Jordan. And then later, that man."

Dr. Lindquist had his phone in hand and was speaking quickly as he headed back out. Together, Jessie and Alex moved back into Jordan's bedroom, taking a closer look at what might have transpired there. Jessie walked around the bed and stopped.

There was a box on the floor.

Alex reached into his pocket and took out a pen. Using the tip, he flipped off the brown top. Inside were a few pieces of clothing. Using the pen, Alex was able to lift a black leather jacket, a couple of sweatshirts, and two pairs of jeans. Beneath those were a toothbrush, a comb, and a valentine's day card. Holding the card open by one corner, he read the inscription. "Forever yours, let's make this real. Signed..." He looked up at Jessie and then back at the card. "Johnny Boy."

Jessie stared at everything. "She packed up his things. She was breaking up with him."

"That could definitely be motive," said Alex. "That's why he was in such a frenzy to get ahold of her. Might also explain that comment he left on her social media."

"That would definitely explain that. But I don't think he killed her."

"How can you be so sure?" Alex asked.

"Because I saw the fear and the hurt in his eyes. He wasn't faking that. And more importantly, whoever killed Jordan has the training that John Bartley just doesn't possess. He's not a fighter. He telegraphed that swing he threw at me by a country mile. He wouldn't have any idea how to dislocate and break someone's joints with his bare hands." She was shaking her head in exasperation. "He was shaking, breathing uncontrollably. No way he could have pulled this off. Whoever did this didn't really care that we found the body. They just wanted to make sure we couldn't find out who they were."

She continued to move around the room, opening the closet door and going through Jordan's things. On a whim, she reached under the mattress of the bed, freezing as her hand closed around something. When she pulled it free, Alex's eyes grew wide.

"Is that Wasp and Hornet spray? What in the world?" he said.

Jessie stared at the spray can. "A lot of women who live alone keep this in strategic places around the house. It's better than mace. You don't have to get close to an assailant, and it can cause severe corneal burns which could lead to permanent blindness." She seemed to think for a moment. "Of course, if Jordan was killed here, in her own home, then that would mean..."

"That she knew her killer," said Alex. "For him to get close enough and her not go for that stuff." Now he was the one who looked around.

Jessie grimaced. "Back at the realty office, Tess said she was seeing someone that she kept a secret. I assumed it was John Bartley. But he said Jordan didn't tell anyone they were seeing each other. Wouldn't even let him come up the main drive for fear of someone seeing him. What if he isn't the person that Jordan told Tess about? Christ. Jordan was dating her killer."

They both jumped as a shout rose from outside the bedroom, followed by urgent calls for the coroner. Racing into the kitchen, they saw a couple of the police officers who had been charged with photographing and securing the rest of the house pale and shaking.

"What is it?" asked Alex.

The first officer turned and ran to the sink, heaving for air.

"No!" screamed Jessie. "If you're going to hurl, go outside, far away from the house!"

The second officer just pointed at the open refrigerator.

Jessie took a deep breath and followed Alex to the appliance. There, on the center shelf, next to a plate of cold cuts, was a human head. It most likely belonged to the man in the bathtub and as she looked at it, Jessie felt the world begin to close in around her and her vision began to tunnel.

"Jessie? What is it?" asked Alex.

"That...that's the man who was impersonating Jordan in the real estate office. He's the man who gave me the keys to my house."

21

ASKING FOR HELP

Asking for Help

J essie stood outside at the end of the driveway, looking out at the dying light of day. Her eyes were unfocused, her body ramrod stiff, arms hugged around her body. The fingers of her right hand were a flurry of motion as she strummed continually, her lips moving in count.

That was how Alex found her, and immediately sensed something was amiss. He approached her slowly, stepping into her peripheral vision, waving a hand as he called her name. "Jessie? You okay?" He frowned, stepping closer, but not touching her. "Jess – you in there?" As a last resort, he placed a hand on her arm, giving her a gentle squeeze.

Her body had been tightly coiled, and his touch set her off. In a blur, she had his arm locked in hers, causing him to throw his head back in pain. The palm of her hand sliced through the air, stopping a hair's-breadth from his nose.

She blinked rapidly as her stupor faded and realized how close she had just come to breaking her friend's nose, and possibly shoving the cartilage into his brain. "Alex? Oh my God, I'm so sorry." She released his arm, watching as he shook the needles that had suddenly imbedded themselves into his bicipital tendon. "I...my mind was somewhere else. I didn't hear you."

His eyebrows dipped as he gave her a stare. "Well, I was calling your name and standing right beside you."

"I'm really sorry. I guess this whole thing has spooked me a little more than I realized."

He looked at her like he only half believed what she was saying. "I was going to ask if you wanted to go with me to take another run at John Bartley. Confront him with what we have found out. See what more he might want to tell us."

She looked away, unable to meet his eyes. "No. That's an excellent idea and you should do it. I need to get home to Blizzard. He'll be starving by now. Plus, I might have an idea about someone who can help us get a better grasp on who we are dealing with here."

He worked the last kinks out of his arm by opening and closing his fist a few times. "Let me guess. You know someone who has a working knowledge of anesthetic drugs and knows how to break people's joints?"

She offered a wan smile. "I just might. Not sure how willing to help they might be though. It's been a while since we spoke. But you should definitely speak with

Bartley; see what you can get out of him. And...I'll let you know what I find out. I promise."

"Yeah. Sure thing. Come on. They're wrapping up the scene. I can drop you off on the way back to the station."

She wanted to decline his offer and look for another ride home, but she also knew that doing so might make the wounds she had just created something that couldn't heal.

The car ride back to her house was an excruciating exercise in silence. After spending nearly all of the last few days in Alex's company, Jessie had found it all too easy to converse with the man. To go from such ease to strained and awkward silence was almost more than she could manage. Luckily, the ride ended before the tension became too unbearable. She opened her door to get out and Alex turned to face her.

"You know, if there's ever anything you want to tell me, you can. I don't judge," he said.

Jessie grimaced to herself, turning her face away from him. "I know. Thank you." She stepped out of the car and leaned back in before closing it. "And I really am sorry about the arm. I'll let you know what I find out tomorrow."

He didn't answer, just waited until she was up the stairs and had her key in the lock before he slowly backed out of the gravel drive.

"Great job, Jessie," she mumbled as Blizzard practically knocked her off her feet when she stepped through the door. She ruffled his head. "Look at you! What a good boy. I am so sorry for being gone so long, but you were so good! Yes, you were. Let's get you all taken care of."

She spent the next forty-five minutes walking, feeding and watering the dog. Once she was satisfied his needs were met, she opened the fridge to her meager supplies of left over wine basket foods. The sight of it brought back the image of the fake realtor's head in the refrigerator and she quickly closed the door, her hunger becoming non-existent.

"Okay, no more stalling. Might as well get this over with."

She looked at her watch. It would be eight, possibly nine hours ahead where he was. At least it wouldn't be the middle of the night. She sighed, took out her phone, and fired off a quick text. Then she sat on the couch, phone resting beside her, and waited.

Exactly fifteen minutes later, her phone buzzed displaying an unknown caller. She took a deep breath and answered.

"Jess? What's happened? Are you okay?" The voice on the other end was close to panicking.

"Brody. It's okay. I'm fine. Why would you jump to something being wrong?"

There was an exhalation of relief in her ear. "Well, it's not like you've called to check in on me before. I figured something awful must have happened."

Ouch. She closed her eyes and sunk back against the couch. "I'm sorry for that, Brody." She seemed to be doing a lot of apologizing lately and wasn't exactly proud of that.

When he spoke again, his voice was softer but still guarded. "It's actually good to hear your voice." He paused and Jessie could almost hear him debating whether to continue. "I heard about what happened. The trial, I mean. How are you doing with all of that?"

"About as well as could be expected, I guess. I mean, having your life laid bare before a tribunal and then being summarily stripped of everything you ever worked for...was interesting."

Brody barked a laugh into her ear. "Your idea of interesting is...interesting."

"I missed seeing you at the funeral."

"I know. I am embedded pretty deep here. There was no way I could get out to come to the service."

She was pretty sure that wasn't true but didn't want to press the issue. Her brother's relationship with their father was complicated. No one knew that better than she. "Brody, I assume it's early where you are? Do you have time for me to run something by you?"

"Of course. It's early morning here. I can't tell you exactly where I am...but let's just say the sun's barely up and I'm already sweating."

"I moved to Pine Haven. Dad left Aunt Gina's house to me, so I'm staying here while I decide what to do with it."

Her brother huffed on the other end, but when he spoke his voice was light-hearted. "Of course he did. Not that I care or anything."

He was kidding, but she still felt a tinge of guilt. "You never even liked this place."

"That's not the point. It's just that it might have been nice to be asked if I wanted it."

She digested that for a second, chewing on it along with the ramifications. "I'm not sure yet. Originally, I was going to sell. Use the money to...disappear. But it's not such a bad place. Just has a bad problem at the moment."

"Oh yeah? What's going on? Is that what you called about?" The concern had returned to his tone, and for a moment, he was once again her little brother trying to protect her from the world.

She sighed. "Yes. I need your expertise in something."

She then proceeded to tell him everything that had happened since arriving in the idyllic lakeside community, leaving out only the part that someone may or may not have been in her home one night. There was no point in alarming anyone about that since she wasn't even certain it had happened. She waited a beat after telling him the last of the gory details about the head in the refrigerator. "And that brings me to calling you."

The silence on the other end lasted long enough for her to worry the call had been dropped. "You still there?"

"I'm here, Jess." Her brother's voice sounded small and constricted. "Why are you getting involved in this?"

She'd be lying if she didn't admit to herself that very question had crossed her mind more than once. "I guess the short answer is, because someone must. Whoever this killer is, he's set up shop here in Pine Haven. He's not going to stop until he's caught – or killed. And I'm not sure the police here can do that on their own. They are in way over their head, Brody."

"And maybe you're in over yours as well. Have you thought about that? You're not in the military world anymore. Civilians think and act completely differently from what you're used to."

"I know. But, Brody, whoever is doing this is a psychopath. They are enjoying what they're doing. And we have both seen what happens in situations like that." He didn't answer, but she knew he agreed with her. "I just need you to tell me if you've heard of or seen anything like this. The use of drugs to render someone helpless, and then the whole joint thing...it feels like someone with very specific training is doing this."

Her brother sighed. "Jessie, I can probably request a leave and be there in a few days. I don't think you should be facing this alone."

"No." She had probably said that too quickly, but the last thing she needed was the distraction of her brother and everything that might bring with it. "Like I said, I'm not alone. The police force here is definitely up against something they aren't prepared for, but they're learning. Alex – I mean, Officer Thomas – is a good man. He's competent."

"Oh, I see."

Jessie hesitated. "What do you see?"

"Something in your voice changed when you mentioned the police officer." He let that dangle in the air before giving it a little pull. "Nothing wrong with that, of course. You're no longer devoting your life to the military now, so it's about time you found someone you have an interest in."

I don't have an interest in him. Not like that.

That's what she wanted to say, but it didn't come out. "So, what is your take on everything I told you? Does it sound military to you?"

Brody sighed. "Honestly? If you mean military as in it

sounds like someone who has set their sights on you, then yes. Come on, Jess, someone impersonates a realtor and meets with you and then ends up dead? In the same manner as a body that is found not that far from your house? Doesn't take a rocket scientist to put this together." He paused. "Does your cop friend know?"

Now it was Jessie who paused. "It's something we need to discuss."

"Jessie...have you told him *everything*?"

"I plan to let him know. The time just hasn't been right."

"When will it be right? Over the third body?"

That one stung, and she took in a sharp breath. "I'll deal with that. I just need your help in figuring out what we might be dealing with here."

"Fine. Can you send me X-rays of the first body? And the full tox-screen? I'll look that over and get back to you as soon as possible. And Jess?"

"Yes?"

"Are you sure you don't want me to come help? I'm worried about you."

She closed her eyes, head dropping back against the couch. The fact that he said that meant more than she would ever admit. "No. I'm just tired. I'll be fine. You concentrate on doing whatever horrible thing it is they have you doing. I'll handle things here."

They said their goodbyes and the line went dead. She held onto her phone for a moment before heading upstairs to bed. As she climbed under the sheets, she resolved to have the conversation with Alex tomorrow.

Closing her eyes, she hoped sleep would be peaceful;

but she knew better. She'd rather face a hundred murderers than disclose the truth to him.

22

REVELATIONS

Revelations

The next morning, Jessie felt like she had been hit by a train in her sleep. Her body ached from tossing and turning most of the night. Her brain felt fatigued from images of headless torsos and broken limbs flooding her third eye.

Blizzard was lying at the front door as she made her way downstairs. Opening the door, she let the dog out and waited on the porch for him to do his business. As he ran back to her, she smiled languidly at him. "You know what, boy, I am taking you with me today." She reached down and ruffled his fur. "Today, you're going to be my emotional support dog."

She made her way back up the stairs, took a nice, long, hot shower, and changed into a pair of jeans and a short-sleeved white tee shirt. Once she was ready, she led Blizzard to the Jeep and the two of them headed into town. One stop at the coffee shop later and they were pulling into the police department parking lot.

Carrying a bag of croissants and two boxes of donuts, Jessie made her way into the station. There was an officer she didn't recognize working the reception desk, but she didn't hesitate to smile and greet him, offering him first choice of the donuts. Honestly, it was a bribe for the man to keep an eye on Blizzard who had plopped down in the waiting area. Then she made her way to the break room, placing the boxes and the croissants on the center table for everyone to enjoy.

Just as she was about to leave the room, Alex entered.

"I heard you were here." Immediately, Jessie sensed something was wrong based on his tone.

"I am. What's the matter?"

He seemed agitated and shrugged. "Not sure. The chief said he has something he wants to address. He has that smug look on his face, so whatever it is, it can't be good."

He led her into the conference room, and immediately she was struck by the tension in the air. Todd seemed extra fidgety, and even the mayor's face was tighter than usual. Only the chief appeared at ease.

And for some reason, that worried Jessie. Especially when his eyes seemed to light up when they landed on her.

"Ah, there's our special guest," he said.

Jessie tensed, making her way to the back of the room. Whatever this was, it couldn't be good.

The chief continued. "I understand you had a tussle with John Bartley."

Jessie stared at the man. "Is that a question or a statement?"

Chief Walker's upper lip quivered as it drew back in a snarl. "Do I need to remind you that you are not a sworn officer of the law? You are a consultant. You don't interact with *anyone*...and you certainly don't attempt to break their arm."

"I did what the situation called for. We were attacked by someone at the scene of a crime. I didn't stop to think about how a consultant should handle the situation," Jessie replied, letting her annoyance at the man show.

He glared at her. "Well, I hope you know that as a result of your actions, we've had to cut Bartley loose. He was threatening to sue the department for allowing an unlicensed officer of the law to physically assault him."

Jessie felt her mouth drop open and her fists tighten at her sides. "You what?" She gave Alex a glance, but the officer didn't – or couldn't – meet her gaze. "That is an egregious breach of protocol."

"First, you don't know our protocol. This ain't the big city or wherever you cut your teeth."

Jessie grimaced, unable to believe what she was hearing.

The chief wasn't done as he narrowed his eyes in her direction. "This is a community; and we do things a little differently here. From what I understand, you don't even think John is the killer, so wasn't no point in keeping him behind bars and risking a lawsuit."

Jessie wasn't sure what she was more angry about. That he was proving himself to be an A-1 level asshole or that Alex had told him what they discussed. "He may or may not have been the killer. How I felt was irrelevant in the course of the investigation. But whether he did it or not, he was still a suspect in an ongoing murder investigation. You had probable cause to hold him for at least forty-eight hours." Now she was the one who narrowed her eyes. "Unless, that is, you had another reason for letting him go."

"What exactly are you implying, missy?" His voice was shrewd and cold.

Jessie swallowed hard. "It seems that this isn't the first time you haven't wanted to deal with John Bartley from a legal standpoint. From what I learned, he was the number one suspect in an arson investigation. An investigation that was mysteriously closed and signed off on by you."

That one hit home. She saw him visibly flinch as a red flush spread up from his neck. A vein on the side of his head throbbed with the increased blood flow. She could practically feel the heat rolling off the man. She'd seen the look in his eyes before; in the military personnel she had helped to convict when she confronted them with irrefutable evidence that would earn them time in a prison or dishonorable discharge at the very least.

Those men usually erupted in acts of violence aimed at her, and judging from Chief Walker's body language, it appeared he was about to learn the same painful lesson they did.

He stood, drawing himself to his full height in an effort to intimidate her. She braced herself, already seeing at least three different ways she could have him on his ass before he could lay a finger on her.

Despite her readiness, there was no defense against what he ultimately hit her with.

"Well, I can certainly see why they kicked you out of the military. You just don't believe in playing well with others, I see."

Jessie stared at the man. He hadn't laid a finger on her, but it felt like she'd just taken a gut punch from him. Blood pooled in her temples as she stared daggers his way.

He raised his eyebrows, widening his eyes to a comical degree. "Oh, I'm sorry. Was that not supposed to get out? That you didn't so much retire from the military as you were *kicked out.*" His expression changed and his face became deadly serious. "Do you think I'm going to let someone walk through my doors and not find out everything there is to know about them?"

Jessie felt everything start to fade from her. She refused to give into the anger and humiliation she felt. She wanted to run from the room. Go back to her house, board herself in, and climb under the covers of her bed with a hundred-pound dog.

That was an option she had. But it was not an option for Jordan Myers. And whoever killed her sure as shit wasn't going to go crawling home due to embarrassment. She swallowed hard and met the chief's eyes, unwilling to give him any satisfaction.

She lifted her chin in full defiance of his attack. "I agreed to help you solve a murder and bring the killer of a member of your community to justice. What may or may not have happened in my personal life has no bearing on that. If you are saying you don't want my help, then that's fine. Call in the FBI and let them take this over." She turned and headed for the door, only to be stopped by the mayor's voice.

"I don't think we are at that point. From what I understand, the team here is making progress.".

"Mag— Mayor," began the chief. "How can we trust someone who turned their back on the United States government? We don't even know what she did to piss off Uncle Sam, but it must have been pretty bad."

Jessie swallowed. At least that told her that her records had indeed been sealed by the government. Thank God for small favors. She turned to see all eyes in the tiny room on her.

Again, it was the mayor who spoke up. "And that is not our concern, Chief Walker. I'm sure, if there is something Ms. Night feels we need to know, she will tell us. Until then, does anyone have a problem working with her to catch this killer?"

There was an uncomfortable silence in the room, but no one dissented. Jessie fully expected to hear the chief voice his opposition, but he just stood there, face beet-red, as he clenched and unclenched his jaw. Of course, it didn't matter that he had been silenced. One glance at Alex told her the damage had been done.

"So, can someone please update me on next steps?" said the mayor, smoothing nonexistent wrinkles from her perfectly pressed pantsuit.

Todd cleared his throat. "Well, it looks like we were able to retrieve a laptop from our victim's house, and we have sent it off to the forensic lab down in Rowan County to see what they can pull off it. We should hear something back by end of evening or tomorrow at the latest. That might help shed any light on what may have happened to Jordan Myers."

The mayor stood, the ever-present Will Mason mimicking her moves as he stuffed his notepad and pen into his pocket.

"Good," she said. "I look forward to hearing more. In the meantime, I expect there will be some...brainstorming, or whatever it is you do." She moved to leave, but then turned back to the room. "I'm having Will draft a statement. Rumors are starting to fly about what happened to Jordan. People are getting scared. I'm holding a town hall tomorrow to address the situation and reassure the community that we have everything under control."

Jessie's mouth dropped open. "But, Madam Mayor, we don't have everything under control. To speak out now—"

The mayor held up a hand. "Don't worry, I will leave certain details of the investigation out. Unlike some, I do know how to perform my duties." She didn't have to glance the chief's way as she left the room.

Jessie headed out as well, Alex close on her heels. She stopped in the waiting room, trying to regain control over her breathing as she bent to rub Blizzard's head.

"Are you okay?" asked Alex.

She had expected him to blast her as well. He had every right to. "Not really. I want...I want to hit something."

Alex nodded before a smile spread over his face. "You know, I may just be able to help you with that." He pulled out his phone and a second later, Jessie's own phone pinged. "Go home, put on some sweats, and meet me at that address in thirty minutes."

Jessie looked down at her screen, and for the first time, found herself unable to contain a brief smile as a sense of elation spread through her.

23

OPENING UP

Opening Up

"Not this time, boy," she said. "And don't give me those sad eyes. You stay here and I'll see you soon." She gave Blizzard a pat on the top of the head and headed out to her Jeep.

She keyed the address from her phone into the navigation system and headed out. According to the nav, her destination was about a twenty-minute drive away, just across the railroad tracks to the outer edge of town. Pulling into the gravel parking lot for an auto repair shop, she questioned if it was the right address. Then she saw the tiny, wooden sign above a door to the left of the garage that read "Marty's Cross-fit". Her eyes swept the tiny parking lot, finally landing on Alex's squad car. This was the right place alright.

Inside the gym, the smell of leather and canvas punching bags, the sharp, metallic tang of perspiration, and the clean scent of antiseptic products used to wipe down the mats and equipment assailed her nostrils. She closed her eyes and breathed the air in, a smile breaking across her features.

The place smelled like hard work, discipline, and the raw physicality of combat sports. Jessie felt right at home.

As she moved deeper into the space, her eyes adjusted to the harsh fluorescent lighting. High ceilings accommodated long, sand-filled heavy bags. Around the room there was the usual assortment of tractor tires, ropes suspended from the ceilings and pull-up bars mounted to the walls.

The gym was vibrating with energy. It was a symphony of exertion – the rhythmic thud of glove against bag, the grunt of effort, the soft scuffle of bare feet against mats. All coalescing into a greeting that welcomed Jessie into an arena she had missed more than she was willing to admit. This was a world she was familiar and comfortable with. Unlike the strangeness of the civilian realm, this place was dedicated to sculpting one's body and mind. A place where everyone was judged on their skill...not their sex. No one in here would dare call her 'missy'.

However, looking around, she realized something she was not prepared for. She was the only female in the gym.

Of course she was. Why had she expected anything different?

"Jessie!"

It was Alex, and she turned to face him as he trotted up to her from one of the corners of the space where the floor was covered in wrestling mats. "Hey, you made it."

Her smile was genuine. "After that last meeting, I

really needed to let off some steam. So, it was either this or I was going to drag Blizzard on a ten-mile run around the lake, and I'm not sure he would have enjoyed that."

Alex smiled and nodded as they began walking back towards the mats. "Believe me, I understand." He stopped and turned to face her. "Hey, I'm sorry about what happened in there. I don't even know how things went that sideways. I mean, I sensed something was up with the chief. We were going over our debriefing and he just kept acting more and more strange. And that made me nervous, and when I get nervous, I tend to ramble and talk too much, and that was probably when I said more than I should have. I'm sorry for that."

His breathing was already rushed and now he appeared to be on the verge of gulping for air. Jessie placed a hand on his forearm, letting him know to stop and try to calm himself.

"It's okay. You were doing your job. And I suppose the chief was doing his as well." Her tone was begrudging but cordial. She needed Alex and didn't want to alienate him. "So, you didn't strike me as a cross-fit type of guy." She stole a quick glance at his physique. He was wearing sweatpants and a sleeveless tee that emphasized his toned torso. Until now, she had only seen him in his uniform and that bulky shirt he had worn the night they had dinner. All the cuts and bulk on display now had been hidden away. She mentally gave her head a shake, reminding herself not to ogle the man she was building a work relationship with.

"Oh, I'm not really into all that...at least not to the level these guys are. But I've been into boxing for the last few years as a way to keep in shape. And tonight is freestyle night, so some of the area martial arts guys and wrestlers come in to practice on each other. After you said you wanted to hit something, I thought this might work for you." He winked at her. "Maybe you can show me that trick you pulled with John Bartley's arm. He said it felt like you were about to rip it out of its socket. You must be a lot stronger than you look." His eyes widened as he considered what he had just said. "Not that you look weak or anything. That's not what I meant to say at all."

Jessie laughed. "It's okay. I understand. In the military I trained in judo and jujitsu. I'll be the first to admit I can't go toe to toe with men...especially ones in the military. But judo isn't about trying to match someone's strength. It's about using leverage and restraining techniques that rely more on timing and precise technique to take an opponent down."

Alex frowned. "Kind of like what our perp did to his victims' limbs?"

"No. Nothing like that. That was way beyond anything I was ever taught. But I did get ahold of someone that I think can provide some more insight."

Alex tensed slightly. "The person you were going home to call last night?"

She nodded. "Brody knows way more about what it would take to do damage like we saw. I sent him some of the pictures of the X-rays of Jordan Myers to take a look at."

They made their way to the padded area where two men were using towels to mop up sweat stains that had been sprayed with liberal amounts of sanitizer. Alex nodded to them in thanks before stepping forward and motioning for Jessie to join him.

She looked around, noting that there were only a couple of men still standing around the mats as she walked up to Alex. "So...you want to spar?"

He shook his head. "No. I want you to show me how to restrain someone. The stuff we learned in the police academy here was a bunch of fake karate stuff that I'm pretty sure the instructor learned from watching old Bruce Lee movies."

Jessie frowned. What kind of training were they providing these officers up in the mountains? Although until now, he was pretty sure none of them had ever had to get physical with anyone. Let alone someone that could probably kill them in the blink of an eye. That was what Alex was asking her for. He wanted to learn how to protect himself against the type of person that could kill a woman they knew and desecrate her body.

They stood facing one another, shoulders squared. Jessie nodded to the larger man. "Okay, well, first, show me how you would attack me."

Alex pondered her request for a moment then shrugged. He dropped his right leg back and moved into a typical boxer stance, leading with his left hand. Sliding forward, he extended his right fist in a jabbing motion, stopping just before he would have made contact with Jessie's chin.

She rolled her eyes at him. "No, not in super-slow-motion. Throw a punch."

· He frowned but nodded, dropping back into his

stance. He launched forward, this time moving far quicker than before, his fist arching in for the side of her jaw. Jessie stepped aside while simultaneously grabbing his wrist out of the air. With a deft tug, she had him bent double, his hand bent around at an odd angle as she controlled his upper body.

He grunted in surprise, dropping to one knee as she released him. "I didn't even see you move. That was pretty cool. Show me how to do it."

They resumed their positions, and this time, as he moved forward slowly, Jessie explained what she was doing. "The secret to judo is balance and positioning. Mastering how to maintain your own balance, while disrupting your opponent's. Get them off balance and stumbling, then apply a grappling lock." Again, she maneuvered him onto the floor, before letting go of his arm. "There are various throws at the heart of judo as well, but those can get tricky and not something you want to attempt without adequate training. Then there are more advanced grappling and ground fighting techniques we can get into that would definitely aid you in a street fight."

Alex nodded, and then slid forward, moving behind Jessie and grabbing her around the torso. "What if I did this?"

Jessie grimaced. "Then I would do this." She bent her knees and lowered her hips. "This drops my center of gravity in case you thought about picking me up to slam me on the ground." One of her legs slipped back slightly between his. "This helps me further stabilize myself and prepares me for this—" She squatted down and very quickly stood back up, causing Alex to loosen his grasp on her slightly. It was enough for her to slam an elbow into his side, eliciting a sharp grunt. At the same time, she pivoted until she faced him, and slid her arm under his left shoulder as she threw her right hip into his midsection, bending sharply at the waist.

The hip throw worked perfectly, and he slammed to the floor, knocking the wind from him as he stared up at Jessie.

She leaned over him, smiling. "You're in a very vulnerable position right now. There are so many... unpleasant things I could do to you."

Alex tried to smile, wincing as he struggled to catch his breath.

Jessie plopped down on the mat beside him. "Alex, I'm sorry."

The officer groaned as he sat up to face her. "No, it's all good. I asked for this, remember?"

"No, not that." She dropped her head, focusing on her folded hands in her lap. "I...I was going to tell you all the stuff the Chief brought up. That's what I wanted to talk to you about this morning. I knew at some point it would come out, and I wanted you to hear it from me." She sighed, unable to meet his gaze.

"So, then why don't you tell me about it in *your* words."

The fingers of her right hand started to strum, and she immediately grasped it with her left before placing it under her thigh. "What he said was true. I was dishonorably discharged from the military. I lost everything I had built; my retirement, my savings. My plans for the future.

That's why I'm here. Because I had nowhere else to go. I came here, hoping it was far enough away from my old life that I could start fresh...somewhere away from my past."

She stopped talking and glanced up at Alex. His green eyes were locked on her, and she knew what he was about to ask.

"Do you want to share why you...were dismissed?" he said, cautiously.

She gave him a half smile. She liked the way he worded that. It was the least hurtful way, and she appreciated his thoughtfulness. "As a military investigator, my primary job was to gather evidence and build cases the prosecutors would ultimately try. They would base trials around what I presented. Investigators work on any number of cases, ranging from drug use and possession to sexual assault and harassment to misconduct. In my case, I specialized in espionage and treason as well as war crimes and homicides. I investigated military personnel who had potentially been turned by enemy states or had committed particularly heinous crimes during times of war. And I was – *am* – proud of my conviction rate. I was responsible for locking up a considerable number of really bad people who committed atrocities in ways you don't want to know." She paused, looking around the gym. The two men who had been watching them from beside the mat had moved off to another area and seemed to be in a competition to see who could do the most pull ups.

"It's alright. No one here is associated with the department." Alex said, sensing her reluctance.

Jessie fought through her discomfort and forced herself to continue. "As I told you, my father was a career military man, and his father before him. It was pretty much a foregone conclusion that me and my brother would follow in his footsteps. My father retired a colonel with full benefits, but he was forced to retire early due to his health. He was diagnosed with lung cancer as a result of chemicals he inhaled as an infantryman." She looked away, focusing on the few remaining members in the gym before continuing. "He wasn't the only one. Most of his platoon suffered from exposure and received the same diagnosis. He wasn't bitter about it. If anything, he was just pissed that his time in the army had been cut short.

"At the time, my brother was assigned to a special forces unit overseas and shipped out, leaving me to take care of our father. Daddy refused any home health care – said it made him look too weak – so I took on the role of his caregiver while also maintaining my workload in the office. That was when I was handed a case involving a potential whistle blower who had been leaking details to the press about the United States' involvement with an off-the-books black site used to interrogate political prisoners into giving up secrets on their country's military plans and capabilities.

"My investigation led me to someone who, by all accounts, was the whistleblower. Of course, they denied being involved in any of it, but the evidence that led me to them – as well as what was recovered on site and in their phone – said otherwise. The trial was fairly routine; an open and shut case. The whistle blower was convicted of treason and sentenced to military prison. One week into their sentencing, they were found dead in their cell. They had hanged themselves. I didn't really think anything about it, until about a year later.

"My father was on his last legs, he was down to a couple of months left, maybe six at the most. He asked me to get his final affairs in order, and I began going through things in his office, taking boxes of documents and files to him to ask what he wanted done with them. I came across a flash drive that, when I showed it to him, he became very distressed and ordered me to destroy it, and not to open it." Her eyes focused far into the distance as she began to relive the moment that changed her life forever. "I sometimes wish I had done as he asked.

"Something just wouldn't let me destroy the drive. Every time I looked at it, there would be this little whisper in the back of my mind. Finally, I popped it into my laptop and opened it. It wasn't even encrypted, which I found strange. On it was a series of correspondences between my father and someone known as Chimera. There were copies of messages between them over a TOR network that, to this day, I have not been able to trace. But in those messages was information about the black site that was the center of the whistleblower investigation.

"It turned out the suspect I had built the case against wasn't the guilty party. They were framed by the real whistleblower. My father."

She heard Alex gasp but still couldn't bring herself to look him in the eyes. Instead, she drew herself to her feet and slowly walked off the mats, heading for the door. Alex followed at her side.

"So, I was torn. I knew what I should have done, according to military law...but I couldn't do it," Jessie said.

"He was your father," Alex replied.

She nodded. "That, and the fact he had months left to live. Did I really want him to spend those last days going through military courtroom procedures? Being locked away in a cell? I just couldn't do it. And I told myself, so what if I did turn it over? It wouldn't bring back the innocent life that was taken because of my actions. So, I locked away the evidence. And once my father passed away, I turned it in."

Alex stopped walking, staring intently at her. "Why would you do that? You had to know what would happen."

She nodded. "I knew. But it was the right thing to do. That person who hanged himself had a family. One that was denied access to their retirement and benefits because of what I had done. So, I turned it over." She shook her head in dismay. "Of course, I had no idea just how many enemies my father had made over the course of his career, or how far they would go to discredit his daughter. Everything I had done, every conviction I had made, was looked at and reviewed, and most were thrown out because I was now a dirty investigator...and who knows how many cases I had tampered with in order to secure a conviction. So, because of me, a lot of really sick individuals were turned loose. Granted, they were still kicked out of the military, but they were no longer in prison."

"Jesus," said Alex, running a hand through his hair. "Talk about painting a target on your back."

She turned to face him. "Exactly."

The officer's eyes grew wide. "You don't...? I mean... you don't think whoever killed Jordan and that impersonator...could be after you, do you?"

She didn't say anything, just turned away and continued toward the gym exit. This was what Brody had hinted at and it was also something that had been in the back of her mind for days now. "I don't know. I hope not."

"But Jordan was killed before you arrived. That business with the realtor was before you arrived as well. Did anyone know you were coming here?"

She shook her head again. "No one."

Other than my therapist, that is.

"Still. The fact that it was the broker for my house who was killed, and then the man impersonating her was killed as well...it can't be coincidence." She turned, looking at Alex. "I'm the only connection we've found between these two."

Alex didn't say anything as they made their way outside into the parking lot. "I think we should grab a bite. This is a lot to take in and I think better on a full belly."

"Actually, that sounds good to me. I still haven't had time to do any real grocery shopping. I've been living on coffee, pastries and the crackers from the welcome basket I—" She stopped mid-sentence.

"What? What is it?" Alex pressed.

"The gift basket I received from the realty company for closing on the house. It was sitting on my front porch when I arrived at the house. If Jordan was already dead, she couldn't have arranged to have it sent. So who did?

Our mystery impersonator? It's a long shot, but maybe he paid with a credit card or wherever he purchased it, the salesperson may remember talking to him." She looked down, shaking her head in annoyance. "That's such a long shot though."

Alex wrinkled his brow in thought. "Was it a wicker basket with gold tinted plastic wrapping? Filled with little jars of jellies and jams as well as crackers?"

Jessie's eyes lit up. "Yes, that's it. Do you know where it came from?"

"I think I just might. And luckily, the fellow who made it is very talkative. We might just get lucky."

24

TIGHT TEES DON'T LIE

Tight Tees don't Lie

The Pine Haven Lakeside Bed and Breakfast sat in a prime location, overlooking the lake. It was a picturesque homage to southern grandeur and charm. Jessie marveled at the beauty of the old Victorian as her Jeep rattled to a stop next to Alex. It was three stories of whitewashed clapboard siding that had weathered gently with time and appeared softened by the dappled shade of the mature willow and oak trees surrounding it. There was a generous wraparound porch replete with white rocking chairs for the visitors to sit and enjoy the sweet tea that Jessie envisioned the Bed and Breakfast provided.

The high pitched, chipped roof was capped with a widow's walk and dormer windows. The front yard was small but elegantly manicured, with a stone walkway that led to the expansive porch. Large, double doors painted a deep green greeted them.

"This is where the basket was made?" asked Jessie.

Alex was climbing out of his car and nodded. "Mark Carmichael is one of the owners. He has a talent for weaving wicker and makes the baskets and the arrangements. But it's his husband, Eric Jensen, who makes the jellies and jams that go in them. They are very popular. Started off he would give them out to the guests staying here, and soon, people all over the area were asking for them to give out as gifts or just keep for themselves. He's made a good penny off packaging them in gift baskets." Alex smiled at her. "Like the one you received."

Jessie spoke up as they headed up the steps to the porch. "You know, I was thinking on the way over here that it's possible Jordan placed the order for the basket well before she was killed. I mean, we had been corresponding by email for a while as she was getting everything ready for me. If that's the case, the basket could have been premade and delivered by anyone."

"It's possible, except that Mark doesn't allow for delivery services to touch the baskets. He either delivers them personally or he insists on them being picked up by the ordering party. He's a stickler about that."

He opened the wooden door and allowed Jessie to step through. Inside, she was greeted by the soaring ceilings that were characteristic of grand Victorians, and large windows that flooded the space with natural light. Polished hardwood floors in the entry spilled into a large, open living space dominated by a large, wood burning fireplace with tastefully maintained antique furniture arranged to take advantage of the mantel's charm.

Off to one side of the entryway was a small, built-in

desk that blocked entrance to a darkened doorway behind it. There was a ledger and a tiny silver bell sitting atop the desk, and Alex wasted no time in walking over and tapping the top of the bell. Immediately, there was a flurry in the room beyond and then a figure appeared, stepping up to the desk offering the two of them a beaming smile.

"Alex!" he said, "What a pleasant surprise."

"Mark," replied the officer. "It's good to see you." He turned in Jessie's direction. "This is Jessie. She's new here, just arrived not long ago from Colorado."

"Well, it's nice to meet you, Jessie," the man said, extending a hand. He was on the shorter side, about the same height as Jessie, with thinning hair so blonde it was almost white. His features were sharp, and his dark brown eyes pierced into her as she shook his hand.

"Thank you. Likewise," she replied.

He dropped her hand and immediately turned to Alex; his dark eyes gleaming. "Alex, we heard about that awfulness with Jordan. I can't believe she's gone. You know the rumor mill is churning about what happened to her, but no one has heard the official story." He leaned over the desk slightly, dropping his tone to just above a whisper. "You know, if you need to share the details, I won't tell a soul."

Alex grinned. "Now, why would I need to share that, Mark?"

The man smiled broadly. "Well, if we knew what happened, we might know what to look out for until the killer is caught. You know...to keep our clientele safe."

Jessie made a show of looking around the large

bottom-floor space, before turning to Mark, her eyebrow arched.

He waved a hand at her. "Oh, it's slow now, but just wait...the summer rush is right around the corner."

Jessie knew what he was saying was true. In a matter of weeks, the town would be crawling with more out-of-towners flocking to the lake. That didn't give them a lot of time to solve this case. More bodies meant more opportunities for the killer to slip away.

Or blend in.

"You know, Mark, it's interesting that you bring that up," said Alex.

The man's eyes widened. "It is? You're going to tell me what happened?"

"Not exactly," replied Alex, "But we do need your help." He turned to Jessie and nodded.

"Mark, when I moved into my house, there was a welcome basket sitting on the front porch for me. It was beautiful. Filled with a couple bottles of wine, some crackers and cheeses, meats, and some delicious-looking little pots of jams. Alex seems to think that basket came from you."

Mark seemed to blush as he waved her off. "Well, yes, that would be one of ours. But I can't take all the credit for it. My husband is the cook in the family, and he came up with the jams everyone is so crazy over."

Jessie smiled and glanced at Alex. "Well, that's good to know. Do you happen to know who placed the order? Was it Jordan?"

The man frowned for a moment. "I don't remember exactly. But it had to be. She always asks for one when she makes a sale. I believe…" He moved to the laptop sitting on the desk and keyed in a couple of strokes. "The order for it was placed by email. Yes, here it is." He pointed to something Jessie and Alex couldn't see. "I remember thinking it was odd that she did that because she usually calls when she needs one. Or stops by in person. "He leaned in and again dropped his voice. "Between you, me and the four walls, I think she has a bit of a crush on Eric. Oh my. Excuse me – she *had* a crush." He shook his head, closing his eyes. "So tragic what happened."

Alex cleared his throat and spoke up. "Do you remember who picked up the basket when it was ready?"

"No. I wasn't here when that happened. That was the day I had gone to the hardware store to get some new paint brushes. We are updating the kitchen and trying to get it finished before the place fills up. But Eric was here." He leaned back and shouted, calling the other man by name. His voice cut through the first floor of the house, and Jessie had to fight the urge to place one finger in her ear to stop the ringing. "Eric! Can you come here for a minute!"

Soon, a shuffling noise from behind Jessie and Alex caught their attention, and another figure appeared out of the living room. Compared to Mark, he was a giant of a man. Standing at least six and a half feet tall, broad shouldered and dressed in denims and a tee shirt that struggled to contain his biceps, Eric marched up, nodding to Alex with a grunt. "Alex." Then he turned to Mark. "I was right around the corner in the kitchen. What are you yelling about now?"

Mark rolled his eyes. "Alex and his friend Jessie are here—" He stopped, looking at Jessie. "I'm sorry, I didn't catch what you are to Alex..."

"She's consulting on the case with us," said Alex.

"Oh," replied Mark, giving her a newly appreciative stare. "Well, they have questions about the order Jordan placed for the last gift basket we did for her. It was for Jessie."

Eric turned to face them. "I'm sorry to hear what happened to Jordan."

Out of the corner of her eye, Jessie saw Mark grimace, his eyes rolling yet again. She filed that away and instead focused on Eric. "Thank you. But we were wondering who picked up the order. Do you remember?"

Eric nodded. "Sure do. It was her boyfriend."

Jessie felt a tingle move down her spine. "Are you certain?"

"Well, that's how he introduced himself," Eric answered. "And he had the receipt that Jordan had paid online and a copy of the emails. Said she told him to pick up the basket because she had a meeting with a new client that had popped up." The big man shrugged. "I didn't think anything about it."

Alex reached into his pocket and took out his phone. He pulled up a picture of John Bartley and showed it to Eric. "Was this the man?"

Eric shook his head. "What? That's John Bartley. No way she would have had anything to do with someone like him."

Jessie didn't say anything but pulled out her own phone and showed him a picture of the man who had been impersonating her. "What about this man? Ever see him before?"

Eric studied the photograph. "No. That wasn't him and I've never seen that man before."

"Do you think if we can sit you down with a sketch artist you could describe the man who picked the basket up?" said Jessie.

"I suppose. I mean, it's been a week almost, but I could give it a shot."

"That would be great," she replied. "One more thing... when was the last time either of you saw Jordan in person?"

Eric and Mark exchanged quick glances.

"Maybe three weeks ago?" said Mark. "I ran into her at the coffee shop. She was all excited about a vacation that she was about to take." His face went stern, and he lowered his voice again. "You don't think...I mean...that man that was in here and picked up the basket; do you think he was the *killer*?"

Alex jumped in quickly. "We did not say anything like that, and don't you go repeating it. We just want to make sure we speak to everyone who may have had contact with Jordan before her death."

As they headed out, Jessie turned to Eric. "I'll have our sketch artist reach out to set up a time to meet with you. Thanks again for making time for this."

"You're welcome," said Mark. "Oh, and you guys should come by for dinner after you wrap this up. We'd love to get to know you better, Jessie."

She hesitated before giving them a smile and walking out the door with Alex.

"What did you think?" Alex asked.

"Something about the look they exchanged when we asked when they last saw Jordan didn't sit right. Also, I saw Mark's reaction when Eric mentioned it was such a shame what happened to her. I'm not saying they're hiding anything, but I don't think they told us everything they could have, either."

Alex took in a deep breath as they reached their respective cars. "What now?"

Jessie thought for a moment. "Why don't we pay John Bartley a visit?" She saw the look Alex gave her. "Not to press him. Just to check in on him since his release. See if he needs anything."

Alex gave her a smirk. "Well, I guess it can't hurt to check in and see how he's doing after the trauma he's been through. Losing the love of his life and all. Follow me."

25

THE DEAD'S JOURNAL

The Dead's Journal

The Gray Eagle was located across the railroad tracks, and as far on the outskirts of Pine Haven as you could be and still qualify as having a Pine Haven address.

While technically open to all, the array of motorcycles of all makes and models sitting in the gravel parking lot made sure that anyone venturing too close knew exactly what they would be in for if they decided to walk into the bar.

Jessie stood beside her Jeep, surveying the entrance to the bar as Alex walked up. "I don't see any lookout."

"Nah, you won't. There's really no need for it. Nothing illegal happens out in the open here, so John and his boys really have nothing to be worried about. The bar is really a front for everything else that they might have their fingers into."

Jessie nodded. "Could be a front for money laundering. Lots of cash in and out of a place like this."

Alex looked at her appreciatively. "Exactly what I always thought. But the chief always said there was no need to go poking a bear that was hibernating."

Jessie frowned. "You know, I'm no expert on civilian police departments, but it sounds to me like your chief is awfully tight with someone who could potentially be a crime boss."

Alex didn't respond, only narrowed his eyes at the bar before heading towards the entrance. Outside the doors, they could hear a wall of sound inside – raucous laughter, loud, inebriated conversations, the clinking of glass bottles. But once inside, all of that gradually quieted as steely eyes turned in their direction. While Alex appeared not to notice, Jessie was immediately hit by the thick, stifling air. The smell of stale beer mingled with fried foods, cigarette smoke and something rank and acrid that she couldn't place.

The interior of the bar was a shadowy maze of narrow halls and dark corners stuffed with worn, wooden tables and chairs. The low ceiling seemed to trap the smoke, creating a haze that dimmed the already low lighting. The bar itself stretched along one side of the room. It looked to be carved from a single, mammoth piece of scarred timber and was lined with cracked leather stools.

Around the space, men and women, dressed in varying degrees of denim and leather, watched the duo with hardened eyes. Jessie had seen the looks being shot their way before. In military bases around the world, she was seen as trouble. The principal stopping in to view a class. The Internal Affairs agent swinging by the precinct haunt for a glass of beer with the fellas.

It was a look of silent unity among the people. One that said, be careful, *they've* breached our territory.

Jessie followed Alex to the bar, eyes forward as she ignored the daggers being stared her way. The bartender was a particularly mean-looking man, with a large beard and a scar that ran from the top of his forehead down to one milky white eye.

"You need something?" His voice was gruff, matching the rest of him. "Or maybe you're just lost."

Alex mustered a smile. "No, not lost. We need to speak to John."

The bartender's good eye trailed over to Jessie. "Who's *we*?" He turned back to Alex. "And John's not here."

Alex didn't reply but leveled a hard look at the man. "Really? Cos I'm pretty sure that's his hog out there. Or maybe I'm mistaken. Maybe I'll go take a closer look at it. I think I might have seen a busted tail-light…"

He motioned over his shoulder towards the front entrance, and multiple people in the bar stiffened; a few of the men started to rise to their feet.

"Josie, that's enough."

The bartender's face went red as Jessie looked over his shoulder. John Bartley was standing in the opening to a dimly lit hallway that led away from the bar space. He looked at the two of them, then motioned for them to follow him as he turned and headed back down the hall.

Alex gave the bartender a smirk as he and Jessie made their way around the bar and down the hall. They followed John through a doorway at the end of the hall marked 'Office' in green lettering. Inside, the space was the opposite of what Jessie had experienced in the bar.

It was a large, windowless room, filled with sleek furnishing and state-of-the-art security monitoring equipment, and dominated by a large, steel and glass desk in the middle of the room. On the desk were multiple computer screens and a single, closed laptop. A full bar made up the back wall behind the mahogany leather desk chair, and John motioned towards it. "Can I get you guys something?" He saw the look on Jessie's face as she took in the space. "What? A little more than you expected?" He motioned to the couch that sat opposite the desk as he plopped down in the chair. There was a short, stylish glass tumbler filled with an amber liquid sitting next to the laptop. John scooped it up and took a large gulp from it.

"Looks like someone keeps a closer eye on their businesses," Jessie said.

John winced as he swallowed the whiskey. "Someone has to."

"How you doing, John?" Alex asked.

The man waved his hand at him. "You can dispense with the pleasantries, Alex. We both know that's not what you're here for. What do you want?" He eyed the officer, a glint passing through his eyes. "Did you find who did that to Jordan?"

Jessie stared hard at the man, watching his every move.

Alex cleared his throat. "John, did Jordan break up with you?"

The bar owner visibly flinched, looking away from

the two of them. He reached for his drink and exhaled sharply. "Yeah. She did."

Jessie raised an eyebrow. She had half expected him to lie about it. She watched as the man seemed to deflate, his body sinking into the chair.

"So, what were you really doing at her house?" Jessie asked.

He stared down into his nearly empty glass, swirling around the few drops that remained. "I wanted to find something – anything – that would tell me who the bastard was that she had started seeing." Like the rest of him, all the energy had fled his tone at that point. He looked up at Alex. "Whoever he is, she took up with him while we were still together. That was why I was there. I swear."

"And did you?" said Jessie. "Find anything that told you who she was seeing?"

John looked sullen, chewing at the inside of his jaw. "Hell no. But I'll find him." He narrowed his eyes. "And if you're thinking he was the bastard that did Jordan...well, you won't have to worry about a trial if I get to him first." He looked at Alex with defiance, daring the officer to tell him differently. Jessie caught his eye and he quickly looked away.

"But you did find something, didn't you?" she asked. "What was it, John?"

His face reddened a bit before he finally blew out an exasperated breath. He reached into the top desk drawer and pulled out a piece of paper, slamming it before them.

Alex picked it up, scanning the printout. He passed it

to Jessie, giving John a hard stare. "That what I think it is?"

John's only response was a shrug.

"Where'd you find it?" asked Jessie.

"Jordan used to keep a journal that she was always scribbling in. One I wasn't allowed to see. I knew where she kept it and figured it might have something in it about the guy she was seeing. But when I saw it was just *that*...I tore the most recent sheet out and kept it."

Jessie gave a curious look to Alex. "Was a journal on the list of things removed from the house and tagged as evidence?"

Alex frowned, scratching at the back of his head. "Not that I recall. Definitely something to check into. Who knows what else might be in there." He glanced down at John. "We are going to need this."

John sighed. "Take it. I have a copy."

They left the bar, each breathing a sigh of relief as they stepped out into the open, fresh air.

Alex turned to Jessie. "I know it's probably not your favorite place right now, but do you feel up to heading into the department? We need to examine that and see why there's no record of a journal being removed from Jordan's place."

Jessie took a deep breath but nodded. Every instinct she had told her why there was no record of a journal. Someone in the precinct didn't want it seeing the light of day. And now they had the smoking gun that might prove why.

26

NOT IN KANSAS

Not in Kansas

The door to Chief Walker's office was open as Alex and Jessie stepped inside. His eyes immediately cut to Jessie. "What are you doing here? I figured you'd have crawled back to Colorado, tail between your legs after everyone learned who you really are."

She gave a half laugh, determined not to give him any satisfaction. "You would have liked that, I'm sure. But that wouldn't have helped with this town's problem. Or helped solve Jordan Myer's murder."

The big man's eyes narrowed. "You're a consultant I hired. That means I can also fire you."

"You could. But I don't think you will. At least not so long as I have the mayor's blessing to continue working this case." Her tone was rising, and she sensed unease creeping into Alex's frame as he stood beside her. "And honestly, you have some nerve criticizing me for doing what I had to in my career. What about you? What have you been doing with your career?"

He sneered, his lip rising as if he suddenly smelled something rotten.

Alex intervened before things could go from bad to worse. "Chief? We found this when we were chasing a lead." He placed the journal paper on the desk in front of his boss. "It's torn from Jordan's personal journal. Everything was supposed to be removed and tagged from her house, but it appears this journal isn't among the evidence."

The man frowned and glanced at the paper. "And what? I'm supposed to know what this is? A bunch of... addresses? And numbers?"

"This is a handwritten ledger page," Jessie said. "The addresses are for properties Jordan has sold, and the numbers correspond to their selling price, and her cut... which is considerably higher than what she would have received as a legitimate commission. We believe that these are off-the-books clients she was working with."

The chief studied the paper, but Jessie could see that he was doing it to buy time for whatever excuse he was about to come up with to tell them to drop the issue. Instead, he looked up at Alex. "And you? What do you think?"

Alex cleared his throat. "I agree. We already cross referenced these addresses with the master list of Jordan's work we got from the realty office. None of these match."

The chief sat back in his chair, his bulk causing it to screech slightly on the floor. "What do you need from me?"

Jessie's lips pressed into a thin line as she tried to figure out his angle. Still, his willingness had disarmed her for the moment.

"We need access to your Computer Aided Dispatch system," she said. "It will let us see who the owner on record is for these addresses, as well as give us access to any 9-1-1 calls that may have come from the address or one next to it. We can look for anything abnormal involving the property."

The chief glared at her, then turned his attention to Alex. "You can have access. She doesn't have that kind of clearance, so she can only watch. Got it?"

Alex didn't even hesitate. "Absolutely, Chief." He turned, ushering Jessie quickly out the door.

"And Alex?" the chief called. "Be sure and keep Todd updated."

"Will do," Alex called over his shoulder as they headed for his cubicle. "Pull up a chair."

From her seat beside him, Jessie had a good view of his workstation screen. He pulled up a locked screen with a password box showing, and Jessie couldn't help but laugh when he lifted his keyboard to reveal a piece of yellow paper taped to the bottom. "Tell me that is not your password."

He smiled sheepishly at her. "What? I'm not a dispatcher. It's not like I access the part of the system that houses the CAD every day."

Jessie shook her head. Everything was so different from what she was used to in the military world. What was it that her father used to love to say?

Looks like we're not in Kansas anymore.

She watched as Alex slowly hunted and pecked his way into the screens they needed. While she waited for him to enter the first address, she carefully waded into the mine field. "So, that was weird the way Chief Walker just gave in on this, huh?"

Alex's fingers hesitated only slightly before returning to their play across the keyboards. "I...don't know. Maybe it's because he really wants us to find this killer and is doing what he can to help." He paused and looked over at her. "Or maybe it's his way of saying he's sorry for being a dick to you earlier."

Jessie twisted beside him. It made perfect sense. But she knew Chief Walker wasn't the type to apologize for anything. The only thing she was sure of was that if he agreed to let them look into this, he had ulterior motives. Before she could press the issue, Alex's back went ramrod straight.

"What is it?" she asked, leaning in.

"I put in the first address on the list, and it just returned the name of the owner." He stared at the screen. "This can't be right. It says it's registered to a Jebediah Thompson."

Jessie's eyes widened as she stared at Alex. "You mean Jeb? As in Blizzard's owner?"

Alex was nodding. "The one and the same." He clicked out of the window and opened another, entering a new address before staring dumbfounded at the name that came back to him. "Jebediah Thompson." He plopped back in the desk chair in exasperation.

Jessie's mind was whirling as she encouraged him to try another address. Same results as the previous two.

This time, she had Alex dig deeper, looking at the closing dates, bank statements and pulling the notarized deeds.

"All of these are cash transactions," Alex said, staring at the screen. "The signatures on the paperwork are all up to date. Everything is above board. What is going on?"

Jessie's mind wandered. There had to be something they were missing. "Is he secretly wealthy? Could he have been making these purchases to one day sell to a developer?"

Alex was shaking his head. "He is the nicest man alive, but he lives paycheck to paycheck, clearly dependent on his social security checks."

"Can you see the banks the money came from?" she asked.

Alex moved the mouse around, clicking and typing in boxes. "No banks on record. It was literally cash. Like, he walked into the closing with a bag of money and handed it over. No idea where it came from."

"That's not easy to do. Sounds like a laundering service to me."

"Yes. That's what I was just thinking."

Jessie thought for a moment. "Hey, enter the rest of these and then check the utilities. Maybe we'll get lucky there. I'll run to the break room and get us some coffee."

The feel of the chief's eyes on her as she walked past his office burned her skin. It took every ounce of control she had not to flip the man off. She had to remind herself he was still Alex's boss, and while there wasn't really anything he could do to her, he could certainly make Alex's life a living hell if he had to. Stepping into the break room, she was greeted by Todd and one of the police officers she recognized from Jordan's house. His name escaped her for the moment, but he was the officer that Alex had remove John Bartley from the house and escort him to the police station.

"Jessie," said Todd. He appeared slightly surprised, but quickly recovered and offered her a wide smile. "What are you doing here?"

"Hi, Todd," she responded, glancing at the other officer. "I'm working with Alex on something. Did the chief loop you in?"

"No. But he did tell me Alex had a lead on something. I was just on my way to find him. I didn't expect to see you back here, however."

Jessie swallowed the blush she felt rising. "Yeah, well, that makes two of us. But I'm not a quitter. Despite what you might have heard to the contrary."

Todd's eyebrow shot up. "Hey, I'm sorry about that. I did have a talk with my uncle after that meeting." If he was going to elaborate on the conversation they had, he stopped, seeming to think better of it. "I just want you to know that not everyone thinks like he does." He moved to stand next to her at the coffee maker as the police officer he had been speaking with left the room.

"Sorry, I didn't mean to interrupt," Jessie said. "I know that officer, I think. He was at the last crime scene."

"Oh, yeah, Wesley. He's new to the department. Just transferred here from out of state," Todd offered.

"Really? What state?" Jessie said, filing the information away.

Todd hesitated briefly before hitting her with another smile. "Tennessee, I believe. Why?"

She shrugged. "No reason. I just like to know the names of everyone I might cross paths with." She took the two cups of coffee in her hands and started to leave the room. "Hey, who works the evidence locker here? I need to get a look at everything logged in from Jordan Myer's house."

Todd frowned. "You just missed him. We all wear multiple hats here, but Wesley typically handles the evidence locker."

Jessie forced a smile. "Great. Thanks for that." She nodded and left the room, making her way back to Alex.

"Perfect timing," he said, looking up. "That was a good idea about utilities. There was a hit on three of the properties. They are the only ones on the list with water and electricity."

Jessie frowned, handing him the coffee. "Are they close to one another by chance?"

Alex shook his head. He reached into his desk drawer and retrieved a folded map. Opening it, he proceeded to draw a circle on the map for each address he had looked up. "None of the addresses are located within the same immediate vicinity. It makes no sense."

Jessie studied the map. "They are all on the far outskirts of town. None seem to be within the town limits. Strange."

Alex took the cup of coffee she offered him and folded the map. "I say we pay a visit. Maybe if we're lucky, someone will be home at one of those sites." He sipped at the coffee. "Also, on the way over, I can put in a call to see if Jeb is awake yet. Maybe he can help shed some light as to why he's buying up so much property."

"Good idea," Jessie said. "Oh, hey, what do you know about that officer from the crime scene? Wesley."

Alex shrugged as he stood up. "New guy. Solid reputation. Ex-military. Why?"

Ex-military. The words caused a tiny flag to shoot up in the back of Jessie's mind. "He's in charge of the evidence locker."

Alex slowly shut off his computer before turning to Jessie. "Interesting. He's also very close to Todd as well."

"And through Todd, the chief I'm betting. Hey, maybe we check this lead out before you bring Todd in on it."

"That's just what I was thinking," Alex replied grimly. Together, they headed out of the station. "Why don't you ride with me? You can reach out to the hospital on the way."

Jessie nodded. She felt eyes on the back of her neck as they headed for the parked cars. Something was off with the police department. She could feel it.

Judging by the way Alex white-knuckled the steering wheel, he could as well.

27

A BRAND NEW DRUG

A Brand New Drug

The first address turned out to be a bust. It was little more than a ramshackle, dilapidated old building that sat at the end of a winding, dirt road on the far reaches of town. The yard was filled with rusted-out cars, their hollow shells now home to families of rats that darted in and out. What lawn they could see, was little more than waist-high sawgrass and weeds.

The door to the house was dry-rotted and lying half off its hinges. One peek inside told them no one had been there in years.

"You sure the power is on in this place?" asked Jessie. "There's literally nothing here."

Alex shrugged, looking around the front porch. He took a tentative step to the side, careful of sagging floor-boards that would give way under the slightest pressure. Satisfied, he returned to Jessie's side. "You're right. Maybe the utilities were never shut off in the first place. Come on, let's get out of here."

As they headed back to his patrol car, Jessie's phone pinged. "It's the hospital. No change for Mr. Thompson. He's still in a coma."

"So much for questioning him," said Alex as they climbed back into his vehicle. "This next place is all the way across the lake. Should take us about twenty minutes or so to get there."

Jessie climbed in, her eyes still on the nearly falling down house that receded as Alex backed out of the gravel drive. "It just doesn't make sense. First, why would Jeb buy this place? There is nothing out here. It's way too far from town and the lake. Second, why keep the power on?"

As Alex eased the car onto the main road, Jessie's phone rang. She looked down, and the smile she gave it caused Alex's spine to straighten as he adjusted his grip on the wheel.

"Hey, Brody, what's up?" Jessie said. There was a pause as she listened to the reply. "No, I'm in the car with Alex now. We are following up on a couple leads. I can talk." A moment of silence followed. Jessie was nodding her head along with what was being said. "Hold on, I'm going to put you on speaker." She touched the screen of her phone and then held it out between her and Alex. "Can you still hear me?"

"Sure can," came the reply, even though the call quality from his end sounded like he was at the bottom of a well.

"Okay, can you start over again? I want Alex to hear

everything as well."

"Hey, Alex, nice to meet you," Brody said.

"Likewise. I understand you're somewhere in the Middle East. Thanks for taking time out to help us with this."

"Happy to do what I can. But hey, you guys have a problem on your hands. As I was telling Jess, whoever killed that woman is highly, highly skilled."

"And you can tell that, how?" asked Alex.

"There are a few things I saw on the X-rays. First, there is the fact the joints are dislocated *and* broken. The location of the breaks on each bone is very precise and in the same spot, which, in martial arts, are known to be weak points. This indicates that the attacker knew exactly where to apply force to cause a break. Second, the breaks are clean and well-defined. In many cases, forceful trauma causes comminuted or spiral fractures. The presence of clean breaks suggests a controlled application of force, consistent with someone who has a high level of skill. Next is the similarity of the fractures; the breaks on the different joints are almost identical. This indicates a precise, repeated technique, suggesting someone who has practiced this technique extensively. Lastly, there is the lack of collateral damage. In many violent attacks, one might expect to see additional damage, such as other bone fractures, dislocations, or soft tissue injury. The absence of such injuries might suggest a level of control and precision consistent with a highly trained individual." He paused, letting his words sink in. "Jess, you're dealing with someone who has spent their life learning how to hurt people."

"Christ," said Alex. "What would someone like that be doing in Pine Haven?"

Jessie took a deep breath, fearful of the answer to that question. "Tell him the rest, Brody."

"Oh, there's more?" said Alex. "Great."

"The tox screen Jessie sent me was interesting, to say the least," Brody said.

"Well, we know the killer used a form of anesthetic to immobilize the victim. We are already looking into the possibility of a pharmacy or hospital theft to obtain it," said Alex.

"You won't find any," Brody replied. "I took the liberty of having someone I know at one of the labs in Bethesda reach out to your medical examiner's office to get a sample of the victim's deep thigh muscle...it's one of the largest muscles in the body and can store a lot of toxins that wash out of the rest of the body."

"You did what?" interjected Alex. "On whose authority?" He turned to Jessie. "Did the doc tell you about that?"

She was just as dumbfounded as Alex and shook her head.

"Well, it might not have been completely above board, and honestly the less your coroner knows about it the better. But the lab at Bethesda is the best in the country, and I was hoping they'd find something to give you a leg up on this killer."

Jessie could see the muscles in Alex's jaw clenching as he gripped the wheel harder.

"If the chief finds out about this he's going to have both our heads. You know that, right?" he said to Jessie.

Brody broke in before she could answer. "Hey, I don't

want to cause any trouble. I can make it so that nothing ever happened. I can keep this to myself so you have plausible deniability if anything comes up."

Jessie shrugged. "It's your call, Alex. There's nothing your chief can really do to me."

Alex released a long sigh. "Fine. Let's hear it. What did they find?"

When he spoke again, there was an excitement in Brody's voice. "Okay, so the anesthetic compound that your lab found in the victim's system wasn't really enough to create the kind of immobilization that would be required to do what was done to her. As a matter of fact, Bethesda thinks it may have been administered after her death, in order to mask the real agent that was used." He paused, giving them time to digest his words before continuing. "So, Bethesda not only has one of the world's largest databases of chemicals, but they also have some state-of-the-art equipment used to analyze them. Not to get all technical, but they used something called a Gas Chromatography-Mass Spectrometry unit. It's a sensitive lab technique that separates chemical mixtures and generates a fingerprint of the distinctive mass-to-charge ratios of compounds present. It's used to find unique molecular signatures of substances meant to be untraceable. And what it found was an agent known as XR-572."

Jessie frowned. "I'm not familiar with that. What is it?"

"I'd be worried if you had heard of it," continued Brody. "It's a cutting-edge neuromuscular blocking agent that is still in clinical trials and not FDA approved. It was developed for some rather...clandestine uses in black site detainment facilities."

"How the hell would something like that make its way here?" Jessie wondered.

"Only two places it could have come from. Either the military or through corporate connections involved in its development. All of this points to one thing, Jess. You have a highly trained, government assassin on the loose in your quaint little town," Brody said.

Neither Alex nor Jessie spoke as the car ground to a stop. Surprised, Jessie looked up to see that they had arrived at the second address on their list.

Alex cleared his throat. "Hey, Brody, if this chemical agent is so rare, is there any way it can be traced to someone? If it was stolen, maybe there is a record of where it came from, or something like that."

"Great idea. I can do some more digging and get back to you guys with what I find. Look, Jess, I can speak with command...see how quickly they can get me out of here. I don't like the thought of you facing something like this alone," Brody said.

"She's not alone," Alex quickly snapped.

"Brody, thank you. But we both know you can't get out of whatever you might be doing, that easily. You've done so much and I – *we* – are grateful. But we got this. But do me a favor, keep all of this quiet on your end."

There was a moment of silence followed by a sigh. "Fine. I don't know how long the lab can keep it quiet that someone has access to experimental pharmaceuticals and is using them to commit murders. But the tech who did this for me owes me in a big way. I'll do what I can on this end. Just promise me you'll be careful and touch base with me when you can."

"I will. Promise. Look, we need to run. But let me know what you find out about that chemical."

The line went dead, and Jessie turned to Alex. "Looks like things just went from bad to worse with this case."

"It also looks like another bust with this place." Alex gave a nod in the direction of the house. It was another ramshackle, rotting siding and broken windows overlooking an unkempt yard. He shook his head as he slammed the car into park. "Do we even bother?"

Jessie was already opening her car door. "Of course we do." She climbed out of the car, her head locking on a structure off to the side, behind the main house. "Looks like this one has a barn. How fun."

"Should we search it or the house first?"

She shrugged. "Why waste the time. You take the house; I'll take the barn. Yell if you see anything."

"Fine. Watch out for rats," he teased as he headed for the front door.

Jessie headed for the barn and stopped a few yards before reaching it. There was a light shining through the broken wooden walls, and for just a moment, she thought she saw a flicker of movement coming from inside.

She took a cautious step forward as she looked back over her shoulder, checking to see if Alex was still in view. Before she could reach the barn door, she caught movement from the corner of her eye.

A figure darted out of the back of the structure and bolted for the woods beyond.

"Alex!" she cried, before sprinting after the person.

28

BLACK AND BLUE AND RED

Black and Blue and Red

Jessie plunged into the forest after the fleeing figure. Branches lashed at her as she tore through the thick underbrush. Her breaths came hot and fast, but she pushed on, bounding over fallen logs and ducking under snagging limbs.

Up ahead, she caught flashes of her quarry – a dark, fleet-footed silhouette slipping between the towering trees. Every time she gained ground, the figure would vanish again into the knotted shadows.

"Stop!" Jessie shouted. Her voice echoed between the dense trunks. "You're only making this worse!"

No response except the drumbeat of fleeing footsteps. Jessie grimaced. Her lungs burned as she tried to close the distance. Ahead of her, the shadowy figure ducked into a particularly dense patch of foliage. In the distance, she could hear Alex calling her name, but she couldn't tell if he was off to one side or trailing behind her.

Barreling into the foliage, Jessie came to a stop, her eyes sweeping the shadows for any signs of movement. Holding her breath, she listened for anything that might tell her which direction the person had fled, but it was hard to hear anything over the pounding of her heart.

The snap of a twig behind her caused her to spin, just as the end of a very large branch was headed towards her face. Instinct caused her to dive to the ground as it passed within inches of where her head had just been. Her foot shot out, making contact with her attacker's knee. He twisted to the side at the last possible moment, avoiding what would have been a crippling strike, but the blow was still enough to make him drop the stick with a grunt.

Jessie rolled to her feet to get some distance between them. He was tall with a wiry build. He was wearing a neck gaiter, pulled up to cover the lower part of his face. He dropped into a fighter's crouch, leading with his right fist. A straight jab came at her face, and Jessie sidestepped while grabbing his leading wrist. She pivoted in, throwing her back against his. She felt his weight shift as he dropped a leg back, expecting her to attempt to throw him.

Instead, she twisted at the hips and struck backwards with her elbow. There was a satisfying crack as she made contact with his cheek. He staggered, letting go of her as one hand reached for his face. With the other, he reached into his jacket and pulled out a snub-nosed revolver, pointing it at Jessie's head.

She backed up, raising both hands in surrender. His arm stiffened as his finger moved to squeeze the trigger.

"Drop it!"

The man froze in place as Alex slowly stepped forward, his own gun aimed at the man's torso. "Don't make me say it again."

Jessie watched the attacker's eyes as they locked with hers. They were wide and filled with desperation. He knew he was in a no-win situation. It was just a matter of what would come next. He let out a sigh, his shoulders slumping slightly as he slowly turned to face Alex. With a flourish, he pointed the gun at the policeman, and Jessie flinched at the impossibly loud crack of gunfire.

The man dropped to the forest floor; Alex's shot having struck him firmly in the chest.

Neither Jessie nor Alex moved. Finally, Alex made his way to the man and kicked the gun away from him. The man lay face down, and Alex reached around to feel for a pulse. Nothing. Jessie walked up slowly as Alex carefully rolled the body over. He looked up at her before pushing down the cloth covering his face.

Jessie gasped. "Wesley?"

Alex stumbled backwards, shock threatening to overcome him.

"Hey," said Jessie, moving to his side. "You're okay." She grabbed him by the hands, forcing him to look at her, taking his eyes off the body of one of his fellow police officers. "You did what you were trained to do. You saved me."

Slowly, he came around, nodding to her. Then, he reached for the small radio attached to the shoulder of his uniform. "This is officer Alex Thomas, requesting assistance. Officer-involved shooting and...and we have an officer down." His voice shook as he gave the address.

Jessie looked at him and then at the body. There wasn't a lot of time for her to explain what she did next; she could only hope Alex would understand. Moving quickly, she bent down next to the body and began going through Wesley's pockets.

"Jessie, what are you doing?" Alex's tone was one of shock and disbelief.

She didn't look up at him, just kept rifling through the dead man's pockets. "He was here for a reason, Alex. Do you think it's a coincidence he was in the break room when I was talking about our leads, and then he gets here before we do? Plus, he isn't in uniform, so he had a change of clothes with him. He's involved in this somehow—" She stopped talking, looking up at him as she pulled a single key from the man's pocket, holding it up. "Is this for handcuffs?"

Alex shook his head.

Jessie stood up. "Listen to me. I'm going to go check the barn. He was doing something in there when we arrived. You can wait here for backup if you need to." She glanced down at the body. "I completely understand."

"No. Whatever is going on, you can't be wandering around in a potential crime scene by yourself." He held a hand up quickly. "Not that you can't handle yourself. But from a legal standpoint. I have cause to go into the barn, and, well...you'll be with me."

She could have debated that but knew there wasn't time. Together, they made their way back to the shed and quietly entered.

"Pine Haven Police!" shouted Alex. "If there is anyone

in here, I need you to step forward with your hands in the air."

They held their breath, but there wasn't so much as a creaking of old timber in answer. Together, they stepped inside the dim and dusty building that consisted of splintery wood walls and a dirt floor littered with debris. Shafts of light streamed through gaps in the weathered siding, illuminating swirling motes of dust. The air smelled of old hay and wood rot.

Other than a few gardening items scattered through the barn – some propped along the walls, others lying here and there – the place appeared empty. Jessie focused on the floor, noting fresh breaks in the dirt. Wesley had left tracks in his haste. Looking around, her eyes fell on a mound of hay. She and Alex followed the scuff marks on the floor, leading to the haphazard mound of straw.

Kicking some aside, she saw a raised edge of white enamel sticking up out of the ground about three inches. Bending down, she swept aside enough hay to uncover the door of a buried refrigerator. It was an older appliance; the kind with only a single door. There was a new, gleaming metal chain latch that had been welded to it at some point and was secured across the handle with a large metal pad lock.

"This normal?" she asked, looking at Alex.

"The fridge, yes. A lot of folks bury them to keep potatoes and such cool during the summer. It's a cheap alternative to electricity."

"Speaking of...do you hear that?" Jessie cocked her head to one side. There was a hum in the air. "If that was what this is used for, why would there be electricity running to the fridge?" She fished in her pocket, taking out the key which she had liberated from the dead policeman lying in the woods.

Alex shrugged when she looked his way. The key slid smoothly into the lock, popping it open with a satisfying click when Jessie turned it. She carefully set the lock aside, and flipped the metal latch up, freeing the handle. With a heave, she pulled it open.

Her breath caught as she stood quickly, her eyes not leaving the open refrigerator. "I could be wrong, but that sure as shit doesn't look like potatoes."

29

SCARED PEOPLE DO SCARY THINGS

Scared People do Scary Things

The head of Jordan Myer was wrapped in plastic and had been placed inside the buried refrigerator. Jessie and Alex left it where it lay and waited outside for reinforcements to arrive.

Chief Walker had called in nearly all the off-duty deputies at his disposal. Even for a town the size of Pine Haven, Jessie thought the number was surprisingly small. Half were sent to work the scene of the shooting with Wesley's body, while the rest spread out around the barn and the main house, securing and investigating the area to the best of their abilities.

During the commotion, Alex and Jessie had been moved to the bumper of an ambulance as they told the paramedics for the fifth time that they were both alright, while trying to keep an eye on anything possibly being removed from the crime scene.

"We should be in there," Jessie said, her eyes darting from the barn to the house and back again.

"Well, I can't because I'm officially on administrative leave pending the results of the officer-involved shooting," Alex replied. He shook his head when Jessie looked at him, concerned. "Don't worry. It's standard procedure. Just a way to force us to take some time to understand and process what happened. I'll be back at my desk in a few days."

Jessie frowned. "How many officer-involved shootings have there been in Pine Haven?"

Alex shrugged. "Just one. And that would be now...with me."

Jessie exhaled sharply as the chief walked up to them. He stared; his eyes emotionless as they settled on Jessie. "Are you guys okay?"

It wasn't what she was expecting. All she could do was nod in response.

"Good to know," Chief Walker continued. "Doc Lindquist is processing the scene. He'll confirm the head you found belongs to Jordan Myer. Not that we need his confirmation...but we kinda do." His eyes broke away from Jessie's as he looked around the ambulance before finally returning to her. "Look, I want to say thank you. I might not have agreed with having you on this case, or your methods, but...I can't deny that you were instrumental in helping us close this."

A jolt passed through Jessie's body. "What do you mean *closed*? This case is far from being closed, Chief."

He gave her a stern look, sucking in a deep breath before answering. "Jessie, not only is the victim's head onsite, but we also uncovered what looks like the murder weapon. There was a serrated knife in the house with traces of blood on it that the doc is pretty sure will match our victim's. That has to be what was used to cut her head off. That, combined with Officer Wesley's presence here, and his attempt on your and Officer Thompson's lives, will probably be all that is needed to convict him. You said yourself there was a traitor inside the Pine Haven PD. Well, it's looking like Wesley was not only a traitor, but a killer as well." He gave her a curt nod. "The town will sleep better tonight knowing a murderer has been stopped."

Before Jessie could respond, the sounds of tires crunching on gravel caught her attention as a black sedan pulled into view. Mayor Beaumont stepped out of the back of the car, followed quickly by Will, his camera flashing as he captured picture after picture of the mayor as she made her way towards them.

"Oh no," breathed Jessie, looking at the chief and then Alex. "What have you done?"

The chief turned away from her, an ear-to-ear smile spreading over his face. "Mayor Beaumont. Great as ever to see you." He shook her hand, and they both turned to smile at the lens of Will's camera as it clicked away.

"Chief Walker," she said, "Tell me this nightmare is over."

He sighed deeply. "It was a tough one. But thanks to the endless dedication Todd showed to this case, and the crack team he helped assemble...well, it was only a matter of time before the guilty party slipped up and was caught." He cast a glance in Alex and Jessie's direction.

"Thank the Almighty," the mayor said, clasping her hands together and looking towards the heavens. She held the pose just long enough for Will's camera to snap a few times before turning her attention to Jessie and the officer sitting beside her. "Thank you. Both." She reached out and clasped their hands.

Her words were heartfelt and seemed to carry so much relief with them, that Jessie found herself swallowing the words she was prepared to say. Chief Walker gave her a look that was borderline pleading, and all she could do was find herself attempting a half-smile and shaking the mayor's hand. Alex did the same, his face reddening as he accepted her praise at a job well done.

She turned to face the house and the barn behind it to one side. "So, this is it, huh? The house of horrors." Her eyebrows shot up at the same time as Will's. He took out his trusty pen and began jotting down what would undoubtedly become the next day's news headline.

"I just can't believe it was one of your own," the mayor continued, turning to Chief Walker.

"I can't believe it either. I guess you never really know someone, but I always had a weird feeling about that one. He was so quiet. I figured it was a military thing...but I guess not."

The mayor clasped her hands together and turned to Will. "Come on, let's go down and get some pics inside the barn and the house." She spun back to the chief, interrupting him before he could protest. "Don't worry, won't touch anything or take pics of anything too gruesome."

Before she could be stopped, she was off, her photographer and the chief in tow.

Jessie whirled to face Alex. "Did you hear that? You know as well as I do that we are in no position to call this investigation closed. We need to establish motive, there are connections to find and explore, and—"

"Jessie," Alex said calmly, interrupting her. "I know. There is still a lot to do before calling this case. And deep down, I think the chief knows that as well."

"Then why the hell is he letting the mayor think that it's all over and done with? Do you know how dangerous a position they are putting everyone in if they go through with announcing the murder has been solved?"

"Two murders have been committed in a town where, up until now, being caught drinking beer on Sunday was just about the most serious crime committed. The people are scared. And scared people do scary things," Alex said.

Jessie gave him a questioning look.

"The local hardware is reporting a serious uptick in the sale of ammunition," he continued. "The chief knows it, and so does the mayor. They need to do something to calm everyone's nerves before they start seeing the boogeyman around every corner and taking action into their own hands."

Jessie sighed. "And I can understand that. But there is a difference in coming out and saying that considerable headway has been made in the case, versus stating that there is no longer a threat because the killer is dead." She began to fidget nervously. "Can you at least get them to hold off on making an announcement? Tell them you need to completely finish examining the crime scene, or doing paperwork, or...I don't know, just tell them something. Slow down the announcement. Buy us some time to dig into what's really going on and find the real killer. Because I guarantee you, he is still out there."

Alex thought for a moment. "The chief won't listen to me. And he sure as hell won't listen to you. But I know someone he might listen to."

Jessie's eyes lit up. "Todd." The thought of depending on him for help would not have crossed her mind. But the fact was, they were desperate. And desperate times made for uncomfortable bedfellows. "Fine. See what he can do. But..." She hesitated, locking eyes with Alex. "Just remember; while I am pretty sure Wesley isn't the killer, we don't know if the real killer is someone in the department working with him." She didn't say any more but could tell from the look Alex gave her that he was thinking the same thing.

"I'll reach out to him before the chief can get back to the station. What about you? Where to next?"

"I've got a hungry dog to feed. But I think the first thing we need to do in the morning is look into Wesley. We need to search his place. Find out what his connection is to all this."

"Hey, I shouldn't do this, but—" He looked around to make sure no one could see them, then lifted his trouser leg to reveal a compact Glock 26. He took it out of its holster and handed it to Jessie. "Take this. Until we can catch the man behind this, I'll feel better knowing you're armed."

Jessie hesitated but then took the firearm from him, slipping it into her jacket. She nodded at Alex as he walked away before heading to her Jeep. Just as she was about to open the car door, she stopped, looking around. Maybe it was paranoia. Or maybe it was just the come down from the action of the day, but she felt eyes on her. Someone was watching her; she was sure of it.

Good. Whoever it was, let them come for her. It was time to end this once and for all.

The drive back to her house was uneventful, only the occasional static of the radio seated next to her for company. She was exhausted, her arms heavy and her legs felt like weights had been tied to them. But as she pulled into her driveway, all of that vanished.

The lights were on inside her house, and the front door was sitting open.

30

WITNESS TO AN ATTACK

Witness to an Attack

Jessie stood there, her body tense. She tried to whistle, but her throat felt like it had been coated in sand. "Blizzard. Here, boy." Her voice wavered as she patted her thigh loudly. No answer from the dog. Only silence and dread greeted her as she slowly walked to the steps of the front porch.

She reached into her pocket and withdrew her phone. Quickly, she tapped out a text to Alex as she watched her front door closely. There was no sign of movement beyond the opening, but that didn't mean the house was empty. Suddenly thankful for Alex's gift, she gripped the handle of the compact Glock, and slowly took the steps leading to the porch. Her phone was buzzing nonstop in her pocket, and she ignored it, focusing instead on the feel of the house as she stepped silently across the threshold.

She stopped; gun pointed at the floor in front of her

as she strained to hear anything that might not belong in the house. Satisfied there was no one walking around upstairs, she slowly crossed into the kitchen. The cabinets doors all sat open, and the drawers had been pulled out as well. She looked around, her eyes settling on the closed refrigerator door. A wave of apprehension passed through her, leaving her body cold and her mouth dry.

Taking a deep breath, she made her way to the appliance and flung the door open. Thankfully, there was nothing in it except for her meager rations and half bottle of wine. She was about to take the stairs when flashing lights and a siren caught her attention. Seconds later, Alex squealed to a stop next to her Jeep and had sprinted up the steps to join her in the living room.

"What the hell, Jessie?" His eyes were wild as he looked from her to the gun to the room around him. "Why would you come in here alone? And why send me a text saying someone might be in your house, and then not respond to the – oh, I don't know – hundred messages I sent back?"

She could see the annoyance in his eyes, but there was something else there as well. Something she wasn't quite ready to address.

Both whirled around, guns up, at a sound coming from the vicinity of the kitchen. Jessie frowned, nodding to Alex as they eased forward. A knocking, followed by what sounded like something small hitting the floor, raised goosebumps on the back of Jessie's neck. The noises were coming from behind a closed door leading to the mudroom. Jessie cursed herself for not having checked the entrance from the back patio.

That would have been a perfect way for someone to sneak inside.

She looked at Alex and nodded, mouthing a countdown to him from three. On one, she pulled the handle, throwing open the door.

There, on the other side, was Blizzard, his head happily buried in a bag of his kibble that had been placed on the floor and overturned for him. His tail wagged incessantly as he looked up at Jessie, gave her a curt bark, and promptly returned to his buffet.

Jessie released her breath and turned to Alex. "Let's sweep the second floor, just to be certain."

Together, they climbed the stairs, and methodically cleared the floor, room by room, before returning to the living room. Blizzard had apparently gorged himself enough and was sitting at the foot of the steps, ears trained on them.

"Did you leave his food out like that?" Alex asked. "Could he have gotten in there and maybe closed the door somehow?"

Jessie raised her eyebrows. "Would that be before or after he went through all the kitchen cabinets and drawers?"

Alex just shook his head, giving her a smile of relief. "Joke all you want, but it won't make up for the fact that you entered this house alone. Especially after what we've been through today."

She didn't answer. He was right of course. It was a bone-headed move that could have ended up disastrously. She reached down and scrubbed at Blizzard's head, running her hand down to scratch under his chin.

Her fingers touched something metallic, and she froze.

There, hidden by all his white fur, was a collar. And on the collar was a tag with his name and what she assumed was Jeb Thompson's phone number on it. For the second time that day, she felt the onset of an attack threatening. When Wesley had drawn a gun on her, sheer adrenaline had fought the impending feeling of helplessness off. But now, in a space where she should have felt most secure, to suddenly be confronted with the fact that someone had violated her space and *laid hands* on a creature she was coming to care deeply for, was too much. She felt herself sinking slowly to the floor.

"Jessie? What is it? What's happening?"

Her vision began to tunnel, taking her hearing with it. Alex, who was right next to her, sounded like he was speaking to her from the opposite end of a tunnel. "Water...please...I need some..."

She was aware that he left her side but couldn't turn her head to see him. His touch on her arm was feather light, and the feeling of the glass on her lips was cold and alien to her. She felt herself slipping, the world she knew sliding farther away from her.

Then she felt it. The heaviness on her thigh. The wet nose and soft, cloud-like fur that made its way under one of her hands. She felt herself being grounded as her senses slowly started to return. She was aware of Alex squeezing the hand that wasn't on top of Blizzard. She couldn't yet move, but she could feel the strumming of her fingers under Alex's hand. He loosened his grip, letting her fingers dance through their rhythm as needed.

A wet, cool towel pressed gently against her forehead and the back of her neck. She began to make out the words Alex was whispering to her.

"It's okay. You're alright. You're safe."

Her eyelids were once again under her control and she began to blink rapidly, bringing her vision back into focus. She relaxed, letting the room around her come back. She knew where she was and who was around her. Her neck ached as she slowly turned her head in Alex's direction. "How...how long?" Her mouth felt like it was filled with cotton balls as she took the glass of water from him.

"You were out for about twenty minutes," he said.

Twenty minutes? How was that possible? It felt like she hadn't even closed her eyes.

"I was going to call the medics, but you kept squeezing my hand harder every time I said I was going to call." He sat back, the concern on his face evident. "That was some kind of anxiety attack. I've never seen anything like it. Can I call someone now?"

She shook her head, still finding her voice. "No. Please. It's not necessary." She took a deep breath, looking around. Blizzard had raised his head and was staring intently at her. "It's not an anxiety attack." Slowly, almost painfully, she pushed herself up off the floor and onto the couch. Blizzard curled up, lying on the floor across her feet. The weight and warmth of the shepherd was strangely comforting to her.

Alex watched her as she composed herself, drawing a few deep breaths as she clenched and unclenched her fists. She turned to him and gave him a tired smile. "I have a condition called catatonia. It's a behavioral syndrome typically expressed in an inability to move. The actual onset of an attack can vary, however. Sometimes, it's fast or strange movements, lack of speech, or other strange occurrences where I can't control my body."

Alex sank back into the couch, his eyes not leaving her. "I'm sorry to hear that. It sounds terrifying."

She nodded slowly. "It can be. To be locked inside your own body. Sometimes, I know everything that is happening around me. Other times, it's like being in a dream where time makes no sense."

"I've never heard of something like this."

"I would be surprised if you had. It's very rare. Something like twenty thousand cases a year are diagnosed."

"Is there a cure for it?" His tone was tentative. Jessie could tell he was trying to be respectful while demonstrating compassion at the same time.

She took another sip of water. "There is no cure. It can be treated." Her tone dropped, a look of distaste flooding her face. "With medication that I am not a fan of. Typically, tranquilizer medications, like low doses of Valium or Ativan. But I couldn't do my job with those in my system; I always felt just a hair off. So, I found a therapist that I worked with, and we used a combination of meditation and stress control techniques to fend off the attacks."

He frowned. "Is that what you're doing with the finger movements? I noticed you doing that at Jordan's house where that first head was found."

Jessie glanced down at her left hand, unaware of the pattern her fingers had been drumming into her thigh.

"Yes. It's a coping technique my therapist taught me. The pattern was originally developed by piano teachers so that their students could master moving their fingers quickly over the keys and having their left and right hands operate without conscious command. It's a pattern that calms me when I'm stressed and can often bring me out of a catatonic state."

"Interesting. Show me," Alex said.

Jessie laughed, feeling a flush creep up her neck and color her face. "What? You're serious?"

"Yes. It will help to calm you and it will make me feel like I know something about you that no one else does."

She didn't hesitate. Instead, she reached out, taking his hand and placing it on her thigh. Then, laying her hand over his, she began the delicate strumming of her fingers on top of his, urging him to match her rhythm. Over and over, he followed her until he could replicate the pattern himself, with only a few mis-taps along the way. Jessie laughed and applauded, grateful that he was actually succeeding in taking her mind off what had just happened to her.

"So, if I may ask, what sets it off?" Alex asked.

She shrugged lightly. "Usually, it's something stressful, or a shock to my emotional state that comes out of nowhere. I can usually feel it coming on. I haven't had a full-blown attack out of the blue in years."

"And what was the stress factor for this one? You were rubbing on Blizzard and then—"

She sat upright as if a bolt of lightning had struck her. "Blizzard! That's it." She bent down and dragged the shepherd to his feet before feeling around his neck. "He didn't have a collar when I found him. No ID tag. But now, look." She motioned to Alex. "He's got a metal tag on that identifies him by name and the owner's number. *Jeb's* number."

Alex stared at her and then the dog, his eyes widening as the meaning of her words settled in. "Whoever was in your house was also in Jeb's house the day he suffered that heart attack."

"They took Blizzard's tag off and probably locked him outside. And now, they break in here and return it. Makes no sense...but it has to be connected somehow."

"Who would get close enough to a hundred pounds of protective claws and teeth to remove the collar?" Alex wondered.

Jessie was nodding, her mind racing a mile a minute. "Someone who knew him. Someone comfortable around him. Someone Jeb knew."

There was a ping just as Alex started to speak. He held up a finger and took out his phone before looking up at Jessie. "Well, looks like we'll be able to dig a little deeper into that. Jeb just woke up."

31

SURPRISE NEXT OF KIN

Surprise Next of Kin

S leep was the last thing Jessie expected to come to her; but sleep she had.

Like the dead.

When Alex received the message that Jeb Thompson was awake, she had immediately jumped up to get her things, assuming they would head to the hospital. Alex had given her a stern look. "Where do you think you're going?"

"Um, to the hospital to ask Mr. Thompson about—"

He stopped her by holding his hand up. "After what just happened, and the day we had, no you aren't. You're getting some rest."

She frowned deeply at the officer. "If you think I'm going to just sit around here while you go and—"

Again, he held up his hand. "Now, normally, I wouldn't cut a lady off while she's talking. And I apologize because I just did it for the second time. But let me save you some time. You're not going anywhere. End of story. And neither am I. There was an intruder in your house that this giant wolf dog won't try to stop. So, I'm staying here tonight to keep an eye on things. In the morning, we can head over to the hospital and speak with Jeb."

She opened her mouth to complain, but he wasn't hearing it. Finally, she nodded in agreement. "Well, I haven't had time to make up the guest room yet so..."

"Not a problem at all. I planned on staying down here next to the door anyway. The couch will be just fine."

Jessie knew there was no point in arguing. She also knew he was right. If Jeb was just coming out of a coma, chances were he would not be up for being badgered with questions anyway. Let the poor man recover a bit. He'd still be there in the morning.

Despite the thoughts racing through her mind, everything shut down the minute she pulled the covers up to her chin. Maybe it was the fact that Blizzard had curled up against her, his steady breathing and body heat soothing to her frayed nerves. Or maybe it was knowing Alex was downstairs and had her back. But whatever it was, she had slept better than she had in weeks.

The next morning, the sun hitting her eyes dragged her awake. Her internal clock told her it was later than her usual wake up time, and for a moment, she was flooded by confusion. Then, everything from the night before came flooding back to her.

The break-in. The shock of knowing someone had been in her house.

Alex.

The onset of catatonia. That explained why she had slept so deeply. Her body was always drained after an episode. More often than not, it made her muscles ache and her brain a little foggy the next day. She looked around and noticed that Blizzard wasn't on the bed or in the room.

As she hit the landing of the stairs, the smell of fresh coffee hit her like a locomotive. The kitchen was flooded with light, and she found Alex sitting at the table, scrolling through his phone, a cup of coffee next to him.

"Good morning, sleepy," he teased. "You really need to hit the grocery store. I was going to make you breakfast, but there was literally nothing to make."

Red lightly colored Jessie's cheeks in response. "I'm sorry; I've been a little busy." Blizzard came trotting up from behind the island, burying his nose in her hand. "Hi, boy! How's my big fella?"

"I've taken him out for a walk already. He's acting like he's hungry but judging from the way he nearly cleaned out his food bag last night, I'm not so sure it's the best idea to feed him again just yet. Hey, do you want some coffee?"

Jessie shook her head. "As much as I would love some caffeine, it's not the best thing for me after an episode. I'll grab some OJ once we're in town. And you were right not to feed him just yet."

Blizzard had his head cocked to one side. He knew when he was being spoken about. Jessie reached out to pet him. "Looks like it's almost the end of the road for you and me, huh, big boy. Your human is on the mend it sounds like." She suddenly had to swallow a lump in her throat at the thought but could only imagine how elated Jeb Thompson would be once he and Blizzard were reunited.

"Speaking of," said Alex. "Do you want to head over to the hospital? The sooner we speak with Jeb, the sooner we can get some answers."

Before he had finished his sentence, Jessie was already pulling on her boots and had grabbed her jacket. After saying goodbye to Blizzard, she climbed into Alex's car, pulling the belt around her. The gravel crunched under the tires as they eased out of the drive and onto paved road.

Alex shifted his weight around uncomfortably as they drove, adjusting and readjusting his hands on the steering wheel multiple times until Jessie finally turned in her seat to look at him.

"Okay, whatever it is, just ask. You've seen me at my most vulnerable, so...I've nothing more to hide from you," she said.

Alex cleared his throat, clearly uncomfortable with his next topic of conversation. "You said that these attacks – er – episodes, don't happen that often. But from what I've seen when it does happen, it can be rather serious. You go through this...alone?"

Jessie stared at him and noticed the blush creeping up from his collar. "Why, Officer Thomas, are you asking me if I'm in a relationship?"

The deepening crimson that clouded his features was all the answer she needed.

"I mean...it sounds personal, and it is. So, you don't

have to answer that. I just wondered is all," he stammered.

She sat back in her seat, glancing out the window. "I am not involved with anyone. I've had one relationship in my adult life and...well, it didn't end up like romantic movies would have you think."

Alex gave her a brief glance. "What happened?"

"Well, if you really want to know, it all boiled down to my condition. The person I thought I was in a very serious relationship with realized that coming home and finding a living corpse for a girlfriend just wasn't in the cards for them." Even though she wasn't facing him she could feel Alex's shock and the jolt that ran through his body. "Oh, I'm not being hard on myself. Those were his exact words after he witnessed one of my episodes. A living corpse...kinda summed up how suffering from catatonia made me feel at the time."

Alex gritted his teeth. "Christ. That pisses me off, someone having that kind of reaction. You know you're better off without them, right?"

She dodged the question. "In the long run, it was for the best. It made me dig in and concentrate on my career, on what was really important to me at the time." She half turned in her seat to face him. "Why did you ask? Did you have someone in mind you were thinking of setting me up with?"

The blush deepened and he cleared his throat. "That might depend on if you've made up your mind as to whether or not you're staying in Pine Haven. Or selling your aunt's place and pocketing some quick cash."

Ouch.

Now it was her turn to blush. Luckily, she was saved from answering as they pulled into the hospital parking lot. Once inside, they made their way to the bank of elevators that would take them up to the small, cardiac care unit.

Stopping at the front desk, Alex let the receptionist know they were there to see Jeb Thompson and, if possible, the doctor taking care of him as well.

"You're in luck," the receptionist said. "Dr. Karni is still making rounds." She nodded in the direction of a woman who looked to be in her late fifties, wearing a set of blue hospital scrubs with a long, white coat over them. She was standing outside of one of the four medical rooms that comprised the unit, writing on a chart and addressing another, younger woman also dressed in blue scrubs. "She's just finishing her rounds. She should be over in a second."

They waited there until the doctor walked over to them and stretched out her hand. "I'm Dr. Elizabeth Karni."

"Dr. Karni, I'm Alex Thomas and this is my friend Jessie Night. She's consulting with the Pine Haven Police Department. I'm the officer you reached out to last night about Mr. Jeb Thompson. Your message said that he is awake."

The doctor was nodding. "Yes. Mr. Thompson. He is awake, but he is far from being out of the woods."

Jessie cleared her throat. "Do you think he would be able to have a conversation with us? A brief one, of course."

Dr. Karni considered her request for a moment. "You

can try, but I must warn you, we are still evaluating the effects of his heart attack. He's also suffered a stroke and, well, the prognosis, while still pending, is not the best."

Jessie and Alex exchanged glances.

"I didn't realize it was so severe," said Jessie.

"Mr. Thompson was in fairly good shape for his age," continued Dr. Karni, "but he was unconscious for quite a while. The damage done to him is most likely permanent, I'm afraid." She gave them both a stern look. "If he makes it out of the hospital, he's going to need long-term, around-the-clock care."

"You mean an adult care facility?" Jessie asked.

Dr. Karni frowned slightly. "Possibly. We are trying to find his next of kin. So far, we haven't had any luck on that front."

Jessie turned to Alex. "Did you know he had next of kin?"

Alex shook his head. "As long as I've known him, he's always been alone. Just him and Blizzard out there."

"Mr. Thompson has been my patient for many years," Dr. Karni said. "He has a granddaughter who lives out of town as his only known descendant. I've never met her, but my office has been trying to get in touch with her. She is also listed on his advanced directive as being executor in charge of his healthcare."

Alex let out a deep breath. "May we speak to him?"

Dr. Karni nodded, walking them to door of one of the medical rooms. "I can't promise you how cooperative he'll be, he can still get confused at times. Try not to tax him."

Jessie nodded. "We won't. Oh, do you think you could get us the name of his granddaughter? Alex might have some resources at his disposal that might make tracking her down a little easier."

Dr. Karni looked elated and gave them both a smile. "I'll go get her contact information now and bring it to you." She left them, heading back towards the receptionist's desk.

"Okay," said Alex. "Let's hope Mr. Thompson can shed some light on why his name is appearing on title deeds to property all around town."

Jessie's face was determined as she followed him into the room. "And maybe tell us what really happened to him the day I found him."

32

BLIZZARD'S HUMAN

Blizzard's Human

Walking into the relatively small room, they were greeted with a wave of antiseptic sterility. The space was windowless, every square inch of the beige wall space was dedicated to blinking monitor equipment, outlets and various read-outs and dials all dedicated to one common goal. Keeping a patient alive.

A bed was placed close to the far wall, the head elevated to aide in Mr. Thompson's breathing. The only sound was the soft hiss coming from the plastic tube that snaked from under his nose, feeding the man life-giving oxygen, and the electronic beeps from the ECG monitor reminding them life persisted inside the frail form.

Dark bags under his closed eyes, slack, pallid skin highlighting his sunken features nearly made Jessie do a double take. He looked like her father had in his last days. The resemblance was striking and, for a moment, she was back in Colorado, standing at his bedside, listening to the slowing of his breathing, the space between the monitor beeps growing further and further apart.

"You okay?" Alex asked, his voice barely above a whisper.

Jessie nodded, shaking away the memories and walked to the side of the bed. Gently, she laid her hand on one of Jeb's. Her touch was feather light. His skin was cold under hers and as delicate as tissue paper. Cloudy eyes fluttered open and tried to focus on her. He stared, confused as he tried to blink away the medically induced fog that no doubt surrounded his brain.

She leaned in close to him. "Mr. Thompson...Jeb? Can you hear me?"

He sighed, struggling to raise his head a bit off the pillow. "Of course I can hear you. I had a heart attack, not an ear attack." His voice was weak but filled with defiance. He glanced down at her hand on top of his. "I can't feel that side of my body."

Jessie withdrew her hand. Somehow, his statement made her feel guilty about the touch, sparking another flashback to time spent with her father. "Jeb, do you know that man?" She nodded for Alex to move closer.

"Lady, I don't know you. So, I sure as shit don't know who he is," came the reply. Still, his eyes drifted lazily to Alex, and he frowned slightly.

"Mr. Thompson, it's me, Alex. Officer Thomas."

The old man squinted, licking his dry lips. "Nadine's boy? How is Nadine? I haven't seen her around town in weeks."

Alex glanced at Jessie, his hands clenching at his sides. "She's...Nadine passed, Mr. Thompson. It's been a while now."

The man looked genuinely confused, and Jessie decided now was as good a time as any if they were going to get any information from the man. "Jeb, Alex is with the police department, and I'm helping him to solve a horrible crime. We think maybe you can help us." This seemed to get his attention and his eyes wandered in her direction. "Did you buy a bunch of houses and property in Pine Haven? Maybe as an investment?"

He scoffed at her, his raspy voice turning to a harsh cough. "Buy them with what? All my good will and intentions?"

His wit was cutting, and if things weren't so dire, Jessie might have laughed with the man.

"Sir, someone has been using your name and signature to buy up a lot of property in town. Do you have any idea why someone would do that?"

A look of sudden terror crossed the old man's face, and he began to struggle in the bed. Alex rushed to his side and joined Jessie in trying to calm him down.

"Where...where's my boy?" he was saying. "Where is Blizzard? Is he hurt? He can't be left outside like that."

Jessie placed a reassuring hand on his shoulder, trying to ease him back against the pillow. "He's fine, Jeb. Blizzard is at my house, and I am taking the best care of him."

The man seemed to calm down a bit, the confusion starting to leave his face. "He...he mustn't overeat. He has a tendency to pretend like he's hungry but don't fall for it.

Such a good boy. I don't know why he let him out like that."

Jessie froze, looking at Alex. "Who let him out, Jeb? Was someone there the day you got sick? Did they let Blizzard out of the house?"

He stared at her, his eyes looking beyond Jessie at something only he could see. "Where...where's my granddaughter? Is she here?"

Alex swallowed hard. "No, Sir...she isn't."

"But we're going to try and help find her; bring her to see you," Jessie quickly added. "But, Jeb, back to the person who let Blizzard out. Do you know who it was?"

He frowned, his lips moving as he tried to call blurry memories into focus. "Yeah, I know him. Didn't much like him, but my granddaughter liked him. Said they were going to get married. But he was mean...I could see it in his eyes." Jeb's own eyes grew large at memories that seemed to come rushing back to him. "I remember! He... he was going to hit me! Only...he didn't. But where is Blizzard? Dear God, did he hurt my Blizzard?"

The monitor was starting to go crazy; the beeping was coming hard and fast now, and Jeb doubled over in a coughing fit. Two nurses rushed in, and Jessie and Alex stepped back giving them room to work.

"Okay, that's enough," said Dr. Karni, her voice floating in from behind Jessie. "We need to calm him down." She nodded to one of the nurses, who then produced a syringe and plugged it into the rubber stopper of one of Jeb's IV tubes.

"I was afraid of this," Dr. Karni continued. "You have to leave, now."

Jessie protested slightly. "Just one more question, please."

Dr. Karni waved her hand. "Not happening. His body can't handle the stress in the condition he's in. You'll have to try again tomorrow. If he's still here tomorrow."

Jessie nodded, backing away.

"Oh but stop by the front desk there. My office sent over the contact information for his granddaughter. If you reach her, tell her she might want to get here sooner rather than later."

There was a sliding screen to one side of the door and Jessie pulled it halfway shut behind them as they exited the room. Alex made his way to the nurses' station and leaned in, speaking quietly to the receptionist. She handed him a sheet of paper that she pulled from the printer. He walked towards Jessie slowly as he stared at it.

"Well, this is weird," said Alex.

"What is it?"

He handed her the printout. "See for yourself."

Jessie's eyes flitted over the paper before looking up at Alex. "Next of kin is listed as Jordana Lawson. Okay."

"Look at the address for her."

Jessie read further down the page and froze. "This is Jordan Myer's home. Jordana Lawson is Jordan Myer."

33

UNANSWERED COMPLAINTS

Unanswered Complaints

Jessie nervously tapped her fingers on the plastic of the car door as they sped away from the hospital towards the police station. "Surely this information will be enough to convince the chief to keep this case open. I mean, there's definitely a connection there. No way it is a coincidence that Jordan Myer was buying up property all over Pine Haven in her grandfather's name, and then ends up dead. And this mystery boyfriend of hers seems to somehow be linked to her and a possible attack on the grandfather."

Alex was shaking his head. "Connections are not proof of anything. Not in the chief's eyes at least. We need to find hard evidence."

"And why is Jordan's last name different on her grandfather's executive orders than what she goes by now? Has she ever been married?" Jessie asked.

"Not that I recall seeing. If she was, it isn't in any of the paperwork we have on her."

"Then the alternative is that Myer is not her real name. Maybe she's been operating under an alias all this time. Maybe she realized that having her real name on her grandfather's legal paperwork might be too easy to trace. Whoever she was working for wanted to make sure she couldn't be found out. Not that it matters in the end, but still curious."

Alex exhaled sharply. "There's something else that bothers me. Why is Jeb still alive? If Jordan's boyfriend is the person responsible for all the killings, then why leave Jeb alive?"

Jessie wanted to think that maybe the killer felt sorry for the old man. But she knew that wasn't the case. Killers like this didn't feel emotions. "Maybe he thought he had killed him. If he was familiar with Jeb, then maybe he thought the heart attack he suffered would be fatal. No one would ever see that as being murder."

Alex was nodding. "True. Jeb said it looked like this guy was going to hit him. Maybe he was, but Jeb's ticker did the job for him."

"Did you get a chance to speak with Todd last night?" She was reluctant to bring up the prior evening in any manner, but with what they had just found out it was more important than ever for the mayor to delay her press release.

Alex nodded, not taking his eyes off the road. "Yes, I was with him when I got your message. He's doing what he can and he's going to funnel any info coming through the department to us as well. Seems like he's onboard."

Good. While she hadn't been overly enthralled with Todd in the beginning, she could see that he understood the stakes and truly had the best interest of the town and its people in mind. Maybe he wouldn't be such a bad replacement for the chief after all. "Do you think the chief seem a little overly enthusiastic about ending this investigation and naming Wesley as the killer?"

Alex's eyes narrowed on the road and he white knuckled the steering wheel. "You know what I was thinking? That the last time I saw him like this was with the arson investigation that was narrowing in on John Bartley. He announced the end to that investigation the same way as this one, stating it was an accidental fire."

"I think we need to look into Chief Walker a little closer, Alex. I know he's your boss, but...something isn't sitting right with him."

"That's not going to be easy. He's a fixture with everyone in these parts. Plus, half the department, including me, owes their jobs to him. We go snooping around, and someone is going to tell him."

Jessie stared at Alex, thoughts spinning in her mind. "Maybe that's the ticket we need. You said the last time you saw him like this was when he closed down the arson investigation. What if there are more cases he's done this with? What if he's protecting or working with a player we don't know about yet?"

Alex's jaw grew tight as he chewed over her words. "You're suggesting we investigate his old cases? Once we do this, there may be no going back."

"He's done his worst to me, so I'm not worried. But I can understand if you want to sit this one out."

They pulled into the station and Alex threw the car into park before turning to face her. "No. If we're wrong, I'll take my lumps like a big boy. And if we're right, and it helps catch a killer, then I'm good with that too."

They climbed out of the squad car and made their way inside to Alex's cubicle.

"Luckily, when we switched over to fully computerized records, most of the old cases were all digitized. We can access them from my computer. I'll have a laptop set up for you that can mirror my access so you can dig through them as well."

The somber atmosphere of the office wasn't lost on Jessie as she settled into the cubicle next to Alex. She could feel the weight of last night's activities practically smothering the department. It wasn't every day you find out one of your own may have been involved in the most heinous crime your town had ever experienced.

It took no time for Alex to set up a workstation for Jessie. And by workstation, it turned out to be an old, fat IBM Thinkpad that he plugged into one of the jacks on the cubicle wall giving her access to the department's intranet.

She took a look at the contraption and then at Alex. "Remind me to set you up with an IT specialist when this is all over. This department is in dire need of an upgraded...everything."

Alex chuckled and sat down at his keyboard. "Alright. So, everything is tagged so we should be able to pull up cases just by searching the chief's name. Anything in particular we should look for?"

Jessie smiled to herself as her fingers began dancing

across the keys. This was her world they were entering, and if there was anything the chief had been hiding, she would find it. "In addition to any abrupt closures of cases, look for sparse documentation, failure to adequately follow up on leads and frequent assignment changes where he may have reassigned an officer investigating a case without probable cause."

The clicking coming from the other side of the partition stopped abruptly and Jessie stood to peek over at Alex. He was staring up at her, his face a mask of concentration.

"What is it?" said Jessie.

"There was a cop who worked here a few years ago. He took a couple of calls about homeowners feeling like they were being threatened. The chief kept downplaying it, and even went out to interview a couple of the callers. But nothing was made of it. But then, the officer – his name was Montoya – said he found something that would prove the homeowners had been telling the truth. Then, out of the blue, Montoya transferred out of state. Just disappeared. Didn't really think much about it at the time. But now..."

Jessie walked around the divide. "What happened to the cases he was working?"

"Well, normally, they would have gone to another officer in the office for follow up." He tapped furiously at the keyboard. "But...this is strange. There's no record of it happening. I'm looking at everything Montoya touched. But nothing about homeowner harassment at all."

"And you're sure that was his name?"

Alex thought for a moment. "Absolutely. Teddy

Montoya. He was new but showed promise." He stood up, looking around the station until his eyes landed on a policeman who had just walked into the main area. "Hey, Miggs, can you come here for a second?" Alex gave Jessie a quick look as the officer walked towards them. "He's old school. A stickler for procedure. I think we can trust him."

The officer walked up, nodding to Alex, and tipping his hat towards Jessie. "Thomas. Ma'am. What can I do for you?" He focused in on Alex. "And shouldn't you be on administrative leave?"

Alex swallowed hard. "I'm not really here. Just filling out some last-minute paperwork. But, hey, do you remember that probie you had for a quick minute? Montoya," Alex said.

The older man's face, already covered in deep creases, wrinkled even further. Finally, he nodded. "Yeah. Good kid. What's he up to these days? I heard he was down in Virginia."

Alex shook his head briefly. "Yeah, not sure about that. I haven't heard from him. Hey—" he leaned in, dropping his voice a little, "—do you remember those cases he caught about the homeowners saying they were being harassed? Do you know what happened to the files on them?"

Miggs didn't say anything, his eyes darted from Alex to Jessie and then to the computer screen Alex had been working on. It was obvious he knew what they were looking at, but he only shrugged. "They're not in there?"

"No. We think it might have something to do with...

what's going on with the murder of Jordan Myer," answered Alex.

Miggs' eyebrows shot up. "I thought that case was closed."

Jessie noticed he didn't mention the name of the dead officer accused of the crime. "We're just being thorough." Her eyes pleaded with him.

The policeman gave her a sideways glance. "Well, I can't help you with where those files are. If they're not in the database, then you're out of luck." He let out a slow breath. "But I can dig around my emails. Montoya was always paranoid about filling out reports perfectly and would always email them to me before submitting. I'm pretty lax when it comes to cleaning out my mailbox. I probably have everything I've ever sent or received since we started using computers. If I still have a copy, I'll shoot them over to you." He gave Alex another nod and headed off.

"In the meantime, let's start looking at another angle. See if you can find any other complaints from home-owners regarding harassment. I'm going to look at those properties under Jeb Thompson's name. I have a hunch about something, and I'll let you know if I find it."

Alex handed her the file containing the addresses and she took out a pen and began making notes in between taps to the keyboard.

After a few moments of silence, Alex spoke up. "Hey, looks like Miggs was able to retrieve the original reports filed by those homeowners." He stood, looking over at Jessie, his face pinched.

"Let me guess. They are by the original owners of the properties now listed under Jeb Thompson's name."

His consternation broke into mild surprise. "How'd you know?"

She held up the sheet of paper she had been taking notes on. "Because I just cross referenced the addresses listed in Jordan's private journal with county records showing what those properties closed for. They all sold for way under what they were valued at. Someone strong armed these sellers into taking less than they should for their homes."

Alex gave her a mischievous grin. "Well, you're right. But that's not all. I just ran a search of all incoming complaints that had not been addressed in the last six weeks. Guess what? I got a hit on one involving Jordan. It was just filed three weeks ago. And guess who called it in?" He gave a dramatic pause before continuing. "Eric Jensen. Seems like someone was pressuring him and Mark into selling their bed and breakfast."

Jessie's mouth dropped open as she slammed the list of addresses down. "Are you serious? Why wouldn't they have told us that?"

Alex walked around his cubicle. "Why don't we go find out?"

34

HELL TO THE CHIEF

Hell to the Chief

Mark was seated at the desk, spread out before him were a stack of cards in one pile and envelopes in another. He looked up, a hint of surprise on his face when they walked in. Jessie saw another emotion make a fleeting appearance as well, before he banished it with his gleaming smile.

"Well, two visits in as many days. To what do I owe the pleasure of your company today?" He stood, reaching out to shake each of their hands.

Alex nodded as he dropped the man's hand. "Mark. Sorry if we're catching you at a bad time." He looked down at the mass of cards.

Mark shrugged and pushed them aside. "No worries. I address all the summer welcome cards for guests that have already booked with us and then arrange them by month in our file drawer. Then I leave them on the guests' beds for when they arrive. Just one more little personal touch that makes the Pine Haven Bed and Breakfast so unforgettable."

Jessie cleared her throat. "Speaking of the Bed and Breakfast, that's what we're here for." She glanced towards the room behind Mark. "Is Eric around?"

"No, he had to run into town. Can I help you with something?"

"I hope so," Jessie continued. "We just need to clear up something. When we were here last, you told us you hadn't really seen Jordan Myer in a while, correct?"

He only hesitated for a split-second before nodding in agreement. "Yes, that's right."

Alex reached into the pocket inside his jacket and produced a folded piece of paper. "Then what is this complaint that you called into the station about? You're saying Jordan was harassing you and Eric."

The color drained from Mark's face and, for a moment, Jessie feared the man was going to pass out. His knees bobbled, and had his chair not been directly behind him, he might have hit the ground.

When he spoke, his voice was weak and strained. "Where...how did you get that? We retracted it."

"We're more interested in why you filed the complaint in the first place," said Jessie. "Can you tell us?"

Mark's hands fluttered across the desk as he shoved the piles of cards from one place to another. His eyes darted everywhere, unable to look at either Jessie or Alex.

Jessie sat on the edge of the desk. "Mark, it's okay. Whatever is going on, we can make sure you're protected if that's what you're worried about."

Mark's mouth dropped open, his eyes round saucers as he grew very still. "We heard the murderer was captured. That it was someone inside the police department. Why would we need protection if that was the case?"

"Where did you hear that?" asked Alex.

"It's a rumor going around town. Are you saying it's not true?" He began fidgeting with the cards yet again.

Jessie gave Alex a slight shake of her head, rolling her eyes. "I wonder how that could have gotten out?"

Alex exhaled sharply, looking at Mark. "We want to double-check some things is all. And we really need to know what happened between you and Jordan. Anything said doesn't leave this room if that's what you're worried about."

Mark's eyes darted from one to the other. He bit hard at his lower lip, and finally leaned forward and spoke in a hushed tone. "Look, I don't know what is going on around here, or what Jordan got herself mixed up in, but we wanted nothing to do with it."

"Just tell us what's going on," said Jessie.

Mark started wringing his hands as if there was an invisible sink in front of him in which he had to scrub them. "I really wish Eric was here for this, but...fine. A little over a month ago, Jordan shows up and said she had a great deal for us. Someone wanted to buy the bed and breakfast. I remember being so confused. We had never once talked about selling this place. No interest in it whatsoever. We told her that. She was very animated and told us what an amazing offer it was and that we should at least consider it." He stopped, his voice starting to crack. He looked around the desk and picked up a glass of water, his hands shaking as he took a sip.

"Take your time," said Alex. "What happened when you told Jordan you weren't interested in selling?"

"She thanked us for our time and left. We thought that was the end of it. But the very next day she came back. And...well, I had never seen her like she was. She was very agitated and worked up over something. She said that the people she represented had presented us with a counter. It was ten thousand *less* than the offer the day before. Can you imagine? I mean, we both looked at her like she was crazy, but she just had this, pleading, scared look about her. She told us that if we didn't accept, we would get another offer tomorrow and it would be lower still. We told her to leave us alone, and not to bother showing up again with what we thought was a bunch of nonsense.

"Sure enough, the next day, she was back again. This time, she was flat out terrified. Of what, we didn't know. But she made the offer – and again it was lowered by another ten thousand – and told us we really needed to accept the offer. That we didn't know her clients the way she did. Eric took this as a threat and said so to her. She didn't deny it. She just said things had a way of happening to people who said no. She seemed...sad."

"Was that the end of it?" Jessie asked.

"I wish. That was just the beginning. From that point on, up until about a week ago, all kinds of messed-up stuff has happened. It started with hang-up calls. Then progressed to some man's voice saying how he couldn't wait to convert the fruit cellar into a dungeon or saying that we needed to be careful with some of the old wiring in the place because you never know when it might spark and burn the place down. And then there was one evening when we came home after going out for dinner and...I don't know, I swear someone had been in the house. Nothing was broken or stolen, but I could just tell someone had been in there. A couple of the cabinet doors in the kitchen were just sitting open, and I know Eric would never leave them open like that."

Jessie tossed Alex a grave look. "And you're sure Jordan was behind this?"

Mark shrugged. "Or whoever her mysterious client was."

"And yet you still continued to make that gift basket for her? The one she emailed you for," said Alex.

"At this point, we were afraid not to. That was also around the time we filed a complaint with the police department. They took our information and said they would send someone out to follow up with us."

Alex frowned. "And did they?"

Mark's head bobbed up and down. "Chief Walker himself came out."

Alex sighed. "Did he take your statement? Give you a copy of it?"

Again, Mark took a drink of water, his hand shaking even more. "Look, Alex, I like you. You seem like one of the good ones. But...I really don't want our names attached to any of this."

Alex placed his hand over Mark's. "I promise you, no one even knows we are here right now. And no one ever will. What happened?"

"The chief took our statement, and then looked us dead in the eyes and said, 'here's what's going to happen next', and then he told us there were some investors looking to make purchases in Pine Haven. These investors were going to bring a lot of money into the town. He then said that we were going to get an email from Jordan with a new offer, and he advised that we take it and not look back. For our own sake. Then, he just gave us this creepy smile and walked out. Oh, but not before telling us that this conversation never happened, and we weren't to call the station again about anything. No matter what might happen moving forward, we weren't to call the police anymore, and if we knew what was good for us, we'd call back and recant our complaint." Mark closed his eyes, shuddering at the memory. "And that was it. Eric and I decided that it was probably time to just pack up and go. We waited for the email, but it never came. Next thing we know, you're asking us about Jordan's death." His eyes hardened for just a moment. "Finding out she had been killed was actually a relief."

Jessie eyed the man. Nothing about his body language suggested he was lying to them. She shifted her weight as an unpleasant thought crossed her mind. "Mark, where did you say Eric was?"

"He went into town to drop off a batch of his new muffins at Angel's Bakery. He's trying a new recipe and wanted her to pass them out." His eyebrows drew together. "Why? Is he in danger?"

Color drained from his face for the second time and Jessie held up a hand to reassure him. "Not at all, Mark. We just want to touch base with him about Jessie's boyfriend. Did he happen to make that appointment with the sketch artist?"

Relief flooded Mark's features as he sank back into the chair. "Honestly, I don't know. He talked about it; said he was. But you'll have to ask him."

Alex opened his mouth to speak, but Jessie cut him off. "Thank you for your time, Mark. You still have our card, so please call if you need anything at all, or remember anything else you think might be helpful. And say hi to Eric for me. Tell him I'll definitely be back for more of those jams he makes."

Mark waved them off before reluctantly returning to the stack of cards on his desk.

Once they were outside, Alex leaned in closer to Jessie. "What was that about? I still had questions."

She was shaking her head as she hurried him to the car. "There was nothing more he could have told us. Besides, we have more pressing matters."

"What's that?" he asked, unlocking both doors with a press of the key fob in his hand.

They settled in and Jessie turned to him. "Think about it. This killer has been very effective at covering his tracks after a kill. For all we know the chief is working with this person. If it is the mysterious boyfriend, he's made sure no one can identify him. The only person who has potentially seen his face, is Eric."

Alex's eyes widened as he started the car. "If he's headed into the station to meet with Will and describe him..."

Jessie's face soured as Alex floored it out of the parking lot. "Chances are he won't make it out of there."

35

CONFRONTATION IS NEVER PRETTY

Confrontation is Never Pretty

The car barely came to a stop in the parking lot and both Jessie and Alex were out of it and running into the building.

"Where's the chief?" Alex said to the officer manning reception.

The officer looked up, stunned. "He's in his office." He started to get up as Alex and Jessie headed for it. "Hey, you're supposed to be on leave, and you can't go in there. He's with someone."

The man's voice trailed off as they rounded the corner and headed down the hallway to Chief Walker's office. Alex swung the door open and stepped into the office, followed by Jessie. The chief was sitting at his desk, a young woman dressed in a casual, mid-calf summer dress and a large, flowery hat stylishly covering long blonde hair stood behind him, looking over his shoulder.

The chief looked up, visibly flustered at the interruption, and slammed the pamphlet he had been holding face down onto his desk. "What the hell? Alex, what are you doing here? You can't just come bursting into my office like this." His face went bright red, the veins on his temples starting to throb in anger.

Jessie looked quickly around the office. She had been expecting to find Eric sitting with the chief and was thankful that wasn't the case. She stared hard at the shocked woman, giving her a curt nod.

Alex moved close to the desk. "I'm sorry, Chief, but there's something we need to talk to you about." He gave the woman a sideways glance. "About the *case*."

The chief exhaled his annoyance then turned to the woman. "Why don't you leave the rest of them. I'll have a look and call you later." The woman standing behind him smiled and reached into a large, oversized purse, pulling out a few more folded pamphlets. She placed them on the chief's desk and made her way out the door, closing it behind her.

Chief Walker stood, drawing himself to his full height, slamming both hands down on the desktop. "Before you open your mouths, you can just turn around and march your asses out of my office. I don't want to hear anything about 'the case' because there is no case. The murder of Jordan Myer was a terrible thing; something that has scarred this town. But it's been solved, and the murderer has been dealt with." At this point his face was moving from red to purple as he stabbed a finger at Alex. "Dealt with by *your* hand. Now, the only thing I want to hear is you telling me you've wrapped up all the paperwork with this and are headed out the door on your mandatory paid leave. Cos if not, I'm tempted to make your leave permanent without any pay, if you get my meaning."

Alex stood there, mouth hanging open.

At this point, Jessie was biting her tongue so hard she was sure she'd drawn blood. She'd had more than enough of this man, and her anger swelled in her chest until she couldn't hold it in any longer. She stormed over to the desk, leaning across it until her face was inches from the chief's, her bluster more than matching his own. "Tell me something, Chief, how much are you being paid to turn your head the other way and allow corruption to take root in this town?"

Alex gasped and took a step towards her. Without breaking her stare with Chief Walker, she held up a hand, stopping the officer in his tracks. She could feel Chief Walker's breath on her face as she watched redness creep into the whites of his eyes.

"Little lady, you are no longer part of this department. I don't think Pine Haven will be in need of your services any longer."

Jessie drew back, shoving her hands into the jacket of her coat as she gave the man a smirk she knew would infuriate him further. "So, why exactly have you been involved in coercing homeowners to give up their property? Is this a side hustle that Jordan Myer was running, and you decided you wanted a piece of her dirty little pie? At what point did you decide you didn't need her as middleman anymore?" She saw his eye twitch as she dangled that bit of bait in front of him. She waited a couple of heartbeats and then gave the line a good yank. "Did you kill her yourself or just give the order?"

The chief snorted, curling his hands into large fists that pounded his desk. "Jordan got in way over her head! I had nothing to do with what happened to her and I won't stand here and be told anything else!"

Jessie laughed, looking down at the pamphlets that had been displaced by his aggression. She snagged one, holding it up. "Brochures for cabins and land on the lake. Interesting. And, oh look, they're mostly out of state. Looking to take your hush money and run, huh? Leave the town to deal with the mess you've helped create."

At this point he was fuming. His eyes all but vibrated as he stared daggers at the woman. "That is none of your damn business. I'll have you know I have put my time in here, given this town everything I have. Where I retire to has shit-all to do with you."

"Yeah, and I'm sure your pension covers the cost of these places alone. Maybe I'll call in a couple favors and have a forensic accountant take a look at your personal accounts. You've nothing to hide, right Chief Walker? Maybe I'll just go have a little chat with the mayor about what's really going on in this department—"

Before she could finish, he stomped around the desk in a flash of rage, towering over her. Alex was at their side in a flash, squirming his way between them. "Chief, calm down. Please."

"Let him go, Alex," Jessie said, goading the larger man. "He wants to take a swing at me. Let him. This'll be fun."

Chief Walker bellowed out loud. "You think I'm that

stupid? Or that kind of man? I've never laid hands on a woman in my life, and I sure as shit ain't about to give you the pleasure of being the first."

Jessie's face tightened as she bit down on her lip. "Just tell us; are you running from someone?"

The chief eyed her, his hands clenching at his sides. "What I am, is done. Done with this town. I just want to take my wife and move somewhere...away from this." He gestured wildly at the space around him. Then he jabbed a finger at Jessie. "And if you were smart, you'd sell your aunt's place and get the hell out of here too."

Now it was Alex who stepped up, his face a mask of curiosity. "Why her? Why are you telling her she needs to get out of here?"

The chief seemed to lose a little of his bluster as he looked around the office, making his way back to the chair behind his desk. "You know...being an outsider and all. This is not the Pine Haven of old anymore."

Sensing an opening, Jessie pressed the matter. "And why is that? You've been in a position of authority here longer than anyone. Which means whatever is going on is happening under your watch." The man looked away from her briefly and there was a slight drop in intensity when he found her gaze again. "That's it, isn't it? Your watch is almost over. You're leaving whatever this mess is to Todd and this department while you run off somewhere with your tail tucked between your legs."

The steel returned to his eyes. "You have no idea what's going on here. And yes, I'm old and I'm tired. I know when it's time to call it quits, but don't you dare try to tell me I'm running from anything."

Alex shifted his weight from one foot to the other. "Chief, I promised him I wouldn't say anything, but... well...why did you visit Mark and Eric and threaten them? Why did you tell them it was in their best interest to accept an offer on their home from an unknown bidder?"

Finally, the chief seemed to deflate, sinking down into his chair. "Christ. I really wish you had just let this go. But yes, I did tell them to accept the offer and move on."

Alex lifted his arms, then let them fall loudly to his sides. "But why? At least give us that."

The chief wheeled on him. "Because the type of people that make offers like this don't accept no for an answer, Alex."

Jessie stared at him, then looked at the pamphlets. "That's how you're making the move, isn't it? They made you the same offer. And you couldn't say no."

He didn't say anything, but she could read the truth on his face. Suddenly, he sagged in his chair. He looked tired, years of silent burdens had taken their toll.

"Yes, I sold my farm to them. We always talked about retiring to a cabin in the woods and starting over. The way I saw it, this just jumpstarted that plan."

Alex was nodding. "That's why you were so gung-ho on getting Todd up to speed and grooming him to take over. You know he isn't ready."

His heavy eyes lifted and looked to the officer. "He better be. Cos I'm not sticking around much longer."

Jessie's lip curled in disdain. "You should be ashamed. You're an embarrassment to the badge." He didn't argue, didn't deny the truth of her words. "Have you at least met these people who are buying up your town?"

This time, something akin to shame crept into the older man's features as he shook his head. "These aren't the type to just waltz in and make a deal in person. No. I haven't met them. But I've seen their handiwork." His eyes cut to Jessie. "And so have you."

She held his gaze until he broke the stare. "Have you ever met Jordan's boyfriend? This mystery guy she was dating? Because right now, I'm pretty sure that's our killer."

"No. From what little Jordan mentioned, he works for the people buying all the land up. In what capacity, I never wanted to know."

Jessie stepped back to stand next to Alex. "Come on. There's nothing more we're going to get out of him." They turned to exit the chief's office and she paused, looking over her shoulder. "I hope you can live with yourself. Wherever you end up."

The door slammed behind them, and she ignored the stares of the other officers in the department. They made their way back to Alex's cubicle just as her phone dinged. She looked down at the screen and saw Brody's name pop up with a message. "Looks like Brody might have some info for us. He's going to call me when he can step away from everything."

Alex wasn't saying anything as he stared at the dark monitor of his computer screen. Jessie knew what he was feeling. More than once she had experienced the hollowing effect of finding out someone you believed in wasn't who they claimed to be. But wallowing in that feeling led nowhere productive, and she needed Alex with his head in the game if they were going to put an end to this investigation.

"Alex, I'm sorry you had to be a part of that," she said.

He huffed loudly, pursing his lips tight. "I don't get it. He is not the man I knew when I first joined the force. What happened to him?"

Jessie didn't answer. She knew all too well what could go through your mind when you were forced to make a decision that could have irreparable consequences. "Sometimes, you get backed into a corner that you just can't come out of swinging. You make the best call you can."

"It's not ethical what he's doing. He needs to be held accountable."

Jessie nodded stiffly. "Once this is over, you can deal with that. But right now, I need your head in the game. We're getting closer."

The officer shrugged. "How? How are we any closer?"

"He told us something, whether he realized it or not." Alex looked up at her, his eyebrows knitted in question. "We don't know who these people are or what their endgame is, but we know what they want. Land. And that takes me back to the list of properties Jordan was securing. What did they all have in common?"

Alex frowned, his eyes drifting to a map of the area that he had tacked up on the wall of his cubicle. He studied all the circled areas of land. "What? They're all outside of town proper."

Jessie was nodding as she pointed to them, tracing the spiderweb of roads next to them. "But they all are on or near a major artery in and out of town. These roads spiral directly into the mountains in many cases." She looked at Alex. "Who needs places that are easily and quickly accessible in and out of town like that?"

"Someone moving something they don't want seen."

She smiled. "Exactly. My money would be on drugs. Wouldn't be the first time a sleepy little town has been used as an exchange hub for transporting illegal substances to much larger cities."

"That would explain why all the sites are so remote. No one around to see or hear what's happening. Well, all with the exception of the bed and breakfast. Why that one?"

Jessie shrugged. "First things first. We need to find Jordan's boyfriend. If he isn't the killer, then he will undoubtedly lead us to who is."

"Right. So, how do we find a ghost?"

Jessie studied the map, her eyes growing wide. "How many of these did you say appeared on the utilities list as having water and electricity?"

He looked at his notepad. "Three."

"And we only checked out two. After encountering Wesley, we didn't follow up with the third one."

They locked eyes, Alex giving her a quick smile.

"The last one is here." He pointed to a circle on the map. "It's the most isolated of them all."

Jessie stepped back. "Well, what are we waiting for? Let's go catch a killer."

36

WHO FOUND HIM FIRST?

Who Found Him First?

They stood on the small rise, looking down a hill of tall grass at the ramshackle cabin below. There was no road or trail leading to the shack, and the only way to approach it was to make their way down the slope to the front porch. The backside of the house was practically nonexistent. It opened directly to a fast-moving stream with dense forestry on the opposite bank. Whoever had originally built the place had wanted to make sure there was only one way in and one way out.

Through the front door.

And that meant there would be no sneaking up on whoever might be inside.

"Maybe I should have called for backup," Alex said.

Jessie narrowed her eyes, shielding them against the glare of the sun. "And how would you have justified it to the chief after the exchange we just had with him?"

The officer sighed at her side. "Well, I'm probably

going to be fired for insubordination anyway. Might as well go out doing something good." He looked over at her. "Ready?"

She raised an eyebrow in response and gave him a slight tilt of her head. Together, they began the descent, taking care not to slide on the loose soil and dry grass. Halfway down the hill, Jessie grabbed Alex by the arm, nodding at the patch of ground next to them. The grass had already been flattened and the earth was churned up by what looked like heavy-duty boots of some kind.

"Well, looks like someone's home," said Alex.

They didn't speak as they approached the sagging front porch, the unstrapped planks bowing in dangerously to either side of the front door. A single, boarded-up window faced the front of the house. The door itself was nearly rotted through and didn't look like it would stand up to even a moderate kick. They took top position, backs pressed against either side of the door. They leaned close, listening for any signs of movement coming from inside.

Muffled voices made their way through the cracks in the house's frame. Jessie held her breath as Alex carefully drew his gun and nodded for her to do the same. She carefully reached into her jacket and took out the small sidearm, holding it at the ready. She pressed the side of her ear against the thin wall, trying to make out what was being said.

There were two voices. Both male. One was low-pitched and calm, while the second was high-pitched and pleading.

Begging.

Alex gave her a hard look and she nodded. He turned his body square with the door and raised his boot. He nodded three times, and on the third, cried out. "Pine Haven Police!" The door splintered open under his boot, and he charged into the room, Jessie on his heels.

The air hummed and Jessie threw her shoulder into Alex's side, pushing him to one side just as a knife whizzed through the air between them, sticking point first into the doorjamb.

Jessie dove to the ground, swinging the barrel of her weapon up as she took in the scene playing out before her. There was a figure, wearing the same dark clothes and face mask that Wesley had been wearing. A ball cap pulled down low on his forehead left only dark eyes visible. He stood behind another man strapped to a chair, his head covered in a black, cloth sack. He faced towards the open door, head sagging, and blocked any shot Alex or Jessie may have had.

Moving fast, the masked man lashed out at the back of the chair with his foot, sending the bound victim and chair flying towards Jessie and Alex. At the same time, the masked man darted for a room off to the side.

Alex was up and on his feet, almost at once. "You okay!"

Jessie waved him off. "Go!"

He was running through the room and disappeared into the same space the attacker had run. Jessie scrambled over to the man now face down on the floor, still tied to the chair. She reached him, pushing hard to roll him onto his side and then his back. He was wearing a white tee shirt that she now realized was stained dark with blood. The tee was slashed in strategic places across his chest and sides.

He screamed, crying out in pain when she rolled him over. A sweep of her eyes told her the issue. His left shoulder was dislocated.

"Try not to move," Jessie said. "My name is Jessie Night and I'm here with the police. You're safe, but we need to get you medical help." She stared at the man, noting the rapid increase in his breathing. He was about to hyperventilate, and she knew she had to get the hood off his face. "I'm going to take the hood off. I know you're in a lot of pain, but I need you to stay still and try to breathe slowly."

She grasped the top of the hood and eased it up and off the man, revealing his face. She gasped as John Bartley's eyes focused on hers. The man's face was swollen, an angry, dark purple bruise under one eye. His lip was split, and he was missing a tooth. She'd seen enough faces like this in the military to know a beating. John had been worked over, and judging from the damage done to him, his attacker had been working him over for hours.

She took out her phone and dialed 9-1-1, giving the operator what information she could. Just as she hung up, Alex returned, his chest heaving from exertion.

He sucked in enough breath to talk. "Sucker's fast. Went out the back window and around the house. I followed him up the break line on the hill, but once he crested the top, he was gone by the time I got there."

"Help me sit him up," Jessie said, motioning to John.

Together, they were able to get the chair back upright. He was secured to the chair by a set of intricately bound bungee cords, his hands duct taped to the arms. His left shoulder dipped precariously, and he screamed in protest when Jessie loosened the cords around his chest. Alex left the room again, this time returning with a kitchen knife that they used to cut the tape binding his wrists.

Jessie looked at John, making sure he fully understood what she was about to ask. "John, the paramedics are on their way. Do you want to wait for them, or do you want me to reset your shoulder?"

Sweat poured down his face as he looked up at her, nodding. The swelling in his eye was spreading across his face and she was afraid that soon he might not be able to see out of either eye. She nodded and moved around behind John.

Alex held out a hand. "Wait. Are you sure you know what you're doing?"

Jessie nodded, not taking her eyes off the man in the chair. "Yes. I've done this before in the military."

John huffed between clenched teeth. "Christ, just do it already."

Jessie reached out and tentatively felt around John's shoulder. He winced in pain, gasping for breath.

"John, I'm just feeling for any other injuries around the shoulder that might prevent it from going back into place," she murmured, concentrating on what she was doing. "It's imperative that you relax as well. I know that's easy for me to say, but don't fight me. I'm going to explain everything as I do it." She slid one hand down to grasp the wrist of his injured arm. "I need to create a little traction." Holding his left arm in hers, she wrapped her right around him so that her palm was resting on the ball of the dislocated shoulder. "Unlike the movies, I'm not going to suddenly yank your arm back into place. I need to slowly guide it back into the socket." While maintaining the traction, she slowly rotated his arm until his palm faced upward while maintaining just enough pressure on the head of his humerus to help gently guide it back into place.

John bucked, letting out a moan of pain, when his shoulder slid back into place.

Once it was done, Jessie walked around in front of him and examined his hand. "Wiggle your fingers for me." He did so, reassuring her that his circulation was still good. Then, she moved her fingers to the man's belt and begun unbuckling it.

"Whoa. At least buy me dinner first," he joked through gritted teeth.

Jessie rolled her eyes as she slid his belt from around his waist. "You wish." She fastened it around his neck and carefully looped it beneath his forearm in a makeshift sling. "This will keep it in place until the paramedics get here and can properly immobilize it. You'll need to keep it still so that it can heal and you don't cause any further damage." She stood upright as Alex steeped closer to admire her work.

"John, what were you doing coming out here?" Alex said, his voice just shy of scolding.

John winced as he looked up, trying to focus through swollen eyes. "I told you I kept a copy of that journal entry I gave you guys. I also told you what would happen if I found him first."

Jessie's lips pressed together in a thin line. "And how'd that work out for you?"

He glowered at her as best he could. "I thought there was no one here when I arrived. Just like the other two sites. But he must have been hiding somewhere expecting me; got the drop on me. That bastard is fast and a hell of a lot stronger than he looked. One punch and I was seeing stars. I reached for him, and next thing I know, my shoulder just felt like it exploded. I must have blacked out for a moment because I came to and was tied to that chair. That was when he started in on me. He was hitting me just hard enough to make it hurt like hell, but not knock me out. I got the feeling he had done this before."

"What did he want?" Alex asked. "I assume he didn't pummel your face just to get his daily workout in."

In the distance, they could hear the approaching sirens. John shifted uncomfortably in his seat before finally speaking. "He wanted to know where the rest of the journal was. I told him the cops took it, but he said he wanted the pages I tore out." His head dropped, turning to one side, away from the two of them.

Jessie squinted. "I assume he wasn't talking about the pages that contained the addresses you shared with us. Did you take something else?" When he hesitated yet again, she leaned in closer. "John, if you did, you need to tell us before the police get here. We know there was a mole in the department, but we don't know if he was the only one. That's how the killer knew what he was after wasn't in the journal at the station. Help us to help you."

John let out a sound that was a mix between a sigh and

a grunt of pain. "Fine. There was another set of pages with information on them. I haven't had time to figure out what exactly it was, but it looked like a shipping manifestation of some kind. Jordan was keeping track of something coming in and out of Pine Haven. That's all I know, I swear."

Alex leaned to within inches of the man's face. "Did you tell this to the man? Where are the pages now?"

John shook his head as the din of the sirens came to a stop along the hillside. Officers and paramedics would be making their way down to them any minute. "No, I didn't tell him. You arrived just in time. He told me he was going to break my knee in a way that no doctor would ever be able to fix, and I'd never walk again. I was going to tell him when you burst in."

"Where are the pages?" said Jessie.

"They're at the bar. I hid them in the bottom of the cash drawer behind the bar. I can get them for you if you take me there." He looked up at them again. "No hospitals."

Jessie and Alex shared a look, but then nodded to the man.

They were helping him to his feet when Todd arrived with two officers in tow and a paramedic.

"We're all good here," said Alex to the paramedic. The young man looked at him questioningly and then cast a glance at Todd. The lead officer just shook his head and pointed out the door with his chin.

Once the paramedic was gone, Todd looked at the three of them. "Do I want to know?"

"This is where the real killer has been holed up," Alex said. "I doubt you'll find much but go over it with a fine-tooth comb. We're running John home. Then we'll swing by the station and fill you in."

They started to walk away, but Todd stopped them.

"The chief has asked me to suspend you. He said Jessie is officially no longer a consultant, and that you are to hand over your badge and sidearm until some things get worked out."

Alex stared at the younger man but didn't speak.

Todd took a breath. "Of course, to do that, I'd have to see you in person. By the time we got here to process the scene, there was no one here. As far as I know it was an anonymous call to 9-1-1 that tipped us off. As far as I'm concerned, I may not run into you for a couple days. On account of you being on administrative leave because of the...incident."

Alex didn't speak but nodded. He ushered Jessie and a limping John Bartley out of the house. "We're on the clock now. The chief is in cover-his-ass mode. The way I see it, we have maybe forty-eight hours to end this."

John Bartley tried to give them a smile. "What do you know. Looks like we're in bed together, folks."

37

JORDAN'S BOYFRIEND

Jordan's Boyfriend

Every bump and pothole the cruiser hit elicited a dramatic moan from the back seat. For the first mile, Jessie was concerned that maybe she hadn't set John's arm correctly. But that quickly turned to eye rolling annoyance as they made their way back into town.

"I've been thinking about it," said Alex. "I don't think there is anyone else at the department involved in this. I mean, I've known everyone for years. Wesley was the new guy on the block, and I'm not sure anyone really got to know him."

Jessie was focusing on her breathing, trying to block out the sounds coming from the back seat. She also noticed the noise stopped whenever the two of them began talking. "Your chief has definitely done some shady, questionable shit that he needs to answer for, but I believe him when he said he's had nothing to do with whoever is behind all this. So, if Wesley was the only other person working with our killer, then we leveled the playing field."

Alex looked over at her, trying to break the tension with a smile. "Leveled? We've more than leveled it. It's two against one now."

"Pssh," came from the back seat.

Jessie wheeled on the man. "Do you have something to add?"

"That guy will wade through the two of you like you're not even there. You gonna take him on, you better call for back up. Like the freaking National Guard."

Jessie rolled her eyes and turned back around. "We can handle ourselves just fine. Besides, this guy is making mistakes."

John grunted. "Oh yeah? How so?"

"You're still alive, aren't you?" she replied.

He didn't answer, just returned to moaning in pain. "Are you sure you did my arm right? It's really throbbing."

"Of course it is. It was pulled out of its socket and shoved back in. It's going to hurt. But if you want, we can drop you at the hospital," Jessie replied.

"No." He shifted back into the seat. "They ask too many questions at hospitals. I'll be fine at home." He saw them exchange quick glances. "What?"

"Are you sure that's the safest thing for you?" asked Alex. "At least until after we catch this guy. If he thinks you have something he wants, don't you think he's either already at your place or he's waiting somewhere for you to pop up on his radar again?"

John didn't say anything. For once, he seemed stunned into silence.

Jessie half turned to face him. "You'll have to stay with one of us until we get this worked out. That is, unless you want to go round two with this guy." She turned back around when he didn't answer. "I didn't think so. Is there anything at all you might have left out that we should know?"

"I told you everything. Whatever that cargo manifest Jordan was keeping is...he wants it bad." He shifted in his seat uncomfortably. "He knew who I was though. Made jokes about how now he understands why Jordan was so eager to break up with me. He said I break easy." His voice trailed off, and he turned his head to study the scenery rushing by the window.

Alex looked up into the rearview mirror at him. "You'll stay with me. I've got a guest room that stays made up."

John didn't turn to look at him when he spoke. "You got something for the pain? Cos if not, I have plenty at my place."

"I'm sure I've got some aspirin somewhere," Alex said.

John let out a sigh. "Do you at least have some bourbon to wash it down with?"

Alex frowned. "No. I don't. I'm not even sure that's safe to do."

John opened his mouth to protest, but Jessie stopped him. "We can stop at the market in town and get you whatever you need. Just, calm down."

The remainder of the short trip back to town was made in silence. Jessie pored over everything that had happened since she arrived in Pine Haven. Something kept nagging at her, picking relentlessly at the back of her mind. She was so close to being able to touch it...but when she tried, it retreated further, leaving the tiniest echoes to tease and mock her.

Alex eased the car into a space just outside the main street grocery store and slammed it into park. "Okay, let's make this quick."

Jessie turned to him. "I'll go. Better that he doesn't get out of the car and be seen. Stay with him." She swiveled to face John. "What do you need?"

"Bourbon. But nothing below the second shelf. And something stronger than freaking aspirin if you can find it."

She rolled her eyes and climbed out of the car, making her way across the sidewalk and into the store. She found the pharmacy section and grabbed a few things, including a cloth sling. Then she hit the alcohol aisle and grabbed one of the only two bourbons they had. She wasn't sure if it was any good or not, but figured at this point beggars shouldn't be choosers.

Luckily the store was almost empty and there was only a couple of people with a few items ahead of her in the check-out line. Standing there, her phone dinged again, and she used her chin to secure the bourbon and first aid supplies against her chest as she dug into her pocket.

Brody's face flashed on the screen again.

He would have to wait as she reached the register and put everything down for the cashier.

"Jessie?" came a voice from behind her. She swung around to see Eric Jensen's smiling face.

Jessie gave the man a genuine smile. "Eric, it's great to see you. I stopped by the bed and breakfast earlier."

"Yeah, Mark told me you were there." He glanced down at the few objects he had in his basket. "Needed some fresh herbs for a sauce recipe I'm working on. Hey, I meant to call you. I reached out to that sketch artist you told me about but was told the case had been closed and there was no need to sit down with him."

Jessie frowned, making a mental note to discuss that with Will. Although she knew he would not have made that call, so that meant it had to come from Chief Walker. "Thank you for letting me know. I'll make some calls and see what we can do. So far, you're still the only one who can provide us a description." She stopped there. No need to explain what that could possibly mean.

The cashier cleared her throat, letting Jessie know she needed to pay. "Oh, sorry." She took out her phone and slid the front of it over the customer-facing display until it dinged, before turning to Eric once again. "Eric, I know I don't need to tell you, but please be careful until all of this is worked out."

"Don't worry. We thought it was over, but...apparently not."

Jessie nodded, gathering up her things. "I'll call you once I figure out what is going on."

She left and Eric dropped his things on the conveyor belt just as the cashier looked towards the door, waving her hand.

She held up the phone Jessie had left on the checkout counter. "Miss. Your phone."

Eric reached for it. "Oh here, I'll run it out to her." He made it through the door just as Jessie was about to step off the sidewalk. "Jessie!"

She turned to see him waving her cell.

"You forgot this," he said. He walked towards her just as it rang. Laughing, he handed it over, but stopped in his tracks before she could take it. His smile fell and his eyes grew wide.

Jessie reached for her phone. "What is it?"

He handed it to her, still ringing, and pointed to the screen. "That's him. That's Jordan's boyfriend."

It took a moment for his words to pierce the shock and register with Jessie. She took the phone and looked down. For a moment, the world receded, and she felt sand fill her throat. She looked up at Eric, trying to control the pounding in her chest. "Are you sure?"

He nodded, fear clouding his eyes. "Absolutely."

The phone stopped ringing finally and the picture and number displayed on the screen disappeared, leaving on a message box.

One missed call. From Brody.

38

A KILLER UNMASKED

A Killer Unmasked

Jessie dropped the bag of groceries she was holding and began pacing feverishly back and forth, her hands on her head.

Alex was out of the car and rushing to her side. "What is it? What's going on?"

Her face was a mixture of hurt and panic as she turned to Eric. "Go! Don't bother going back into that store. Go home, get Mark, and get out of town until you're told it's safe to come back."

Eric looked at her in surprise. "But, what about—"

She cut him off with a sharp snap of her hand at the air. "Don't argue. Pick up Mark and go somewhere, anywhere, right now. Now!"

A jolt passed through Eric as he ran off towards the parking lot, not looking back.

Alex's voice trembled as he spoke up. "Jessie, you're scaring me. What's happened?"

Her eyes told him something terrible had happened as she made her way to the car, leaning her weight onto the hood, her head dropping. John, seeing what was transpiring, stepped out of the car, his swollen eye darting from one to the other. "What's going on, guys?"

Jessie wheeled on him. "Get back in the car. Now!" Her tone left no room for arguing and John moved as quickly as his injuries would allow, throwing himself into the backseat.

Turning to Alex, Jessie held up a finger as she tried to center herself. Everything was closing in around her and it took every ounce of willpower she had to hold the walls at bay.

She needed to think. To focus. What Eric had said couldn't possibly be right. There was no way. It couldn't possibly be him. Her brother was somewhere in the Middle East running ops for the government. He wasn't hanging out in Pine Haven killing people.

Was he?

She called up memories from earlier in the day. At the tiny shack. There was something...something about the way the attacker threw that knife at them. The casual ease with which it flew from his hand. It seemed somehow familiar to her.

The look in the killer's eyes as they cut away. Did those eyes look familiar?

No. It simply wasn't possible.

What she needed was proof. Eric was wrong. It wasn't Brody he had spoken with. It was someone who might have *looked* like Brody; but it wasn't him.

She started pacing again, aware she was muttering to herself but not caring.

What she needed was to prove Eric was wrong. That would do it. She needed a second opinion. But how?

And then it hit her. She moved to the back door of the car and threw it open. She stabbed a finger at John. "You. Don't say a word. Do *not* speak."

She took a deep breath to center her thoughts and calm her shaking hands. She nodded, more to herself than anyone else, and unlocked her phone and hit the call back button.

She held the phone to her ear and waited. Brody picked up almost immediately.

"Hey, Jess, where have you been? I've been trying to reach you," he said.

She listened hard to the timbre of his voice, the cadence...anything that might betray him. But there was nothing. "Yeah, I'm sorry about that. We've been really busy with this case."

There was the slightest of pauses. "What's wrong, Jess?"

She pinched her eyes shut; clenched her fist so hard she felt her knuckles crack under the pressure. "Nothing, I'm fine. Just a little tired is all. Haven't slept much."

Another pause. "You don't sound fine."

She swallowed, willing herself to calm down. "Never could hide anything from you. This case has me on edge. This killer...he's more than we expected. Hey, what time is it there? I hope I didn't catch you too late."

"No...you didn't. It's late, but I'm all good." This time

his voice changed, his tone becoming a little more cautious. Not much, but Jessie could hear it.

"Hey, look, I'm here with Alex. I'm going to put you on speaker, and you can tell us what you've learned."

Her hands shook as she pressed the speaker button and held the phone out.

"Okay. Hi, Alex. Um, I just wanted you guys to know that my contacts in the government are still working my request. But I'm pretty sure I can have some names for you this time tomorrow."

The whole time he spoke, Jessie's eyes never left John. The man had grown pale and sweaty. Even the purple bruises on his face had drained of color. He covered his mouth with one hand and was backpedaling away from the phone, clawing his way to the far side of the car. When he was pressed against the opposite door, all he could do was point one shaking finger at the phone, his mouth wide in terror.

Jessie's pounding heart threatened to leap out of her chest.

"Hey, you still there?"

"Um, yeah, we're here, Brody. Um, thanks for the update."

"So...what kind of headway are you making with the case? Have you found out anything more about this killer you're tracking?"

Jessie pursed her lips, pacing slowly back and forth. Her mind raced. How much had they told him before? What had they given away? "No. Nothing more. But I'm confident we'll catch a break. It's a small town. Can't hide all the time." Silence met her from the other end and immediately she cursed herself. "Say, how are you holding up over there? Where are you again?"

"You know I can't discuss that, Jess. Hey look, my CO is calling for me. I have to run. But hey...we'll talk again. Soon."

And with that, the line went dead.

"Holy shit!" screamed John. "That was the psycho who just threatened to kneecap me with his bare hands!"

Alex was breathing fast as he stared at Jessie. "Jessie. What the hell?"

She was shaking out her hands as she gulped in a lungful of air. "I...I don't know. I need to think." No matter how she spun this in her mind, it didn't make sense.

Only, it did make sense.

"Okay, first thing's first. We need to get John into protective custody while we work through this," she said.

The man's bruised face turned into a scowl. "What's that mean?"

Alex turned to him. "It means you're spending the night in jail. Until we can figure out how exposed we are. I can't risk taking you back to my place."

"Fuck that," the man growled. "I'll take my chances at the bar. I'll get some of the boys to sleep there tonight. This guy shows up, we'll make him wish he was dead."

Jessie spun around. "No, you will do nothing of the sort to him." She took one menacing step forward only to be blocked by Alex.

"Not the time, Jessie," he whispered to her, placing a hand lightly on her shoulder.

She spun angrily away from him. He was right, and

she knew it. "If we take you back to your bar, you'll be vulnerable."

John shrugged. "I heard you guys talking. You don't know for sure that I'd be safe inside a jail cell either."

"Get in," Alex said, ushering her to the car.

They made the drive to the motorcycle bar in under a half-hour. John was out of the car and heading for the building before it came to a full stop.

"Hey, are you sure about this?" Alex said out the driver's window.

John just raised his good hand, waving them on.

"Your funeral," Alex breathed as he slipped the car in gear and headed back out towards town. He glanced over at Jessie; her fingers were tapping furiously on the passenger side door. "Jessie, you're not going to like this, but you need to consider stepping back from this case now."

She didn't answer, her eyes fixed on the horizon.

Alex gripped the steering wheel and continued. "He's no longer an unsub – we have a concrete description we can send out. We know who we're looking for now. Pine Haven is a small community. We'll find him."

Finally, she swung her head in his direction. "He's managed to stay hidden and practically invisible for who knows how long. This is what he is trained to do. You and the rest of the department aren't trained in military MOs. If he doesn't want to be found, he won't be."

"Jessie, he's your brother."

She swallowed hard. "And that's why I have to see this through. Something must be wrong. He must be working something on the books...there's no way he...that he did these things." She whipped out her phone and tapped out a quick message.

"What was that?" Alex asked.

"A message to a friend. One that hopefully can help shed some light on what might be happening." She slammed the heel of her hand into the dashboard. "Damnit! This...if this is happening, how is it not my fault?"

"Whoa, whoa, now. There is no way you are responsible for any of this. You're not the person who killed Jordan. You didn't have someone impersonate her and then kill that person as well. You're the person trying to right a horrible wrong that happened. But look at what it's doing to you now. Because of whom it could potentially be? No one would think less of you for sitting this one out. I know I wouldn't." Alex pulled into the police station and parked, turning to face her. "You know we have to tell the chief."

Jessie couldn't speak. Her throat felt like it was filled with thumbtacks. All she could do was follow Alex in, fighting to hold back tears of anger and betrayal.

This time, Alex knocked on his door before entering. Chief Walker looked up, his face immediately souring. "Damnit, Thomas, that's it. You're officially canned. Leave your badge and—"

Alex cut him off. "I'll be happy to do that. After you hear what we have to say."

As Alex began to recite everything that had happened, Chief Walker's eyes drifted to Jessie and locked onto her. Alex continued talking, ending with the revelation of who the killer they were chasing might potentially be.

"You're telling me that this homicidal lunatic is your brother? And he followed you here to commit these atrocities?" the chief said, still staring daggers in Jessie's direction. "I knew you were nothing but trouble."

She shook her head. As much as she hated to admit it, his words had cracked her shell in a few places. "I don't know. But it doesn't make sense that he followed me here. Everything was already in play by the time I arrived."

"But you're the central piece in this puzzle, right?" the chief said. "Could it be that he's just after you?"

Something in the tone of his voice drew Alex's ire. "And what if he is after her? Would you suggest we just let him have her and then hope he moves on?"

Jessie raised her hand to try and calm him. "Alex, it's alright."

He huffed at the chief. "The hell it is, Jessie." His eyes were blazing as he took a couple of steps towards the chief. "You know, we took an oath. To protect and serve the people of this town. And that means everyone. Including her. She has done more to help this department in the last week than some in this office have done in years."

The chief narrowed his eyes. "Careful with what comes out of your mouth next, Alex."

Jessie snapped. There was no more fight in her, just resignation. "Alright, enough. Chief, you've never wanted me here. And now, I'm starting to see why. You don't want whatever little side hustle you have going on to be meddled with.

Well, guess what? I don't care about it. I don't care what it is. Keep it. All I care about is making sure that nobody else in this town dies a gruesome death. Because let's face it...none of us know who could be next. Let me put an end to this, and one way or another, I won't be around anymore, and you can go back to doing whatever shady things you were doing."

Alex opened his mouth to protest, but she silenced him with a look.

The chief tapped at the top of his desk with his knuckles as he seemed to mull over her words. "This guy – your brother – he really as dangerous as you claim?"

Jessie took a moment, her eyes scanned the chief's, assessing just how much she should tell him. "Chief Walker, my brother is a member of one of the most secretive, deadliest special operations team this country has ever produced. He has run ops that aren't on any books. He is a master strategist, martial arts and weapons expert, and a survivalist. Our father drilled him to be the hardest, toughest man he could possibly be. And while the Brody I knew was empathic, thoughtful, and kind, he was also prone to great bouts of rage and blind violence. Our father thought that was a good thing, and at times even encouraged it. Then, when he was eighteen, my father handed him over to the military, where they stripped away whatever part of his humanity remained and turned him into God knows what. If he's here in Pine Haven and working for...whoever it is that you are working for, then no one in this town is safe. All I want is to bring him in and find out what is really going on."

For what seemed like the longest minute of Jessie's life, the chief just stared at her. Finally, with a gruffness in his voice that seemed more put on than genuine, he addressed them. "So, if I agree to let you continue this, what next?"

"We send out a BOLO with his picture attached," she said. "You pull in as many officers as you have and send them out to all the properties on Jordan's list. See if we can't rattle him; flush him out into the open."

The chief was nodding. She could tell he liked the plan. His eyes glinted as he looked at her. "And if we find him?"

She swallowed hard. "Your men will do what they have to in order to protect themselves, I'm sure."

"And what are you going to be doing?" he asked.

She looked at Alex. "The same thing. We're going to go back to the shack where he was torturing John Bartley. That's where he's set up camp, and while it's not likely, he may return there."

The chief seemed to consider her strategy and nodded in agreement. "Fine. But I'm not risking my men. If they see him, and he resists in any way…"

Jessie only nodded as the chief lifted his phone and called Todd into the office. As they were speaking, Jessie sent the most recent picture of her brother that she had to Todd's phone. Then, she left the building with Alex, heading for his squad car.

Once away from the building, Alex turned to her. "You don't really think he'll go back to that shack, do you?"

She shook her head. "No. that place is burned for him. He'll never set foot there again."

"Okay, what's the real play then?"

She swallowed, her eyes growing hard. "Simple. As soon as that BOLO is issued, he'll know we are on to him. We don't need to find him. We have something he wants, so he'll come to us, and one way or another, we will end this."

39

FLUSHING OUT A MURDERER

Flushing out a Murderer

After gulping his food down, and a quick walk down to the lake and back, Blizzard plopped himself down on the stone hearth in front of the small fireplace and exhaled contentedly.

Alex came down the stairs after his second sweep of the house. "The place seems secure."

Jessie sat on the couch, watching Blizzard. "I told you, there's no one here. The windows are locked, and the back patio doors are bolted and blocked. He's not getting in."

Alex wasn't so sure. "How long before you think Brody's aware of the BOLO on him? And why do that? We lose any element of surprise we might have had over him."

"Did you see the chief when I suggested that? I gave him a way out of his situation."

Alex nodded appreciatively as realization hit him.

"Good play. Brody won't be the only one alerted by the BOLO."

"Yep. And I'm betting the chief was telling the truth when he said he doesn't know who's behind the land grab and what they're up to. And if Brody is after the shipping manifest that Jordan had, I'm betting he's working directly for someone. And whoever they are, they won't be too happy with their asset being put on blast."

"Everyone will panic and hopefully get flushed out into the open."

The sudden ringing of her phone made them both jump. Jessie scooped it up off the coffee table, and immediately answered after glancing at the screen. "Jasmin. What did you find out?" She laid the phone down and clicked it on speaker.

"Well, hello to you too," came the response.

"I'm sorry, I just...time is of the essence here."

"Jessie, what is going on? Your message scared me—" She paused. "Am I on speaker right now?"

"Yes, but it's fine. Alex is here with me. He's the police officer working this thing with me."

"Alright, well, I'm not going to beat around the bush. I hope you know I had to pull a lot of strings to find this out. And I may have fibbed a little about it being a possible medical emergency...but I made some calls to find out where your brother is. And Jessie? I don't know how to say this, but Brody was discharged. Not sure what the conditions of the discharge are either. So many of these special ops guys are handled differently."

Jessie folded her arms across her body and sank back into the couch. "When did this happen?"

"Looks like it was a little over nine months ago."

Vertigo washed over Jessie, and she had to close her eyes to stop the room's spin. Nine months? How was that possible?

"Jessie? You still there?" Jasmin asked.

Jessie started, forcing herself to sit upright. "I'm here. Were you able to find out anything else? An address he's maybe using? Anything?"

"No. His file is locked down like nothing I've ever seen. Medical records, everything; it's like he's a ghost."

Jessie swallowed hard. "Okay, thank you, Jasmin. I owe you."

"Yeah, you do. Just, whatever you've stepped into...be careful."

Jessie hung up and looked up at Alex, her face a mask of disbelief. "Nine months? My God, do you know what he could have done in nine months?"

"Well, that explains how he was able to charm his way into Jordan's life. He had time to work on her. I just don't know how he could have been operating in Pine Haven for so long without anyone seeing him. Let alone dating Jordan Myer for who knows how long."

Jessie exhaled sharply. "Please, she was seeing John Bartley before that. Did anyone know about them?"

"Good point. But still, this changes things."

She had an uneasy feeling as to what Alex meant but couldn't bring herself to ask him to continue.

Turned out, she didn't have to.

"Jessie, what if he isn't working for anyone? What if he's calling the shots? Maybe he needs that cargo manifesto back because it can incriminate him?"

She didn't answer. As much as she hated the path Alex was steering her down, something told her he might be onto something. "He would have known I would come here. After everything that happened with my – with *our* – father. And my discharge. There really was no other choice. Damnit. The timing adds up."

Alex was shaking his head, pacing back and forth. "But why would he do this to you? That makes no sense."

She swallowed hard, pushing back against dark memories that fought to be heard. Long forgotten ghosts rattled their chains once again. "We didn't have the best upbringing. But we don't have time to go into that. We need to find him."

Her phone buzzed again, startling Blizzard out of his slumber. The shepherd's head bobbed up, looking around to make sure all was still in order before returning to his nap.

Jessie's jaw tensed as she glanced at the screen and the incoming video call. She looked up at Alex, and he knew.

She picked up the phone and held it out in front of her. "Hello, Brody."

Her screen blazed to life and was filled with the handsome face of her brother. "Hi Jess. Long time no see."

Jessie blinked rapidly, trying to steady herself. "Brody, what is going on?"

Brody gave her a broad, toothy smile. "You really shouldn't have let them send out that BOLO. Cos officially, I'm not supposed to be here. So that created some problems for my employer."

"Brody, whatever you're into, let me help you. Please."

He sighed, looking down and then back up into her face. "Yeah, because helping me is what you're good at, right?" She felt like he had slapped her in the face. The phantom sting brought tears to her eyes. "I do need your help though." His smile faded and a hardness crept over his features. "The cargo manifest that Mr. Bartley took. I need you to give it to me."

"Brody, we don't have it. I swear," she replied.

"Maybe. But I'm betting you know where it is. John knows. He was just about to tell me when you interrupted us. So now, I'm betting he either gave it to you or he told you where to find it. Either way, bring it to me." His smile returned. "I mean, I could go find John and get it myself, but thanks to your little all-hands-on-deck scenario, I need to lay low for just a bit longer."

Jessie didn't like the way he said that. Her mind raced as she ran through delaying tactics.

"And before you try to buy yourself time to figure out what to do next, I'm giving you an hour to get it to me," Brody said.

Alex had been standing to Jessie's side and at this point he'd had enough. He leaned in, sharing the camera's space with her. "Enough of this, you psycho. I don't care who you are or what you're capable of. We both know there are only two ways this ends. Turn yourself in now."

Brody's grin broadened. "Alex, my man. It's good to see you in person. Well, I've seen you a couple times. Stood right next to you once in line at Angel's bakery. I really should have introduced myself." His features were deadly serious again. "Jessie, did you know that the Pine

Haven police department is rife with corruption? Did you think that good old Wes was the only one?"

Jessie swallowed as a cold sweat began to break out down her back.

Brody smirked. "I mean, you really need to be careful who you trust." He feigned a sudden look of concern. "There's going to be a turnover at Pine Haven PD soon. And that turnover is going to create a lot of openings for some new blood. Some new Wesleys."

Alex was fuming. "Never going to happen."

"See, here's the thing. A police officer that everyone trusted turned out to be very, very, nasty. He committed an awful crime." The camera slowly panned away from Brody, and Jessie gasped at what was revealed.

The room he was in was not well lit, but she could clearly make out a chair in the middle of it; and tied to that chair was the mayor.

Black duct tape stretched across her mouth, bits of her dark hair were caught in the edges and trapped against the sides of her face. Her eyes were wide and pleading, her tears leaving dark tracks as they ran through her mascara and down her face. She was hyperventilating, her chest heaving with effort. Blood poured down part of her face from trauma to one side of her head.

The sight made Alex cry out. "I swear to God, if you hurt her—"

The camera swung back to Brody's face. "Me? I'm not even here. But as I was saying, this police officer apparently took the mayor of this peaceful town hostage, and then brutally murdered her." He paused, placing a finger on his lips for a second. "That is, unless I get that manifest. Then, maybe the mayor makes a miraculous escape." A flash of glee shone in his eyes. "Maybe. We'll have to see. But one thing is for certain. In one hour, if I don't get what I need, the officer is going to slit the mayor's throat from ear to ear. Bye." He reached forward, and Jessie's screen went black.

"Damnit!" she said, throwing the phone onto the couch and running the fingers of both hands through her hair.

"We need to get that manifest from John, now," Alex said, starting for the door.

Jessie stopped him. "It won't matter, Alex. He's going to kill her anyway."

Alex looked at her dumbfounded. "What do you mean?"

"Her eyes weren't covered. She's seen his face. We don't have time to get what he wants from Bartley. We need to get to the mayor's house and—"

Alex was shaking his head. "I recognized that room they're in. He isn't holding her at her house. That's my place. He's setting me up to take the fall for killing her."

40

A SHOT IN THE DARK

A Shot in the Dark

"**W**ill he fall for it?" Alex's voice was tense as he looked at Jessie.

She glanced at the pieces of folded paper in her hands as they sat in the car. "No. Not at all. But I've a feeling it's not about the manifest."

"It has to be a trap of some kind. I don't care how good he is, it's still two of us and one of him."

They had driven to Alex's house and parked downhill from the drive that led to the small, white farmhouse-style home. Under normal circumstances, Jessie would have found the place charming, with its perfect picket fence and manicured lawn. She wasn't sure what to expect when it came to where the officer lived, but she was pleasantly surprised.

But she also knew that what was undoubtedly going on inside was anything but pleasant.

"He'll never believe you came alone," Alex continued

as they stepped out of the car and made their way silently through the brush.

"I know my brother. I only have to see it for a minute, and I can do that. Flanking him is a much better option than both of us walking through that front door."

"Fine." Alex turned to his left to go around the back of the house but stopped. "Jessie, I know he's your brother, but if you have to..."

She nodded with a grimace. "No one else dies tonight." She watched him disappear around the side of his own house before taking the steps that led to the front door. She took a deep breath and steadied her nerves. "Brody! I'm here." She listened, but there were no signs of movement coming from within the house. Her hand shook as she reached for the doorknob. It wasn't locked and swung open with the slightest of creaks.

Taking a breath, she stepped inside.

The front door opened to a living area where she paused, letting her eyes adjust to the low, ambient light. Alex had given her the details of the shotgun-style house. The living room led to the kitchen, and from there, to another, smaller den with two bedrooms beyond that. The den was where he said the mayor was being held, and probably where Brody would be waiting for her.

She made her way to the tiny kitchen.

On your left, just past the stove, there is a set of Trident kitchen knives. I just had them sharpened.

Alex's words played through her mind. She kept her eyes straight ahead as she advanced, one hand trailing along the counter for the butcher-block holder the knives would rest in. She paused when her fingers encountered the wooden casing. Without looking, she felt along the top.

Empty.

Of course. That's what she would have done as well. Removed anything that could be used against her.

Another step and she heard a voice. Faint, but getting stronger once she stepped out of the kitchen, entering the transitional space before the den.

"You're getting warmer..."

He sounded playful, just like when they were children and would play hide and seek.

Two more steps and she would be in the den. The lighting increased, but not by much. Transitioning from the near dark of the kitchen, Brody would have the advantage. It would take her eyes a few extra seconds to adjust. Jessie knew those few seconds could be the difference between life and death.

She took in a breath, steeling herself for what might come next.

Fuck it.

She took the steps boldly, stepping into the light.

"And there she is. Welcome, sister."

The first thing Jessie saw was the chair sitting in the center of the room. She had made Alex tell her every piece of furniture not only in the room, but the house itself. Just as she expected, the furniture had been pushed to the sides of the room. Behind the chair the mayor was strapped to, a cloth couch and matching oversized chair had been shoved together. A floor lamp had been moved next to a large, older, floor model television set.

The last piece of furniture in the room was a two-tiered glass coffee table. It was moved to the shorter wall perpendicular to the couch. She could see rolls of duct tape resting on it, as well as extra bungee cords.

Brody was standing in one of the corners of the room, barely illuminated by the light. He took a step towards the center of the room, flashing his sister a smile. Even though it had been years since they saw one another, Jessie found herself mesmerized by her brother's smile.

It was all gleaming teeth and thin lips. Familiar eyes so dark they were almost black shone from beneath a mop of curly brown hair. His skin was dark, a testament to spending months outside in a Middle Eastern sun. He was wearing jeans and a black tee shirt that hugged his frame. Muscles that were the result of years of physical exertion, not hours spent in a gym, strained at the fabric.

He looked like he could have stepped off the pages of a fitness magazine.

Despite the years, he looked just like the brother she had hugged so tightly just before he had boarded a flight to Georgia to start training to be the best he could be at doing all the government's dirty deeds.

"Brody." Her voice was deep and lost and filled with emotions she couldn't name.

He moved closer, standing before her. He was tall, a full head higher than her. His eyes grew wide as his emotions betrayed him. His nostrils flared standing before her, and she knew he was feeling the same rush of tidal wave emotions that threatened to overcome her.

"Jessie. It's been too long."

She swallowed, trying to find her center. "If I had known you were in town, I'd have had you over to see the place. Hasn't changed a bit since we were kids," she said. "But you know that."

He sighed. "I was hoping that you had hidden the manifesto in the house. It would have saved us both a lot of heartache."

"Somehow, I think we would both end up standing right where we are, whether you found it or not."

He gave her a large, charismatic smile. "You know, for someone with the reputation you developed, I expected you to put all of this together sooner."

The casual tone he had was too much for her. Everything that was bottled up inside her came rushing to the surface in a well of emotions. "Brody, what is going on? You left special ops?"

He laughed. "Well, I wonder who could have told you that? The doctor always did have a soft spot for you."

The last bit was tinged with something bitter. How much did he know about her relationship with Jasmin?

"This isn't you, Brody. Tell me what's going on," Jessie pleaded.

For the first time, his features grew taut and serious. "How do you know who I am, Jessie? The last time we spent any meaningful time together you were ushering me onto a plane and out of yours and dad's lives."

Her mouth dropped. "Brody, that's not true. I mean, yes, you were headed off to basic, but that didn't mean you were not part of my life." Guilt coated her words, and she knew he could hear it. The truth was, the day they said their goodbyes something between them changed.

But wasn't that normal?

He shook his head, walking over to the chair. The

mayor's eyes were so wide that all Jessie could see were the whites of her orbs surrounding her bright blue irises. The woman was terrified, and Jessie couldn't blame her.

Out of nowhere, Brody produced a large Bowie knife with a six-inch serrated blade. The mayor whined as he moved to stand next to her. Brody leaned close, the point of his blade teasing the juncture where her neck met her clavicle.

He stared at Jessie. "Did you bring me what I need?"

Jessie's eyes locked with the mayor's, pleading with the older woman not to move. She nodded. "I did. But I'm not giving you anything until you let Mayor Beaumont go."

Brody frowned, glancing down at the trembling woman whose life he literally held in his hand at the moment. "Now, Jessie, that wasn't the deal, and you know it."

"Brody." She leveled her gaze at him. "Did you kill Jordan Myer?"

He cocked his head to one side as he weighed her words. "I did. But to be honest she brought it on herself. She really shouldn't have tried blackmailing the wrong people with those lists she started keeping. I mean, I had no choice in that one. We all do what we're told, right?" He straightened his head. "Except for you. You decide when, where and who you're going to do the right thing for, don't you?"

Again, the sting of his words carried extra weight. "Brody, Dad was dying. Which you would have understood had you bothered coming home once during his final days. But I guess you were too busy out here committing murder and setting up drug runners, huh?"

The look he gave her was almost comical. "Drugs? Jessie, it's almost like you don't know me at all. When have I ever been involved in drugs?"

He was right. Even when they were growing up, she was the one that experimented with pot and a lot of other substances. Not him. As a matter of fact, he shielded her from their father, but then would lecture her nonstop about what was being done to her brain. "Most of the best front men and dealers don't use their own product. But isn't that what you're doing? Setting up a smuggling route for someone? Using you military contacts and know-how to help them get a drug trade up and running?"

His attitude turned sour faster than she could register. The jovial cockiness was gone. In a flash he moved away from the mayor and stormed Jessie. He moved so fast that he had his hands on her arms, pinning them at her sides in a vice-like grip, before she could set up a defense. "No. This has nothing to do with drugs, Jess. You need to drop all this." He leaned in close, whispering quickly to her. "You need to let this go and get out of this town. Now."

He drew back and she searched his eyes. For a second, the old Brody she knew, the brother she had grown up with, had been staring back at her. But in a flash, that Brody was gone and replaced by a coldness, an alien likeness that she didn't know.

"Now," he said, letting go of her, "About Alex. Where could he be?"

She opened her mouth to again assure him that she

was alone. But before she could, the bang made her jump. The unmistakable sharpness of a single shot firearm discharging very close by.

Brody smiled wolf-like. "Ah. There he is." He narrowed his eyes at his sister. "I told you Wesley wasn't the only dirty cop in that department."

Her ears ringing, Jessie managed to hear the sliding door opening somewhere in the kitchen, followed by footsteps. She turned to see Todd walking in, holding a Sig Sauer P320 in his hands.

He gave her a grin and nodded at Brody. "He was right where you said he'd be. Got him."

41

WHAT A MONSTER MADE

What a Monster Made

Shock settled in as Jessie looked into the eyes of someone she had trusted. "You. What have you done?"

Todd walked closer, his swagger mimicking her brother's. "I hate to say it, but he was going to have to go at some point. He was too goody-two-shoes. There was no swaying him, and I had a feeling he was going to be a thorn in my side moving forward."

Heat rose in Jessie and her heart was beating so fast she thought for sure it would rip its way out of her chest. "You're not going to get away with this."

"Oh, I've heard that before," he replied. "But so far so good. I only need to get a few more officers in place and we'll be fine." His grin broadened. "And looks like we now have two openings; not just one."

Jessie's mind was racing. Rage was fuelling her,

making it hard to think. "Did you just shoot Alex in cold blood?" She watched the gleam fill his eyes as he took a couple more steps towards her. He was almost in range. Out of the corner of her eye, she saw Brody quietly inch his way back from the deputy. "And the chief? Is your uncle in on this?"

Todd let out a sharp laugh that came out more like a bark. "Are you kidding me? Hell no. The only thing that's keeping him around is his connections in smoothing things out with the locals. A few words from him and those stubborn old coots that refused to sell would see things differently. Well, except for the bed and breakfast. Mark and Eric are dug in like ticks. But we were making headway with them."

Jessie nodded. That was it. She just needed him to keep running his mouth a bit longer. "You're not smart enough to pull an operation like this off. Drug running is a dangerous business, and sooner or later whoever you're working for is going to see you are out of your league. And when that happens, you're going to end up on Doc Lindquist's exam table."

He frowned at her, his hateful eyes growing dark. "Drugs? We're not running drugs. That's chump change compared to what we're going to be making. Once the route opens—"-

Brody cleared his throat loudly, directing it at Todd.

The deputy clamped his mouth shut, giving Jessie a look of anger. "You almost got me, bitch."

That was enough of that. If he wasn't going to tell her anything useful, she had no use for him. And after what he had just done to Alex, she really didn't care if he had useful information or not. In the blink of an eye, she exploded into action.

She shifted her hips, using the sudden transfer of weight onto her left leg to push her forward and close the gap between herself and Todd faster than the deputy could react. One minute he was sneering at her, the next her face was inches from his own. As she expected, he moved to bring the Sig Sauer up, but she jammed the space between them with the side of her body, blocking his ability to lift his arm.

She grabbed the wrist of his gun hand and twisted her body, throwing her back into his torso as she bent his hand down and out, tearing multiple ligaments in his wrist. He let out a high-pitched squeal of pain that was cut short by the elbow that she drove backwards into his solar plexus. With a torque of her waist, she spun to her right, bringing the outside of her forearm into the bridge of his nose. There was a satisfying crunch followed by an explosion of blood from his nostrils.

She reached behind her, dropping her hip into his pelvis as she hooked his waist. He tried to feebly counter her, but at this point he would have had more luck getting a Pit Bull off him that had sunk a death grip into his groin.

With little effort, she pulled, using her lower center of gravity to toss him over her hip and send him crashing through the glass coffee table to the floor. He looked up at her, spitting blood, eyes wide with pain and panic. The kick that she let fly at the side of his face was the last thing he saw coming before succumbing to uncon-sciousness.

A slow clap came from behind her, and she wheeled to see Brody smiling.

"And here I thought you had lost a step," he said, looking down at Todd. "Dad would be proud to see all those hours he spent on us didn't go to waste. He's still breathing. Finish him off, and I promise I'll let you walk out the door. After you give me that manifest, I mean." He saw the look in her eyes. "Jess – I'm serious. Don't get involved in any of this. You have no idea."

She was taking deep breaths, trying to get a handle on the adrenaline that flooded her system. "I don't have the manifest. It's somewhere safe. And without Todd, I'm betting your little gig will blow up in your face. You know as well as I do, he will flip in no time to save his own hide."

Brody's jaw pulsed as he appeared to grind his teeth. Then, he shrugged his shoulders. Casually, he pulled a pistol, one that Jessie couldn't make out, from the waist-band of his jeans, and shot Todd once in the head. "Thanks. You're right. I hadn't thought of that." He gave her a stealthy look. "Or had I? And that just leaves..." He turned slowly towards the mayor.

Mayor Beaumont began to cry, shaking her head violently from side to side as her pleas were cut off by the binding that kept her mouth shut.

"The question is, how do I stage this now?" He seemed to be talking to himself as he scratched the side of his head with the barrel of the pistol. "Damnit, Jessie. See, Todd was going to be the hero here. After stumbling on the kidnapping and bloody murder of the mayor, he took out Alex and saved the day, taking out the serial killer that has been terrorizing Pine Haven. This would solidify his sudden rise to position of chief where he'd begin rebuilding the police department with hard working deputies that he would hand pick. But now... what a fucking mess you've made of things."

Jessie centered herself, tried to ignore the throbbing in her temples. Her vision was threatening to go dim.

Damnit, no. Not now.

She held her breath, now trying to speed up her heart, force some adrenaline back into her slowing system as she fought off the numbness that began to creep in. "Brody, just tell me one thing. Why? Why are you doing any of this?"

He pursed his lips. "I could say it's for the boatload of money I'm being paid. And that would be half true. But I have another reason as well. One that's a little more personal. But that's for me to know."

"And why hire someone to impersonate Jordan Myer? Were they just another innocent pawn in all this?"

He laughed cruelly. "Yeah, that one was my bad. See, the couple that owns the B and B were playing hardball and we needed a backup place with private, waterfront access. Aunt Glenda's house was perfect for that, if it came down to it. But with her gone, the deed needed to be clean. That meant you had to go through with assuming full ownership. But by the time we realized that, I had already killed Jordan. So, I hired an out-of-town actor. But that was just one more little thread I had to make sure got snipped."

Jessie frowned. "I owned Aunt Glenda's house. But if something had happened to me, it would have gone to you. You would have let them kill me?"

His eyes grew large. "No. Absolutely not. Everyone kept telling you to leave, but you didn't listen. I would not have let them hurt you."

She clenched her fist, driving her nails into her palm, focusing on the pain. "It's not too late to come back from this, Brody."

He let out a long sigh, and for the first time, a sadness crossed his eyes that Jessie had never seen before. "It kind of is."

He raised the gun and pointed it at the mayor's head.

"No!" Jessie knew she would be too late, but she had to try. She launched herself at the woman, knocking the chair backwards, her own body covering Mayor Beaumont's. The bang of the gun never happened, and Jessie didn't stop to question why. Instead, she kicked out with her foot, hearing a grunt in response as it caught her brother in the side of the leg, knocking him off balance.

She was on her feet at once, closing the distance between them as she grabbed her brother and drove her knee into his midsection then smashed her elbow down onto his back while he was doubled over. He dropped to one knee and Jessie maneuvered to his side as she wrapped him in a headlock.

Too late, she realized her mistake as he had purposefully let her in close enough that he could grasp the wrist of the arm closed around his throat. With a twisting of his hand, he bent her arm out painfully, before tossing her over his shoulder to the ground. He maintained his grip

on her left arm and with his free hand, stabbed two
fingers into her shoulder and elbow in rapid succession.
Her blood turned to fire and then her arm went
completely numb.

She gritted her teeth and grabbed at her shoulder
with her good hand, squeezing it as she tried to restart
the circulation that his blows had blocked. Slowly, she
rolled over onto her stomach and managed to claw her
way through the table's broken glass until she could sit
with her back against the wall. The world around her
began to slowly spin, threatening to suck her into a catatonic state that she knew there would be no coming out
of this time. Brody moved closer to stand over her, head
cocked to one side, the gun pointing downward.

She looked down at her arm. It was a dead weight,
and try as she might, she could not make it move. As
good as she was, she knew that she stood no chance
against her brother with just one functioning arm. Still,
she wasn't going down without a fight.

The report of a gun was deafening in the confined
room. Brody jerked to one side, diving into a roll and
coming up in a crouch, gun up and aiming at something
to Jessie's left. He squeezed off a shot, and she looked up
in time to see Alex take a slug to his shoulder. He had
been leaning against the wall for support between the
kitchen and the den. Blood covered his shirt.

The bullet from Brody's gun spun him around and he
sank to the floor without a sound.

Brody stood slowly, and reached up, cupping one ear.
When he pulled his hand away, red liquid coated his
fingers. He looked at them surprised then showed them

to Jessie. "Your boyfriend almost blew my damn head off. Should have known better than to trust Todd to finish a job."

Jessie began to pant. It was too much for her and she could feel her body slipping away as she stared at Brody in panic.

His brows knitted together as he watched her intently. "It's happening, isn't it?" He lowered his bloody hand to his side as he continued to watch his sister struggle, losing control of her own body. "I've never actually seen it happen before. I mean, it was kind of hard for me to see anything from my vantage point back then..."

The tunnel began to close in around Jessie's vision as her eyes darted wildly, trying to keep a lock on her brother.

He stepped into the center of her vision. "You're not faking this, are you? Because that's what I used to think it was. I thought it was just some shit you pulled to make yourself feel better for just lying there and letting that happen to me night after night. I even tried it myself a few times when he'd come creeping into our room. I thought if I didn't move, then maybe he'd leave me alone. But I think he liked it more when I didn't move. Good old Charlie and Patsy. Remember how Dad would leave us with them from time to time? Remember the games Charlie would like to play with me and where they'd lead to? How he'd come into the room, whispering, asking if I was asleep? And you would just lie there through the whole thing. Pretending to be a corpse." He huffed, laughing harshly at her. "You were the inspiration for the art I created in this town. How's it feel knowing Jordan Myer died in your image?"

The numbness spread through Jessie's body, and for the first time she wished it would take her completely. Send her into a coma, into the dark embrace of cold death if need be. Anything to close her ears off from Brody's words.

A scraping sound distracted him, and he looked to one side. "Oh look. Your boyfriend's not dead yet. He's trying to crawl over to you. I think he wants his last breath to be at your side. You know what? I'm feeling generous." He moved away, disappearing from Jessie's view. But then she heard the sound of a body being dragged through glass and the thump as it was dropped somewhere close to her.

She looked down and could just make out Alex's arm, covered in blood, lying next to her leg. His hand was twitching, reaching out to her. She couldn't imagine the effort it took for him to raise it and place it on her knee.

"Wow," Brody said. "He really must care about you. I guess that means you haven't told him everything about our childhood, huh?" He straddled Jessie's legs and bent down to make sure she could see into his eyes. "Tell you what. When your little catatonic state wears off, you tell me where the manifest is, and I'll kill Alex quickly and painlessly. If he lasts that long. But if you lie to me, and I'll know when you lie, I'm going to practice breaking a human's neck without killing them on him. Then I'll move on to the mayor."

Jessie stared into his black eyes. She knew he wasn't lying. Her brother, the boy she once knew, was gone.

Tears rolled down her cheeks as she grieved his loss. Anything good that was once inside him was gone; snuffed out by a monster who crept into their room at night when their father was away.

Brody looked down at Alex's hand. "How cute. He's patting your leg, telling you it's okay. I guess he's saying he's not afraid to die."

Jessie swallowed hard, closing her eyes, and steeling herself. She opened them and looked deeply into Brody's features. "He's not patting. He's strumming."

Her brother's eyes grew wide as he looked at the pattern Alex was repeating on Jessie's leg, his fingers dancing in a rhythm that touched the deepest part of her.

In a flash, her hand that was unaffected by his nerve blocks shot up, jamming a large piece of the broken table glass into Brody's side, then quickly pulling it out to re-plunge it into the side of his neck.

He gasped, already choking on his own blood as he stood up and staggered back, reaching up for the shard that had struck his carotid. He fell to the ground, only a couple of feet from his sister, his face turning towards her as he struggled to breathe.

Her body was leaden, and Jessie still couldn't stand, but the disassociation with her own body was starting to fade. She could see the life flowing out of her brother, gushing between the fingers that gripped the gash on his neck.

He opened his mouth, gargling on his own blood as he struggled to speak. "Jess...don't stay here...you...you don't know. Haven't you ever wondered...what...why Dad did what he did? Who he...protected. I know who

Chimera is. They killed Aunt Glenda and will kill... you...too."

And then, with a final heave of breath, he was still, his eyes staring at her without seeing.

Jessie dropped her chin to her chest and began to cry harder than she ever had in her life.

42

TO TRANSITION WITH LOVE

To Transition with Love

J essie refused to leave Alex's side as the paramedics loaded him into the back of the ambulance. Chief Walker was the first on the scene when Mayor Beaumont made the 9-1-1 call. He had surveyed the scene, and not shed a single tear at the sight of his nephew's body.

His voice had broken as he stood with the mayor.

"Maggie, I am so sorry you had to be pulled into this. To think that – maniac—" he stabbed a thumb at Todd's lifeless form, "—could do the things he's been doing."

Maggie had patted the chief's hand. By then, Alex's house was crawling with police and paramedics. Will's camera flashed repeatedly, but purposefully, in the mayor's direction.

"Now, Trent, don't you go apologizing for something out of your control. Besides, all this will almost certainly get me re-elected." She motioned for Will to take some photos of her that showed the now dried blood on one side of her head.

For her part, Jessie refused to look at her brother's body as it was lifted onto a stretcher, covered with plastic, and removed from the house. Instead, she focused on Alex. His breathing came in gasps, and he winced with pain as the paramedics worked to stabilize the gunshots he sustained before they could begin transporting him to the hospital. Jessie kept her hand on his, pouring as much of her will power into the man as she could.

He had saved her life, and she'd do everything in her power to return the favor.

THE SURGERY HAD BEEN touch and go at times, but four hours later, a weary surgeon made her way to the waiting room where Jessie, Chief Walker, and Mayor Beaumont had been waiting. They all jumped at the doctor at once, questions filled their eyes.

"He's going to be okay," the doctor said, holding up both hands. "It was tricky. He had a bullet lodged in his side that barely missed his liver. The one he took to the shoulder was the trickier of the two. It broke his clavicle and nicked the subclavian artery. He's lucky he was bought in as quickly as he was."

"Can we see him?" Jessie asked.

"Soon. He's in recovery and then will be moved to one of the ICU wards just for close overnight observation. But you should be able to talk to him a bit at that point. I need to get back and finish up some things, but I'll make sure a nurse updates you every step of the way." He gave them a weary smile and nod of his head before disappearing out of the room.

Jessie breathed a sigh of relief and wrapped her arms around herself as she made her way to the counter that held a single serve coffee machine and began to peruse the various flavor pods available. She felt someone walking up behind her and turned just as Chief Walker cleared his throat.

He held his hands clasped before him and stared down at his boots. "Jessie – Ms. Night, I mean. I wanted to say thank you. For what you did. You saved Maggie's life, and I'll always be grateful for that. I know what doing that must have cost you, and I'm sorry for your loss."

Jessie nodded in thanks, swallowing the lump that formed in her throat. "Thank you for that. And I'm sorry for your loss as well. How are you doing?"

He sighed, raising his head to look at her for the first time. "I haven't really dealt with it, I guess. My wife and sister-in-law are dealing with everyone. As you can imagine, things are a mess, now that everything is out in the open."

"Everything?" Jessie asked.

His cheeks colored and he started examining the tops of his boots again. "I have offered my resignation to the mayor."

"And I have not accepted it."

Jessie turned to see the mayor contemplating the two of them.

She moved over to stand next to them, shooing them both aside so she could get her own coffee. Jessie tried to hide her annoyance when the mayor took the last vanilla hazelnut flavor pod and tossed it into the maker.

"When the time comes for a changing of the guard, then it will be done the right way; with proper vetting of all candidates and an appropriate amount of mentoring and shadowing so that the chosen candidate is ready to take over the reins." She turned, giving them both a dazzling smile, then focusing on the chief. "I know why you did what you did. You used your position to persuade some of our residents to sell their land maybe against their will." She placed a hand on his arm. "But you did it for their own protection. Who knows what side of the dirt those poor people might be on if you hadn't done what you did. Granted you also harbored and protected a criminal, but I can understand that as well. Todd would have hurt the people closest to you." She looked at Jessie. "Or worse. At some point in our lives, we've all suffered a lack of judgement when it comes to protecting those we love, right?"

The question was rhetorical but brought a glimmer of red to Jessie's cheeks.

"But what about old Davis, and the poor Hendricks family that I made sell?" the chief asked. He was starting to wring his hands, and for a moment, Jessie thought he might be on the verge of tears.

The mayor took his trembling hand in hers. "I happen to know, that those families are far happier now than they were when they were living on all that land, worrying about how they were going to pay their property tax each year. It's amazing how a waterfront condo in another state can make you happy." She gave the

Chief a small smile and wink. "So, no worries there. Especially since I heard a little birdie might have found some discretionary funds to pay the monthly HOA's on said condos. But you didn't hear that from me." She turned to Jessie, her face suddenly a little sterner. "You see, around here, we take care of our own. Always have, always will. The question is, are you going to become one of ours?"

Jessie's breath caught in her chest. The truth was, she had lost count recently of the number of times those words had crossed her mind.

Mayor Beaumont leaned in, her voice dropping to little more than a whisper. "Your brother told me things about you. Things I didn't believe until I saw you in action." She pulled back, smiling broadly. "The truth is, we could use someone like you around. Maybe in a more permanent consulting position, or something like that. At least until we can find out who hired your brother and what he was really up to for them." She picked up her cup of coffee and walked back over to her chair. "I'll leave you two to work out the details."

Chief Walker seemed a little skittish. There was no trace of the swagger and bravado he had exhibited previously when in her presence. "Maggie's right. We could not have done this without you. As much as I hate to admit it, this might be a small town, but it's not the same small town it once was. I don't know what Maggie was alluding to a second ago, but you've more than proven yourself to me. You and Alex are quite the team. And I for one would be honored to learn a thing or two from you."

It wasn't often that Jessie found herself at a loss for

words, but this was one of those times. All she could do was give him a quick nod. "I'll think about it."

He returned the nod. "That's all I can ask."

Two hours later and a nurse popped her head in the doorway. "Hi, I was told to let you all know that Alex Thomas is awake. Groggy, but awake. I can let you in to see him one at a time."

Although they all stood up, Mayor Beaumont and the chief both looked at Jessie, letting her know she needed to be the first to see him.

Inside the room, Jesse was struck by just how frail Alex looked. Propped up on the pillows of the hospital bed, his skin was pale and nearly translucent. For a second, she wondered what kind of makeup they used to create such a vampiric effect.

His eyes were open, and the corners wrinkled in pleasure when she walked in. He must have read in her eyes just how bad he looked. "They say the color is due to the amount of blood I lost. Even though I was transfused, it will be a bit before my cheeks are rosy again." His voice was scratchy and little more than a whisper.

Jessie pulled the lone chair in the room close to the bed, careful not to get entangled in the mass of cords trailing from it to the wall. "You shouldn't try to talk. I just wanted to make sure you were doing okay."

His attempt at a smile was weak at best. "I'm hurting everywhere. But I'm alive. Thanks to you."

She felt her eyes well up and tried to blink the impending tears away. "Nah. Other way around. You saved me. You remembered my strumming pattern. It called to me; pulled me back to myself at the last moment."

"Well, even if I had been in top form, I knew you stood a much better chance at your brother than I did. And I was right."

"So, the Chief is staying on. At least until he can find a replacement the right way. Not by extortion."

Alex sighed, closing his eyes. "And just when I was starting to like Todd. He goes and shoots me in the guts."

Despite herself, Jessie couldn't help but laugh, but immediately regretted it when Alex's attempt at laughter turned into a painful-sounding bout of coughing that started a couple of his monitors beeping. He took some slow, deep breaths and tried to relax back against the pillow.

"I going to leave now. Let you get some rest."

She got up to exit the room, but he motioned for her to wait. "So, will I see you again?"

"Of course. I'll be back tomorrow afternoon."

His stare was intense. "Not what I meant."

She knew what he meant. "The chief and the mayor have asked me to stay on and continue in some capacity working with the department." She gave him a smile. "I'm thinking about it." Her phone buzzed and her face dropped when she looked at the screen. "Alex, I have to go. But I'll see you soon."

"Hey. Visiting hours don't end for the ICU units."

She paused mid-step, looking back over her shoulder. "I know." She gave a quick glance to her phone. "But there's something important I need to do right now."

JESSIE HAD DRIVEN home way too fast. Her return to the hospital was even faster. She wasn't religious in the least but found herself mouthing silent prayers to any deity that might listen, begging them to let her be on time.

She raced through the hallway, ignoring the surprised looks she received. Women and men jumped to the side, little shouts of surprise echoing off the walls behind her as she drove her legs to move faster and faster. At the elevator, the blinking light showed that the car was on the eleventh floor. It would take forever to get to her, and a quick calculation told her she could make it up four flights before it could come all the way down.

Breaking through the door marked "stairs" at breakout speed, she pulled on the leash in her right hand, urging Blizzard to keep up as they pounded their way up four flights. One more race down the hall and she arrived at the nurse's station. Ignoring the pinch in her side, she waved at the first person she saw. "Which room is—"

"Jessie. Over here."

She looked up to see Dr. Karni waving her over to one of the rooms.

"Am I too late?" Jessie breathed.

Dr. Karni took her hand, her voice was calm and smooth. "No. You're right on time." She ushered them into the quiet of the room. The lights had been dimmed; the curtains drawn. The only sound was the slow, irregular beeping coming from the monitor still connected to the old man.

The smell of antiseptic cleaner that filled the air swept Jessie up in a wave of déjà vu, as she moved closer to the frail figure, his tiny head dwarfed by the pillow he rested against. Blizzard hesitated, his tale dropping, his large, brown eyes, taking in the space. His nostrils quivered as he picked up the scent of his human and carefully made his way to the bedside.

The IVs had been removed from Jeb Thompson's arm and one of them rested at the edge of his bed, on top of the lightweight blanket that covered him. With a low whine, Blizzard inched forward and pressed his nose against Jeb's hand before lying his head tenderly in the man's lap. The shepherd reared up on his hind legs, stretching his body until he could snuggle against the old man's chest.

Jeb's breathing was shallow, but as Blizzard settled against him, a subtle change registered in his features. The lines of pain etched on Jeb's face softened and retreated as his hand twitched. He slowly reached out and placed it on his dog's head, clumsily ruffling the thick coat. The start of a smile broke out across his face, and Jessie's eyes welled up as she watched the silent communication between an old man and his best friend.

As the minutes ticked by, the room was filled with a profound sense of peace, love, and finality. Jessie could feel the bond between them. She watched as Blizzard would slowly roll his head on the man's lap, a slight flick of his tongue striking Jeb's hand.

The beeping of the heart monitor slowed ever more, and Dr. Karni reached out and took Jessie's hand, giving it a squeeze.

"Thank you for doing this. It won't be long now. After what you've told me about Jordan, there's no other family on record and that dog means so much to him," she whispered.

Jeb's eyes flickered open, gray and unseeing, but somehow at peace. They tried to focus on Jessie, and the old man's mouth worked silently, trying desperately to communicate as his grip on Blizzard began to fade.

Jessie stepped to the bedside and placed her hand on his. "Don't you worry about Blizzard. I will take care of him. Forever."

Whether he heard her words or understood them, peace seemed to descend on the old man. His breathing grew shallower and the monitor beeping slowed, until finally there was nothing left for it to echo. There, in the silent room, with Blizzard's warm presence to ease his transition, Jebediah Thompson took his last breath, and left this world.

Jessie let Blizzard remain with him a bit longer before taking him gently by the collar and walking him out of the room. He pulled back, looking behind him a few times, before nuzzling against the side of her leg as they walked away.

She had meant what she said. She would take care of him. Always. But now, she realized that extended to more than just Blizzard. Like it or not, Pine Haven had become her home.

And if there was something big and bad and terrible headed its way, then she would be there, blocking its path. "Come on, boy. I think it's time we stop putting things off, go to the grocery store, and stock up. Looks like neither of us is going anywhere anytime soon."

***

Book Two is coming soon and is now available for pre-order!

Night's Descent: Jessie Night Thriller Book Two

ALSO, if you'd like to stay up to date on all new releases, including the third book in this exciting new series, join the author's mailing list, at:

sendfox.com/emberscottauthor

ABOUT THE AUTHOR

Ember Scott is an author of thrillers and mysteries living in the great state of North Carolina. He is a lover of dogs, mountains, lakes...and some people.

He loves to create tale about very bad people that do very bad things and ultimately get their comeuppance.

If you like fast paced thrillers that are built around unforgettable characters, then this is the author for you.

He can be reached at:

emberscottauthor@gmail.com

ALSO BY EMBER SCOTT

Printed in Great Britain
by Amazon